Henry Edward Colvile

The Land of the Nile Springs

Henry Edward Colvile

The Land of the Nile Springs

ISBN/EAN: 9783337367176

Printed in Europe, USA, Canada, Australia, Japan

Cover: Foto ©Andreas Hilbeck / pixelio.de

More available books at **www.hansebooks.com**

THE LAND

OF

THE NILE SPRINGS

BEING CHIEFLY AN ACCOUNT OF HOW
WE FOUGHT KABAREGA

BY

COLONEL SIR HENRY COLVILE, K.C.M.G., C.B.

GRENADIER GUARDS

ILLUSTRATED BY MR. J. BURRELL-SMITH AND MR. TWIDLE
FROM SKETCHES BY THE AUTHOR AND MAJOR THRUSTON
AND FROM PHOTOGRAPHS BY THE AUTHOR

EDWARD ARNOLD

Publisher to the India Office

LONDON
37 BEDFORD STREET

NEW YORK
70 FIFTH AVENUE

1895

PREFACE

I WAS selected a few years ago to write the official history of a campaign, a most valuable work, I am told by the man who read it; and during my stay in Uganda I had to contribute a good deal to Blue Book literature. I trust that the habits acquired during these experiences may be considered a sufficient excuse for any items of useful information that I may have allowed to slip into the following pages.

H. E. COLVILE.

London, *May 29th*, 1895.

CONTENTS

CHAPTER I

THE ROAD TO THE LAKE

CHAPTER II

THE ROAD TO THE LAKE—*continued*

CHAPTER III

USOGA

CHAPTER VII

THE CONCENTRATION ON THE FRONTIER

CHAPTER VIII

CROSSING THE KAFU

CHAPTER IX

OCCUPATION OF THE CAPITAL

CHAPTER XVI

THE CHAIN OF FORTS

CHAPTER XVII

THE RETURN TO UGANDA

CHAPTER XVIII

PARADE AND POLICY

CHAPTER XIX

LIFE AT PORT ALICE

CHAPTER XX

THE MRULI EXPEDITION

CHAPTER XXI

AFFAIRS IN UNYORO

CHAPTER XXII

THE ANKOLI EXPEDITION

CHAPTER XXIII

A BRITISH PROTECTORATE

LIST OF ILLUSTRATIONS

THE LAND OF THE NILE SPRINGS

CHAPTER I

THE ROAD TO THE LAKE

Appointed to Uganda—Companions—Zanzibar—Mombasa—Taru tanks—Taru desert—Voi river—Ndi—Tsavo—An unquiet night—Kibwezi—Besant left behind—British and Hindu East Africa—Prospects of Ukambani—Machako's—Wakamba —Picturesque costumes — Kikuyu — Colonisation — Foodless tract—Open despatches—Decide to hurry—Masai.

ON the 4th of August 1893, I received a telegram from the War Office, asking whether I would accept an appointment under Sir Gerald Portal, in Uganda. I answered "Yes"; and started by the Indian mail leaving on the 11th, accompanied by Captain Gibb (Worcestershire Regiment), Captain Besant (Norfolk Regiment), and Captain Thruston (Oxfordshire Light Infantry). We were being sent out in consequence of a telegram received from Sir Gerald Portal, asking for the services of four Arabic-speaking officers, of whom the senior should have sufficient rank and experience to take control of affairs.

On the 31st of August we reached Zanzibar, where we were each presented with a horse by the Sultan, and I also bought a couple. On the 4th of September we embarked with these, some donkeys, and our porters, for Mombasa, on the s.s. *Juba*, a vessel which, sailors tell me, has many good qualities, but which we were unfortunately not able to discover.

After a day's halt at Mombasa, to pick up more porters, we moved on to Banderini, at the head of the Creek, and encamped there for two days, adjusting our loads, and generally preparing for a start. The result of this adjustment was that we found we had neither enough boxes nor porters, so Mr. Muxworthy, our caravan leader, returned to Mombasa, to make up deficiencies, while we, with half the porters, strolled slowly on to Taru, where he caught us up.

This first forty-five miles of road ran through a level country, either parklike or covered with thick mimosa bush, and, in spite of its being the height of the dry season, we found it sufficiently watered; but I must say that very little of the

TARU

(To face page 3)

remarkable mixture of earth, moisture, and rotten grasses, which we got out of the sluggish streams, proved to be sufficient.

Taru is rather an important place, or may become so on account of its being the starting-point for the march across the so-called "Taru desert," over which water has to be carried in the dry season, and over which the traveller steps out of civilisation.

This water collects during the rains in some large rock basins, in sufficient quantity to last all through the dry weather, and with a very moderate amount of labour might be kept as clean as that in the tanks at Aden. The pools are now, however, choked with mud, vegetation, and general liveliness and its consequences; and as the African traveller does not like being tormented before his time, more than other people, it would be a charity to send a few men with spades and buckets to clean out the tanks, and let him have his stirrup-cup of some liquid not absolutely warranted to produce fever.

On the 16th of September, Mr. Muxworthy and the tail of the caravan having caught us up, I sent on half my party to form a water depôt at Butzuma, and with the remainder, and half of his, followed in the afternoon.   We reached Maungu, thirty miles distant, on the farther side of the "desert," at three the next day.

The march was across a level country, covered with thick thorn bush, which holds a certain amount of game.   I am told that all attempts to get water by boring have hitherto proved unsuccessful, but from the number of streams that run into it from the Teita hills, and the amount of vegetation which it supports, I can hardly think that the case is hopeless.   If it is, there is nothing to be done but make a railway.   Taru and the pools between it and the coast are only just sufficient to supply present wants, and certainly would not suffice for the many teams of oxen which will have to stream inland, if Kikuyu and Uganda are ever to be developed.

From Maungu we moved on next day to Mkuyuni,[1] where a nice little cascade falls out of the Ndara hills, and where we again waited for the tail of the caravan.

On the 19th we made a fair start all together,

---

[1] I only use this form of spelling under protest.   This place is pronounced Emkuyuni, as Ndi is pronounced Endi, and Ntebe, Entebbi.   As Swahili is not a written language, I see no reason why the most intelligible form of orthography should not be adopted

about three hundred strong, and after crossing the numerous channels of the swampy Voi river, camped on its banks. This river has now been bridged, and the bridge has collapsed, but it is nevertheless a good deal easier to get over than when I first crossed it, and as a fair road, or rather ride, has now been cut as far as Kibwezi, a week's work would make that place perfectly accessible to ox-waggons.

On the 21st, wishing to make arrangements for a waterless march which I knew was ahead of us, I rode on with Spire to Tsavo, a station of the I.B.E.A. Company, on the banks of the river of that name, and in charge of a native known as Fundi (artisan) William. This station has since been abandoned, a new one having been formed at Ndi in its stead. William entertained us most hospitably, but, in spite of his exertions on our behalf, we passed rather an uncomfortable night. The hut seemed to have been built chiefly with a view to providing the fullest ventilation, and as I had brought no wraps with me, I was too cold to sleep comfortably, and when I did drop off, was roused by Spire's noisy but ineffectual attempts to drive away the many rats who shared this abode with William. I tried to quiet him with the assurance that it was far better to feel a real rat than see a phantom one, but wholly failed to conciliate him with his strange bedfellows. At nine next morning the caravan marched in, and at three we started off again to Ngomeni, where William had sent on water for us.

The country passed through between the Voi and Tsavo rivers differed but little in appearance from that between Taru and Maungu, but, owing to proximity to the hills, is better watered, and the soil looked richer. After crossing the river, however, a considerable change begins to take place; the ground becomes more undulating, streams more frequent, the thorn bushes are partly replaced by more succulent-looking trees, and as Kibwezi is approached, a zone of cultivation is reached, which has already begun to be tapped by Mombasa merchants, who have established small trading stations in the district.

On the 26th we arrived at Kibwezi, 185 miles from the coast, a Scottish industrial mission station, under the charge of Dr. Charters, who was unfortunately lost, and, it is believed, killed by Masai, while out shooting, in 1894.

Besant, who had picked up fever on the Voi, had been so ill for the last few days, that I was very glad to get some medical assistance, and after considering Dr. Charters' strongly expressed opinion that he was unfit to travel any farther, I very reluctantly felt myself compelled to leave him behind.

About a mile beyond Kibwezi, the road stops short, and we suddenly found ourselves on a tortuous track, in a belt of thick thorn bush, through which we squeezed our way, to the great detriment of our clothes and epidermes. Luckily the bush soon thins off, and an hour's march brought us into a slightly undulating district, sparsely clothed with thorns, euphorbia and baobab trees, teeming with game, and watered by the Kiboko, Makindo, and Ndange rivers. Half a day's march beyond the ford of the latter stream, and on its left bank, Nzoi is reached, a fine rocky peak, some eight thousand feet above the sea, and dominating a very well watered agricultural district, supporting a large population of Wakamba.

This peak may be said to be the boundary mark of true British East Africa. The Daruma, Samburu, and Wateita districts between this and the coast may turn out a Hindu or Chinese East Africa, but will never make homes for English-

men, who, even if they like "roughing it" themselves,—I have never met one who did,—prefer,
that for the sake of peace and quietness, their
wives and families should be able to eat and
drink by day, and sleep by night. Now both
these things can be done beyond Nzoi, whence
the country begins to rise steadily, from 3755
feet at the starting-point to anything you may
like, or otherwise, on Mau or Elgon. Streams
in all directions water the valleys, an industrious,
but not over thick, population produce a sufficient
supply of grain for present wants,[1] but have not
occupied a tenth part of the available land; large
herds of sheep, goats, and cattle browse on the
hillsides; the nights are cool, or even cold : and as
far as I can see, the only objection to this district
is that it is at present only to be reached by
such an anachronistic means of locomotion as
walking. Not being good at descriptive writing,
I think I can best give an idea of the country
by saying that it reminded me chiefly of North
Wales.

On leaving Nzoi, a two days' march along a
sheep-track, with occasional belts of very thick

---

[1] Mr. Ainsworth calculates that at the present moment Ukambani
produces 5000 tons of grain yearly.

KOLUNGU CAMP

(*To face page* 9)

thorn bush, brought us to the junction of the Keize and Kolungu rivers, whence our course lay up the deep-cut bed of the latter stream, to its head waters and the parting between them and the Machako's river. Occasionally wading waist deep, and always trudging through deep sand, our progress was slow, and the twenty miles' march entailed two days' fairly hard work. Flanked by high mountains, furrowed by the affluents, great and small, of the Kolungu, this valley, bad though it is, affords the best route to Machako's; and although there is no impossibility in making a road through this district, it would be an expensive work, and one not likely to be undertaken, until the wants of colonists have rendered it a necessity. However, there is no reason why the up-country road should follow this line; a far easier route can be chosen to the west, neglecting for the present Nzoi and Machako's, and directly connecting Kibwezi with Kikuyu.

Another day's march through a highly cultivated but annoyingly undulating country brought us to the I.B.E.A. Company's post under the hill, which is still named after its late chief, Machako. Here we enjoyed for two days the hospitality of Mr.

Ainsworth, and revelled in the products of an excellent kitchen garden.

Mr. Ainsworth has succeeded in establishing most satisfactory relations with the Wakamba, of whom and whose country he, with me, entertains the highest opinion. Although they are not a race of warriors like the Masai, they have generally been able to hold their own against them, and, judging by the specimens employed at the fort, make smart and efficient soldiers ; the large tracts of land under cultivation and watered by artificial channels show them to be industrious agriculturists, and Mr. Ainsworth told me that he could at any moment get two thousand of them as carriers or labourers. Like most Africans, however, they have an objection to go far from their own country, but under the leadership of an European in whom they had confidence, they could undoubtedly be gradually induced to do so. On the whole, I look upon them as the most promising tribe which I came across in East Africa.

I have written this and my remarks on the suitability of the country for colonisation, urged on solely by a stern sense of patriotism. Were I to follow my own inclination, I would warn all Europeans off the country of the Wakamba,

WAKAMBA   (*To face page* 11)

and postpone for as long as possible the evil day when their picturesque costumes of black skin and bright brass wire will be exchanged for imported horrors from East End slop-shops, and their cheerful and virtuous paganism will undergo the inevitable metamorphosis which follows in the track of the three great civilisers.

After passing through a few miles of pretty, well-tree'd hill district, we descended on to the Athi plains, a broad open prairie teeming with game of all kinds, and as fine a piece of grazing land as could well be wished for, lying a little over five thousand feet above the sea, and enjoying an almost ideal climate. On the northern side these plains are bounded by the Kikuyu forest, through which a fifteen-feet road has been cut, and which leads through the highly cultivated Kikuyu district to Fort Smith, another of the Company's stations, and commanded by Mr. Hall.

The Wakikuyu are quite as industrious as the Wakamba, and their soil is if anything more fertile, but for some unexplained reason they have hitherto been on far less friendly terms with Europeans than is the case with their Wakamba neighbours, and at present I fear colonisation could only be carried on in their district by force. They have, however, lately begun to engage themselves as porters, and there is hope that before long a better understanding between them and the white men may arise.

Between Kikuyu and Kavirondo is an uninhabited tract which takes about twenty-five days to traverse, and which I have often seen described as a desert. No word that I know of could convey a more false impression of this district, which is well watered, and alternately covered with rich prairies or luxuriant belts of forest. Its only tenants at present are countless herds of game, and it is waiting with open arms to welcome the first man who cares to settle in an earthly paradise, but, like that other paradise which we all hope to reach, but are in no hurry to get to, it probably will not be one in which filthy lucre is likely to accumulate, at all events until it is a good deal more closely connected with the outer world than is the case now. Owing to the absence of man, this district grows nothing edible by human beings, and consequently a stock of food has to be taken to meet the requirements of the porters, who, already pretty heavily laden, cannot carry more than ten days' rations extra, so donkeys

have to be procured to convey the food for the·
remaining fifteen days.

As our arrival was unexpected, no preparation
had been made for us, and we had to make a
four days' halt while our necessaries were being
collected ; a rest which the porters thoroughly
appreciated and made the most of, disposing of
all their clothes and blankets to the Wakikuyu in
exchange for a spirit distilled by those aborigines,
and getting gloriously drunk.

As I had left England with orders to serve
under Sir Gerald Portal, I was somewhat surprised
to hear from Mr. Hall that he had passed the
station about ten days before our arrival, and was
then on his way to the coast *via* the Tana river.
I also learned that we had been sent for in such a
hurry on account of a mutiny among the Sudanese
troops.   As in Sir Gerald Portal's absence I
should be the senior officer in Uganda, I opened
some despatches which I was carrying up for
him, and among them found one ordering the
return to India of Captain Macdonald, who had
been left as Acting Commissioner in Uganda.
This news left no doubt that I should have to
take up the duties of Acting Commissioner, and as
things did not seem to be in a particularly

satisfactory state, I determined to hurry on as fast as I could. We had, however, an unusually small proportion of armed men in the caravan, and as Mr. Hall assured me that it would be running an unjustifiable risk to pass through the Masai country with less than thirty guns, I had to make up my mind to stick to the main body until we were clear of the dangerous zone. As it turned out, we never saw a Masai, and I might perfectly well have gone through unarmed.

CHAPTER II

Residential estates—Death of horses—Great prairie—The highway
to Uganda—Rough on clothes—Waggon road—Kedong escarpment—Morandat river—A little Hades—Wadorobo hunters—
Well kept meat—Lake Naivasha—Lakes Elmenteita and
Nakuru—I leave the caravan—A serious obstacle—The
Subugo forest—The Nile watershed—A Scotch mist—Two
bad rivers—The Hingin hills—Kabras—The human form
divine—Unknown tongues—Mumia's—The British flag nailed
to the mast—A health station—A nasty brook—A Kavirondo
hut—The Victoria Nyanza—Berkeley Bay.

ON the 15th of October we got off at last, passing on that and the following day through
a lovely, slightly undulating country, dotted with
clumps of pine trees and large patches of forest,
abounding in pretty glades and glens, every square
mile of which contained a perfect site for a house;
as the agents say, "standing in its own grounds,
beautifully situated and commanding an extensive
view of parklike country," but not, I am afraid, for
some time to come, "within easy reach of an important railway station."

All this district is about seven thousand feet above the sea; and although it was pleasant enough sitting by Mr. Hall's big wood fire in his comfortable room at Fort Smith, we found the evenings rather chilly in our tents, and were generally inclined to walk on as hard as we could to keep warm during the early morning marches.

It looked as if we should soon all have to walk whether we liked it or no. I had already lost two out of my three horses, while those belonging to Gibb and Mr. Muxworthy were looking very bad. Various reasons have been given for the mortality among horses on this road, but I believe it is simply a question of want of care, and chiefly due to chills. Mr. Martin, who has taken up a considerable number for sale in Uganda, has, I am told, never lost one, and I believe his good luck is accounted for by his habit of building a thatched stable for them every night.

After reaching the limits of the Kikuyu forest, we entered the stretch of prairie extending for a hundred miles to the Guaso Masai river. The road across this is most easily and accurately described by saying that there is not one. Narrow tracks, made either by game or wandering Masai, stretch here and there across the grass, and, steering on some distant mark, the leader of the caravan selects the one which for the time being points most nearly in the desired direction, and follows it until a converging path seems to offer greater advantages.

After the passage of the first team this district would offer no obstacles to waggon traffic, and half a dozen in succession would probably make a good road ; but under existing conditions this portion of the route is not a pleasant one to travel over. The track is so narrow that one is forced to walk native fashion, that is to say, with one foot straight in front of the other, while the high stiff grass on either side rapidly wears holes in the knees of one's breeches and sleeves of one's coat. On horseback the wearing process is transferred from the sleeves to the boots, the knees being subjected to it in any case. As the grass is laden with moisture from the heavy dews of the night, we also usually found ourselves by eight in the morning as thoroughly soaked through as if we had been wading up to our armpits in a river.

I have said that this district would offer no obstacles to waggon traffic : there is, however, one impediment which would require all the skill of a Hottentot driver to get up or down, viz. the Kedong escarpment, a very steep bank in rather broken ground, the worst portion of which is about seven hundred feet high. I do not think it is absolutely impassable for a waggon even now, but it is certainly capable of improvement.

The Morandat river is also sometimes impassable for a few days at a time in the rainy season, but I have never heard of a caravan having to wait more than a week there.

I have spoken of all this region as an earthly paradise, but there is one little Hades in its midst into which we entered on descending the escarpment. I mean the Kedong valley. This is a hole (in every sense of the word) surrounded by high hills, stuffy by day and at night swept by hurricanes, which make tent life both precarious and trying to the temper; and I should strongly advise an intending colonist, who values the harmony of his domestic circle, to carefully avoid it.

Although this district is destitute of any permanent inhabitants, it is visited by the wandering Wadorobo, a tribe which has not yet even reached the pastoral stage, and whose members live entirely by hunting. Their favourite quarry is the elephant, and when, after infinite labour, they succeed in

killing one, they call their wives and families to the spot, and, building a rude hut, settle down near the carcase until it is finished, an event which rarely takes place before it has attained a fine gamey flavour.

Luckily, the Kedong valley is not very extensive, and a good day's march from the escarpment brought us to Lake Naivasha, from whose shores, prettily sprinkled with trees and covered with wildfowl, a lovely view is obtained of the Mau range, bathed when we saw it in the purple mist of the evening, and casting dancing reflections in the island-dotted water.

Another fifty miles' marching took us past Lake Elmenteita to Nakuru, the last of this group of three lakes; and fifteen more, still over rolling prairie land, to the Guaso Masai river.

We were now well clear of the Masai, not a trace of whom we had seen, so, packing up provisions and clothes for three weeks into twenty half loads (*i.e.* about thirty lb. each), I started ahead next morning, accompanied by Spire, my servant, and twenty men, of whom seven were armed. We covered three marches that day (a pace which we managed to keep up to the end of the journey), and camped on the farther side of the Eldoma ravine by the edge of the Subugo forest.

As I wished to travel as fast as possible, I left behind most of my rubbish, including the cook, whose duties were undertaken by Spire; thanks to him, and a plentiful supply of hartebeeste, I lived better during this forced march than at any other period of my stay in Equatoria.

After leaving the Guaso Masai river, a wholly different region is entered. At first a forest country dotted with large open spaces and frequently intersected by running brooks, but gradually thinning until it assumes a more parklike appearance. It is flanked to the west by the bold escarpment of the Mau range, deeply scored by ravines and brightened by cascades, while to the east the great prairie stretches like a sea some two or three hundred feet below it.

The Eldoma ravine is the only really serious obstacle to a road or railway between the coast and the Victoria Lake; it is a rocky gorge sharply cut into a grass plain, some 300 yards wide at the top and 200 feet deep, narrowing at the bottom to the width of the roaring torrent which flows through it. For the passage of a railway it would of course have to be bridged, but for the use of carts a road could be cut down its sides; a work requiring a considerable amount of labour and some engineering skill, but by no means an impracticable or even very extravagant operation.

About a mile beyond the ravine is the southern border of the Subugo forest, a dense belt of heavy timber and parasitic undergrowth, extending for twenty miles in a westerly direction, and clothing the face of the Mau escarpment. At present a mere hunter's track leads through the forest, following a straight line over an intervening hill or spur and up the side of the mountain. With a little intelligent care, a road might be led up this without encountering any impossible gradients, but the work of cutting through the forest would be a heavy one.

As the western edge of the forest is approached, a few bamboos appear among the other trees, but no marked change takes place until one suddenly emerges into sunlight, and finds oneself on the watershed of the Nile, looking over a great expanse of rolling downs, fringed on the east by the forest, and gradually losing itself to the west and north among clumps of timber trees and bamboos. Having travelled so far from Egypt by sea and land, it rather fascinated me to think that every little rivulet I saw was surely making its way to join the great mass of water which flows under the Kasr-el-Nil bridge at Cairo.

That part of the plateau which the track passes over ranges to nearly nine thousand feet above the sea level, and being wet through, as usual, from the dew-covered grass, I found it chilly even in the middle of the day, while every wrap I had was insufficient to keep me as warm as I wished at night. That the unfortunate porters, who, as I have said, sold all their clothing at Kikuyu, did not die of cold, must be due to some special providence which watches over idiots and Swahilis.

Another long march, through a cold, driving Scotch mist, took us off the Mau plateau and into the warmer regions of the Nollosogelli valley, which we followed all the next day. On the fourth day from the ravine, we crossed the Guaso Masa[1] and Ekatatok rivers, and camped on the farther bank of the latter.

From the edge of the Subugo forest to the Ekatatok, the track had run entirely across undulating grass land requiring no road-making for an ox-waggon; and although several streams

---

[1] Not to be confounded with the Guaso Masai.

and rivers had been crossed, there were none which could not easily be forded. The two last-named rivers, however, are more serious obstacles, running deep and strong, and although, this being the dry season, we managed to ford them, they often cause considerable delay.

Beyond the Ekatatok the country undergoes a further change; the rolling prairie gives place to grass-covered hills, studded with a low pod-bearing tree, the ground becoming much more rocky and uneven, while its unsuitableness for wheeled traffic culminates in the Hingin range of hills, an impassable barrier to carts until a road has been made.

Our first march from the Ekatatok took us to the outlying villages of Kabras, where we were greeted with the sight of some human beings, other than ourselves, for the first time since leaving Kikuyu. They were not very pleasing specimens of the species, being stark naked, stumpy, and stupid-looking. It is not everybody who can afford to go about without clothes; the Wakamba can, and look very well in their rather aggressive nudity set off by ochre, oil, and brightly polished ornaments; but there is an uncared-for look about the Wakavirondo nakedness; their dead black skins would not even qualify them as advertisements for anybody's blacking, while their utter lack of ornaments conveys the idea that they abjure clothing more because they have not got it, than from any strong sense of the divine beauty of the human form.

However, they had milk, eggs, and vegetables to sell, for the sake of which I would gladly have put up with a far greater shock to my æsthetic sensibilities than I received.

These people talk a language closely allied to that of the Lendus, a low tribe living to the west of the Nile near Wadelai. As far as I know, few strangers talk these languages, which seem to be more akin to that which Professor Garner has made his speciality than any other that I am acquainted with, and consequently their customs and religious views are little known. They live in strongly entrenched villages, very similar to those of Western Madagascar. This is probably merely a matter of habit, acquired in the times when they were subject to Masai raids, as they are not now threatened either by external enemies or much given to internecine warfare.

From Kabras a very long day's march, across a fertile, somewhat undulating country, brought us to the village of Mumia, a rather weak-minded Kavirondo chief, the position of whose head-quarters at the end of the long, foodless march has given him an importance far beyond his personal worth. On our arrival, one of his retainers was hurriedly sent off, and soon reappeared from a hut, bearing a mast, to which a Union Jack had been carefully nailed, and which was then planted in the ground.

During the afternoon and evening my porters struggled in, so dead beat that I saw I must leave some of them behind; so, borrowing a dozen men from Mumia, I placed an equal number of my own in his charge, and started next morning for Berkeley Bay.

The track from Mumia's to Lake Victoria is an easy one, but, the country being thickly populated and much under cultivation, it is unfortunately fenced in on either side by thorn hedges, which are far too close together to admit of the passage of a cart; and when the road is made, a certain amount of destruction of property, and consequent wrangling and remuneration, will be necessary.

Badly as a road is wanted to connect Uganda with the coast, I am not certain that one is not quite as urgently required from Berkeley Bay to

Mumia's, and thence to Mount Elgon. This mountain, a fine volcanic peak some ten thousand feet above the sea, which had been in view for the last three days, is undoubtedly the best site for an Uganda health station. The climate of Uganda, especially near the lake, though pleasant, is decidedly relaxing, and after about a year's hard work in it, Europeans get into a state of depression and bad temper, which makes their companionship a thing to be avoided, and their urgent requests to be allowed to return to Europe the more readily granted. By the time they get to Kikuyu, however, their views on life have changed, and they are as anxious to get back as a few weeks before they were to go away. Now if, instead of having to make up one's mind that one had lost these friends for ever (always to be disappointed), they could be sent for a little holiday on Elgon, they would recover their spirits as easily as they do on Mau, and within a month or six weeks be back again at their posts.

Another good reason for the occupation of Mount Elgon lies in the fact that an important trade route passes over its lower slopes, by which guns and powder go up to Kabarega and the Nile Valley, and slaves come down. During the whole of my stay in Uganda, I was trying to establish this station, but want of sufficient English officers to undertake the work prevented me doing so.

About half an hour out of Mumia's we crossed the Nzoia river by a primitive ferry in charge of a very drunk but amiable old gentleman; and in the next valley we came to a deep brook, which we bipeds crossed by a single plank-bridge, but which nearly finished my only remaining horse. Without taking the trouble to find out its depth, my *syce* rode him boldly in, and when he found that he disappeared under the water, was too surprised even to get off. The poor beast was very tired and weak, and it was only by getting a rope round his head that we kept him above water at all; and even then we could not by any means get him up the steep banks. However, we at last found a place a good way down stream, to which he was towed, and from which we managed to drag him out, pretty thoroughly exhausted. Unfortunately, my camera and dry plates were strapped on to the saddle, and the latter, which held all the latent pictures which I had taken during the last fortnight, were hopelessly ruined, and the former was so disorganised that I was not able to use it again until, after my return from the Unyoro expedition, I found time to devote a day to it.

I did not ride the horse again during that day's march, until, late in the afternoon, a heavy thunderstorm came on, when, seeing a village a few hundred yards off on the other side of a little valley, I jumped on him to hurry into shelter. Unfortunately, the little valley contained a little bog, and into this he rolled over on to the top of me, pressing me down in about two feet of slushy water. The baggage was some distance behind, and as by the time it came up, tents, clothes, and blankets, as well as the ground, were soaking, I thought it better to accept the hospitality of the villagers, and put up in a native hut.

These are built in a circle inside the rampart which I have already spoken of. They consist of a sort of Chinese umbrella about twenty to twenty-five feet in diameter, very neatly made of reeds, and reaching to within about two feet of the ground. Inside the circumference of this is built an elliptical mud wall, traced somewhat out of centre to the umbrella, so that, while its back part coincides with the circumference of the latter, its front is considerably inside it, thus forming near the doorway a fairly broad verandah, which gradually tapers to nothing at the rear. As the umbrella roof is not raised at all near the doorway to form a porch, one has to enter the house almost on all fours.

Having started a good fire, I proceeded to take off my wet things and dry them, clothed in the meanwhile in a primitive costume, which seemed to be highly appreciated by the nearly similarly attired audience which had collected in the hut.

After a five hours' march next morning, in the course of which I again managed to tumble into a bog, we came in sight of the Victoria Nyanza, which, with its horizon screened by islands, did not convey the idea of a very vast sheet of water. Another hour brought us to Berkeley Bay, where I found Mr. Purkiss in charge, busily engaged in building a station and attempting to make a harbour on the marshy shore. Although this spot is a convenient one, as being that at which the present track touches the lake, it is not a desirable one in any other way. The food supply is very limited, timber is scarce, and the marshy shore makes the construction of a harbour a work of some difficulty, and renders the neighbourhood unhealthy. It was at this place that Mr. Purkiss contracted the germs of the disease of which he died six months later.

I had hoped to find a boat or canoes at Berkeley Bay to take me direct to Port Alice, but, hearing that I should probably have to wait three or four days for them, I settled to push on by land.

CHAPTER III

USOGA

STARTING in the early morning of the 2nd
of November, I reached by noon the frontier
of what may fairly be called Uganda. I am aware
that it is called Usoga on the map, and does not
form part of the British Protectorate, but neither
of these circumstances alter the fact that Uganda
and Usoga are ruled by the same king, that their
inhabitants speak the same language, and have
the same appearance, manners, and customs; in
fact, our Protectorate would be most accurately
described as one over Uganda, except Usoga.

Physically, however, the two countries do not
greatly resemble each other, for while Uganda is

(as will be seen later) for the most part a treeless country, destitute of any marked features, and, owing to an insufficient population, sparsely cultivated, Usoga is well timbered, plentifully supplied with picturesque masses of rock and vegetation, and very fully brought under cultivation.

The road through it is a narrow lane passing between a succession of banana plantations, from which it is cut off by high hedges affording a pleasant shade; while instead of journeying, as is the case in Uganda, often for a long day's march without seeing a human habitation, in Usoga little clusters of huts peep through the bananas at almost every turn of the road.

Blessed in their country, however, the people of Usoga are placed at a great disadvantage by their exclusion from the Protectorate. In Uganda, although the native law has not been changed, it is administered under the eye of British officials, to the detriment and probably disgust of the king and chiefs, but to the great benefit of the peasants. Usoga, however, is left to the mercies of Mwanga and his myrmidons, and although he and they would, of course, be brought to book, were any flagrant act of injustice reported, it is very difficult, in the absence of resident English officers on the spot, to bring anything of the sort home, and there is little doubt that the Usoga chiefs are unmercifully bled by Mwanga's tax-collectors. Odd though it may appear to be at first sight, this treatment is by no means regarded by them as an evil, and nothing is further from their wishes than the establishment of a proper administration in their midst. The explanation of this is that it is only by the help of the king's Mbaka, or emissary, that they are enabled to squeeze their retainers. Failing the presence of that official, the people refuse to pay up; but supposing that Mwanga has demanded say 100 head of cattle from a certain district, the Mbaka arrives with all pomp and dignity, demands 200, and the chief of the district, parading the Mbaka as an authority for his demand, collects 300, and everybody is contented except the unfortunate peasants.

This independence of English rule, coupled with the dislike of the chiefs to the impartiality of our justice, has made them rather difficult to deal with, and I had later to persuade Mwanga to replace some of the more obnoxious ones. At present, our water communication between Berkeley Bay and Port Alice being so uncertain, most caravans pass through Usoga, and it is necessary for their safety that the Wasoga chiefs should not think that any crime may be commuted by a suitable present to the king; but I hope it will not be long before we have steam launches regularly running across the lake, and then, as far as our merely selfish interests are concerned, the attitude of the Wasoga chiefs will be a matter of indifference. Nor do I look upon Usoga as of much importance from the point of view of colonisation; its soil is neither better nor worse than that of Uganda, and as the latter country is far less thickly populated, land could be acquired there more easily than in Usoga, and in sufficient quantities, at all events to meet the requirements of the present generation of colonists.

By nine next morning we found ourselves at Wakoli's, still so called after the late chief whose headquarters it was. Although his son, a poor creature, has lost most of his father's power, the place is still of importance as being in the middle of a good food district, and as such is a favourite halting-place of caravans. We halted for a quarter of an hour in a large stockaded enclosure, chiefly remarkable for the number of grey parrots which it contained;

the Usoga forests are full of these birds, which are taken down in large quantities by porters returning to the coast.

My men did not at all like such a breach of convention as passing this place without even making one night's halt, and when, at about three in the afternoon, we found ourselves at nowhere in particular, in the middle of a heavy thunderstorm, they began first to look very reproachfully at me, and then, one by one, to slink away into the banana groves. I pushed on myself till sunset, and then, as the tents and most of my baggage had disappeared, took refuge for the night in a native village, where I was most hospitably entertained, and the population got drunk in honour of my visit.

The hut in which I put up was of the same sort of beehive shape as the Kavirondo one, but contained a great deal more woodwork, and, instead of being supported by a single pole in the middle, was propped in all directions. The outer mud wall of the Kavirondo hut was replaced by a circle of posts, across which reeds were lashed horizontally to hold the thatch of the walls, while the roof near the entrance was raised on props to form a porch, so that one could enter the hut in a fairly upright position. This was an advantage ; but altogether, in spite of the superior civilisation of the Wasoga, their huts did not seem to me so neat as those of their ruder neighbours.

Like that of the Waganda, the Wasoga dress consists of a large sheet of bark cloth thrown toga-fashion over one shoulder, and leaving the other arm free; they as a rule have no head covering and go barefooted. The chiefs, however, of both countries have taken to an Arab dress of white calico, and wear a small turban of the same material, and are shod in spoon-shaped sandals fastened on by bands of beaver-skin.

A short march next morning brought us to the village of Lubwa, on the Napoleon Gulf, out of the north-west corner of which the Victoria Nile leaves the lake. Near this village is a station, then in charge of Mr. Grant, at which caravans halt while arrangements are being made for their conveyance in canoes to the Uganda shore.

Lubwa is the chief who actually carried out the orders of Mwanga for the execution of Bishop Hannington. I do not know what his personal views as to Europeans may have been at that time, or whether he carried out his orders *con amore* or otherwise, but he is certainly now most amiably disposed towards us, and as he is probably the only Wasoga chief who has steadily refused to pay Mwanga more than his fair share of taxes, there is little love lost between them. I look upon him as the most reliable native in or near the Protectorate. That this should be so is fortunate, as he owns a large number of war canoes, which have been very useful for transport purposes, and in the event of any disturbances placing the Sesse island canoes out of our reach, it might be convenient to have his fleet at our disposal.

The Uvuma group of islands also owe allegiance to Lubwa, and as these islands lie in the direct water route from Berkeley Bay to Port Alice, it is important that their inhabitants should be friendly. Unfortunately, owing to our having assisted the Waganda, in the Company's time, in an expedition against the Wavuma, a good deal of resentment was felt by the islanders against us,[1] and at the time of my arrival, boats or canoes containing Europeans could not safely put up on these islands. I am glad to say that before I left

---

[1] I do not question the general expediency of the Company's officer's action, but merely allude to one of the results.

Uganda, thanks chiefly to the exertions of Lubwa and Mr. Grant, that ill-feeling had entirely subsided, and we can now not only count on the Uvuma Islanders to supply us with canoes, but can reckon them among our best friends.

CHAPTER IV

UGANDA

LUBWA soon produced the canoes I required, so, after an hour's halt, I embarked, and slept for the night at Lugumbwa's, a village on the Uganda shore of the gulf. As we were very late in arriving, and our baggage was still behind, I put up in a native hut, by the fire in which Spire began to warm up a tin of soup and prepare a few provisions which we always carried with us. He had not had a mount since my second horse died, and I had noticed for the last day or two that he was getting more and more exhausted, and therefore was not particularly surprised to see him fall fast asleep over his cooking operations and nearly tumble into the fire. Thinking I could not do better than prescribe the remedy which I always take myself on such occasions, I poured him out a good big tot of whisky, and, wakening him up, made him swallow it ; but I suppose his constitution is different from mine, for instead of cheering up, as I expected, he simply subsided into a lifeless mass on the floor, from which I had a good deal of difficulty in carrying him on to a sort of raised platform near the wall. However, he got up from this next morning, apparently none the worse.

After a few hours through the outskirts of the Chagwe forest, we got into typical Uganda scenery. As will be seen by the map, all the principal rivers of northern Uganda rise within about ten miles of the lake and flow northward, only a few insignificant streams flowing into the lake. The watershed between these two systems is the top of a steep ridge, falling abruptly into the lake on one side, and into the great Bulamwezi plain on the other. The road leads over the northern spur of this ridge, crossing a succession of abrupt undulations, whose sides and summits are clothed in coarse grass, while in each boggy bottom grows a narrow belt of trees.

Judging from the surrounding countries, which are all heavily timbered, it is probable that Uganda was at one time covered with forest, which a large, industrious, but inartistic population cleared away, and that this population, overtaken by Nemesis, followed in the way of the trees, leaving huge tracts of staring, uncultivated ridge and furrow as a monument of their exertions. The latter stages of this process seem still to be in operation. On the outskirts of nearly every village, banana plants may be seen carrying on an unequal struggle for life with the overpowering grass, and testifying to the comparatively recent desertion of a *shamba*.

With so much waste land to be acquired for the asking, the destruction of trees has necessarily ceased on any wholesale scale, although, for the sake of firewood, canoe, and house building, a considerable amount of chopping still goes on, without, needless to say, any corresponding planting being done to fill up gaps. At present this is not a very serious matter, but when the country comes to be more thickly peopled by Europeans, and wood-consuming steam launches are plying on the lake, some sort of a " Woods and Forests Department " will have to be created, if we wish to spare Uganda the curse of utter treelessness.

I have mentioned the swampy bottoms of the

valleys, a subject which has already been written on by my predecessors, but only, I fear, with the result of conveying a false impression, on those, at all events, who wished to be falsely impressed. I have seen Uganda described as a " swamp and a desert," or a " swamp and a jungle " (two rather contradictory expressions), but exchanging desert and jungle for a better term, Uganda is not even a swamp and a *veldt*. As I have explained, the watershed ridge falls abruptly to the north and south, and in the former direction merges into the great Bulamwezi plain, across which the rivers flow over an easy gradient to the Nile or its tributary the Kafu. Partly owing to the slightness of the fall, but chiefly to want of artificial drainage on the hillsides, no great rush of water ever takes place to sweep away the weeds, and the rivers have consequently become choked with bulrushes and papyrus. It is through these masses of vegetation which the traveller has to wade, ankle, waist, or chest deep, and feeling no current, and seeing more vegetation than water, has named them "swamps." In the case of large streams like the Maanja, they may be 800 yards wide, in that of small ones they may be jumped over, but they are all the same in character, and are merely incidents, important or otherwise, in the landscape, not, as seems to be imagined, preponderating elements in it. With the advent of scientific agriculture and consequent drainage, and the expenditure of a certain amount of labour in cutting a channel through the weeds, there is no reason why steam launches or stern wheelers should not run from the neighbourhood of Kampala down the Maanja and Kafu rivers to Fovira on the Victoria Nile. Yet a traveller crossing either of these rivers at any point of their course would probably state that he had passed a bad swamp.

This watershed also has a considerable effect on the climate of Uganda; the prevailing winds being from the lake, the moisture with which they are laden is deposited on its southern slope, and it consequently has a far damper climate than other parts of the Protectorate. Unfortunately both for administrative reasons and for convenience of communication, English officials are at present chiefly concentrated on the littoral, with the depressing results to which I have already alluded. This necessity, however, will not apply to colonists, who would probably prefer the rich plains of Bulamwezi or the highlands of Singo, enjoying in the former a drier climate at an elevation of about 4000 feet above the sea, and in the latter the cool air obtainable at a height of 6000 feet.

I had been much interested and amused since we entered Usoga by the peculiar manner of greeting of natives whom we had seen meeting each other on the road. When about twenty yards from each other a short preliminary conversation takes place, which is quickly closed by one of the travellers saying " Eh," a remark which the other answers by a similar one, which is then repeated by the first, taken up by the second, and continued by each in turn, until the voices die away in feeble grunts from the summits of neighbouring hills.

It was explained to me afterwards that this form of salutation is due to extreme politeness. The first traveller saying, " How are you ? " the second replies, " It is I who should ask how you are," to which the first answers, " NO." " NO," replies the second, " NO " the first, and so on, " NO," " NO," " NO," " NO," "NO," until their protests are lost in the distance, and each goes on his way as ignorant as when they met of the state of his friend's health.

On the second day from the Napoleon Gulf, I

had pushed on ahead, always expecting to come on some convenient camping-ground, but found nothing, until half an hour after sunset we walked into a group of native huts. As I had no idea where the porters were, I determined to stop and wait for them, making myself as comfortable as I could in the meanwhile. This degree of comfort was not very great; it had been pouring all day, and I was wet through, all my wraps and provisions were behind, and my boots were too wet to take off; so I sat by a very poor fire of damp wood, and thought of my sins. After about two hours of this amusement, the porters not having turned up, I remembered that I had had nothing to eat but some raisins and a biscuit since four in the morning, and began to think seriously of ordering dinner, and was considerably annoyed to find that the menu consisted of about half a cupful of sour milk. However, as I remarked to Spire, this was a better supper than one generally gets at an English railway station, so, after scrupulously dividing it into two portions (I was sadly tempted not to play fair), we retired to what, for want of a better term, I must call rest; but the thing was not a success; the fire would not burn, my clothes would not dry, I kept wishing that they would look sharp and bring the joint, and out of sheer sympathy the mosquitoes seemed anxious to let me know that they were exceptionally hungry.

Take it all round, I was very glad (and I think Spire shared my sentiments) when the day broke, and we were able to proceed towards Kampala, which we could now see about five miles off.

After marching for about half an hour, I was handed a letter by a native, who proved to be Mr. Arthur's cook, whom that officer had kindly sent to meet me with materials for making breakfast.

It turned out that my porters had passed our halting-place and had pushed on to Kampala, which they had reached at about midnight, and that Mr. Arthur, hearing that I had no provisions with me, had very thoughtfully taken early steps to supply the deficiency.

As we descended into the valley on the farther slope of which Kampala fort is situated, I saw the troops turning out ready to receive me ; and, feeling that I was not looking my best either as regards clothes or features, began polishing myself up as well as I could, and was just beginning to feel that although I was not exactly smart, an imaginative man might guess at the possibility of better things beneath the dirt, when my horse gave a flounder in a boggy stream, which I had been too pre-occupied to notice, and landed me fair on my head in a pool of black mud. Two minutes afterwards, with bugles sounding, drums beating, and the troops presenting arms, I entered the head-quarters of my command, returning the salute with what dignity I could, and then hurriedly rushed into Arthur's hut and plunged my head into a basin of clean water.

CHAPTER V

KAMPALA

Kampala—Dr. Moffat—Hopes for a new broom—Sanitation—
Architecture — Hæmaturic fever — Jiggers — Behaviour of
Kikukuri—Treatment of Kikukuri—Call on Mwanga—His
appearance and character—The palace—Types of chiefs—
An impertinent snake — His fate — Waganda horsemen —
Judicial functions—Order in court—Peculiarities of evidence
—Questions of defence—A savage mode of torture—Decad-
ence of Europeans—Driven out by the *shauri*.

THE capital of Uganda is built on four hills,
Mengo, Rubaga, Namirembi and Kampala,
the three first being occupied by the king and the
Catholic and Protestant missions respectively, while
the last was selected by the officers of the Company
as the site for their fort.   It is commanded on all
sides, but in the absence of any possible hostile
artillery, the position is probably quite good
enough from a military point of view, though its
sanitary aspects caused all doctors who saw it to
begin making arrangements for turning in their
graves.

Doctor Moffat seemed to have made considerable advances in this direction, for he was lying dangerously ill when I arrived, and his state caused Arthur great uneasiness; but one of the missionaries who knew something of doctoring was kindly looking after him, and pulled him through.

Two days after, a stranger walking into the room, whom I took to be one of the missionaries, I asked him if he had come to see the doctor, but he replied, " I am the doctor," and at once began to tackle me on the subject of sanitation, and the necessity of building a hospital hut. I suppose he hoped that something might be got out of a new broom, but even that useful instrument cannot create tools and men, and I was for the time as powerless as my predecessors to do any useful work in this direction. A few days after, he started off to visit Purkiss, who was lying dangerously ill in Kavirondo, and only returned just in time to join the Unyoro expedition.

The fort itself consists of an irregular stockade of wild date-palm stems surrounded by a small ditch; inside it are dotted about the storehouses and officers' quarters, all full of jiggers, and all with thatched roofs and rough mud walls, perforated by many little windows warranted to let in the minimum of light and the maximum of through draughts.

As the causes which produce a cold in England generally bring on an attack of fever, with me, in the tropics, I believe that the structural peculiarities of these huts had more to do with the fever which I always got at Kampala than my friend the boggy stream, which was always pointed out to me as a source of danger. I admit, however, that this was far from perfect, either as a neighbour or a source of water supply. It half encircled Kampala hill, which was clothed every morning in the cold smelly mist which arose from it; while, as the Swahili camp was pitched on the slope between it and the fort, it is pretty certain that every thunderstorm washed into it a good deal of matter which medical authorities tell one is out of place in drinking water.

Hæmaturic fever and jiggers are the two principal curses of Uganda. Malarial fever is of course a nuisance, and I daresay that repeated attacks of it undermine one's constitution, but it has not the same serious immediate effects as the other two, and will probably die out when we get better sanitation and drainage. Hæmaturic fever, however, generally kills after the third, or, at all events, fourth attack, and so little is known about it, that so far doctors have been unable to suggest any preventive measures. It is known to be a disease of the kidneys, and that Hazeline is the best remedy for it, but that appears to be about the sum of our knowledge on the subject.

The jigger, though less serious in quality, is even more so in quantity, for he attacks all sorts and conditions of men alike, and, insignificant little bug though he be, is capable of stopping the march of an army, or starving out a fort by incapacitating the porters who should supply it. He is very small, very active, and is credited with having the power to bore through a pair of thick shooting-boots, but I rather doubt this, and fancy that he gets inside by the, to him, easier way over the top; but whatever the exact route which he may choose may be, there is no doubt that he does get inside, and proceeds to play mischief when he has done so. His (or perhaps I should say her—I am not well up in these matters) motives are doubtless highly praiseworthy, being none other than those induced by that beautiful maternal instinct which we all so much admire when it does not interfere with our own comfort. Unlike the cruel flea thirsting for human blood, the jigger mother is actuated by no base desire to satisfy her own appetites, but when she buries herself at the edge of one's toe-nail, is merely seeking a haven of rest in which to deposit the little ones she is about to bring into the world. Unfortunately there is something about these little ones or their mamma which does not agree with toe-nails, and after a few hours they make their presence felt by producing a violent irritation. After feeling this, the man whom experience has made knowing in these matters will wait a day, and then, calling his boy, tell him, if he is a Swahili, to take out the *funza*, if a Sudanese, the *dūd;* then the operator will squat on the floor, and, taking a needle out of his cap, proceed to dig a trench round the black spot which marks the entrance to the jigger's nest. If he is a fairly good hand at his work, and it is done at this stage, he ought, after a few minutes, to pull out a little white bag, which is carefully burnt, and if some iodiform ointment is then rubbed into the sore, the chances are that no great harm has been done to anybody but the jigger. Sometimes, however, it happens that the preliminary itching is not noticed, and the bag is allowed to grow until it attains the size of a pea and produces a sore; then a very big hole has to be dug, and, unless the extractor is a real artist the nest is very likely to be brought out in bits, and possibly a few eggs left behind. Then a big ulcer forms, the toe-nail comes off, and the victim of the jigger's maternal instincts has to hobble about on one leg for several weeks to come. In spite of all precautions, this happened to me four or five times during my sojourn in Uganda, and is continually befalling the Swahilis, who never wash, and whom nothing short of a man standing over them with a thick stick will induce to take any precaution, or even give themselves the trouble of attending to sores that a camel could hardly disregard. In the absence of doctors, it is the privilege of station commandants to attend to these, and I remember that one of my officers, in addition to his other duties, had at one time to dress sixty of these abominations every morning before breakfast. So extraordinarily careless are some of the Swahilis, that two of them actually allowed jigger sores to spread until mortification or the strain on their system killed them, and many lost one or more toes.

After breakfast and a wash, I had a good talk with Arthur on the state of affairs. Captain Macdonald, he told me, was on his way to Berkeley Bay and Lubwa's in the boat, so that if I had not been in such a hurry, I should have met him ; however, I did not so much regret this, as during his absence some serious news had come in from Major Owen, in command of the Singo district, to the effect that Kikukuri, one of the principal chiefs of Kabarega, king of Unyoro, was threatening our frontier fort in Singo, and killing any of the inhabitants whom he caught supplying us with food. I at once sent a message to Owen, asking him to come in and discuss the situation.

On the 14th of November he turned up, accompanied by M. Decle, a French traveller, who had made a remarkable journey from the Cape, and whom he had found at Port 'Alice. I settled with Owen that he was to get back as soon as possible, collect 200 men at Fort Grant (the frontier fort), and, by making a night march, try to surprise Kikukuri.

Two days afterwards Macdonald arrived, five days later than he had expected, having been becalmed on the lake. He handed over his commission, and consented to stay on for a short time to assist me. In the meanwhile, I had been interviewing the king, chiefs, and notabilities, native and European.

My first call was on Mwanga, the king. I had heard so much against him that I confess that I was agreeably disappointed both in his manner and appearance. His face is a weak one, with half-covered, fishlike eyes, a rather squat nose, and a drooping mouth, but it shows no very marked signs either of cruelty or debauchery, and the points which impressed me most were his extreme nervousness and efforts to appear pleasing. He is a wretchedly weak creature, utterly self-indulgent, a prey to timidity, and swayed by the opinion of the last comer; but after many opportunities of studying him carefully in all his many moods, I am inclined to think that he is not quite as black as he has been painted, and that, politically, at all events, he is harmless, and fairly satisfied with our rule. Of course we have to limit his power in many ways that are distasteful to him, and in fits of temper he may say things about us, the expression of which is encouraged by our enemies, and reported to us by his; but I believe that his leading characteristic is timidity, and that most of his acts are prompted by the desire to escape some imaginary danger.

The palace consists of a number of detached buildings, each standing in a separate enclosure walled with high reeds, and the whole surrounded by a fourteen-feet-high fence of the same material.

The building in which I was received was a room some sixty feet long by forty broad and thirty high, completely open at one end, and with an arched reed roof supported by a double row of wild date-palm pillars. The mud floor was strewn with freshly cut grass. The king was sitting in a large gilt arm chair, presented to him by the I.B.E.A. Company, with his feet on a leopard-skin rug spread over a square of Brussels carpet. He was dressed in Arab costume, over which he wore a light grey tweed jacket; he had a small turban on his head, and Waganda sandals on his bare feet. Like all his race, his hands and feet were beautifully small and neatly kept.

Ranged along the walls to the king's right and left were his chiefs and retainers, the principal among the former being the Protestant and Catholic Katikiros, the Makwenda, chief of Singo, and the Kangao, chief of Bulamwezi.

Katikiro, or agent, is the term given to the principal headman of any chief, and in the case of the king this official performs the duties assigned in the East to the Grand Vizier. Formerly only one person held this office, but by an arrangement made by Sir Gerald Portal between the Catholic and Protestant parties, each of these sects was to be represented by a Katikiro, whose duty it was to try the cases of his co-religionists, and be responsible for order in the districts assigned to them.

People who are accustomed to look upon the "nigger" as an unvarying type, modelled on the appearance of "Mr. Bones," both as regards dress and features, would have been surprised at the four very distinct individualities of these chiefs. Apollo, the Protestant Katikiro, is a great round-faced, boyish-looking creature, a good six feet high, with a swinging walk, a cheery smile, and a very cordial manner; as an Englishman, he would probably be taken for the captain of a football team. On state occasions he generally wears a Royal Artillery tunic over his Arab dress, and occasionally indulges in European abominations in the way of headgear. He is a remarkably strong and able man, and possibly somewhat of a schemer.

Magwania, the Catholic Katikiro, is rather a shrivelled old man with a restrained manner, except when he loses his temper, and wholly lacking Apollo's originality and go, but with a fund of perseverance which makes up for other deficiencies; he is, I believe, a thoroughly honest man, and fills his rather difficult position very satisfactorily. Some gratitude is due to him for discarding European embellishments from his costume.

The Makwenda is a wiry, middle-aged man, with a keen, clever face, an independent manner, and distinctly conveys the impression of a thoroughly practical man, who knows his own mind. He has the reputation of being the most go-ahead landed proprietor in the country; his religious views are said to be rather shaky; and he is not wholly free from suspicion of doing a little slave-trading on the quiet.

The Kangao is an earnest, tubby little man, in every sense, for his figure is barrel-shaped, and his manner raises reminiscences of coloured gentlemen in frock-coats and large white ties, who preach of salvation in Hyde Park, their feet planted on receptacles of the compound which they tell us leads the other way. He has a cooing way of talking, and a deep respect for all constituted authority and any orders that come from the "Queeni" or her representatives. He is an able and energetic little man, and, I believe, rules his large province very well. He did excellent work for me during the Unyoro Expedition, but I always found it rather difficult to take him seriously.

Shortly after my arrival on the 7th, I had received a message from the king, begging me not to be alarmed if I saw a great number of people about with spears, as his horse had been bitten and killed by a snake, and he had turned the population out to slay the reptile. I took the opportunity of this visit to condole with him on the loss of his horse, and ask if the snake had been killed. He replied that it had, at which news I expressed my satisfaction, but felt some doubt whether the real guilty serpent had suffered the extreme penalty, and had not rather allowed some innocent kinsman to be executed in his place.

It really does not very much matter whether a Waganda chief's horse is killed by a snake or not, for he is sure to kill him himself in a very few weeks. Of course the Waganda peasant knows no more of how to treat horses than Tommy Atkins does of "vetting" camels, while the chiefs look upon them as mere galloping machines. It is therefore not to be wondered at that the European traders, who bring up ten-pound ponies and sell them for a hundred and fifty, do a brisk trade, and take down much ivory.

Two days after Macdonald arrived, I had to exercise for the first time my judicial function, the court sitting in my office in the fort. The king was present, and, the first case being a land dispute between a Protestant and a Catholic, the two Katikiros were also in attendance.

The case was on the question of the occupation of certain Protestant lands by a Catholic chief, the Protestant holding that they had been forcibly seized after Sir Gerald Portal's partition, by which they had been declared to belong to the Protestants; the Catholic, on the other hand, claiming that he had been in possession of them some time before the partition. As no one could say within a month when the occupation took place, I dismissed the case of unlawful seizure, but said that the Catholic was evidently now in possession of lands which did not belong to him, and that he had better clear out.

This decision was received with the Waganda equivalent for cheers, which consists in clasping the two hands together, striking them repeatedly on the ground, and emitting sepulchral groans. In the absence of that official, these manifestations of approval were not " promptly suppressed by the usher." I am afraid an usher or any other officially-minded person would have a very bad time of it in a Waganda court. I made some feeble attempts at first to reduce the proceedings to something like order, but soon found that it was very much better to let them go on in their own ways, which consist in everybody—king, katikiros, witnesses, prisoner, and spectators—all talking at once and explaining their views on any subject, whether relevant to the case or not, that may strike their fancy. I think the idea of the prisoner, defendant or claimant, as the case may be, is not so much to produce evidence as to the facts under consideration, as to show that he is an important person, in whose favour it should be given ; while his friends, with the same idea in view, think that the best way of helping him is to show that his is the noisiest side.

Gradually, after many months, as the idea seemed to dawn on them that I was introducing the startling innovation of judging a case on its own merits, they became less demonstrative, and before I left, the court was conducted in a way which, although it would have undoubtedly turned a regular magistrate's hair grey, would not have actually lifted it off his head.

The Waganda ideas on evidence and the manner of giving it were to the last a fearful trial. Nothing could persuade them that second-hand evidence was in any way inferior to first. After having been duly sworn, and having enumerated the events of his life from his early childhood, and all the incidents on his journey to the neighbourhood of (say) the murder, a witness would state that here he met a man driving three bullocks and a flock of goats, and wearing a dilapidated bark cloth, who told him that he had heard that a murder had been committed in the neighbourhood. Then a triumphant smile would creep over the prosecutor's face, the prisoner would clearly show his knowledge that his doom was sealed; and if, failing any other evidence, I pronounced a verdict of "Not guilty," all would sorrowfully depart, convinced that a grave miscarriage of justice had taken place.

I tried at first to somewhat curtail the early reminiscences of witnesses, but soon found that interruption only led to their starting again at the very beginning. I am told that hypnotic subjects cannot make use of a mental flying machine and jump straight to the scene of their investigations, but have to be led carefully, with the aid of Bradshaw and the Ordnance Survey, by the recognised route; the Waganda must have minds somewhat similar to those of these unfortunate persons. They seem unable to leap at one bound from the court-house to the locality they are called on to describe, but in order to reach the latter, must retrace each step which took them there.

After finishing the land dispute, I had my first experience of one of these criminal cases, —an attempted murderous assault,—and the fact that a sharp attack of fever had just come on did not much help me in unravelling its many intricacies.

The evidently hostile attitude of Kabarega, as shown by the conduct of his chief Kikukuri, who certainly would not have acted without orders, forced me to turn my attention to questions of defence; and after going thoroughly into the matter with Macdonald, I was soon convinced that the means at our disposal were hazardously insufficient, and that I must set to work on making a complete catalogue of our requirements for the information of the home authorities.

I had already halted the outgoing mail in Kavirondo to wait for my despatches, but I had no wish to keep it indefinitely, a course which seemed likely to be forced on me as long as I stayed at Kampala and spent my days and nights in interminable *shauris.* I do not like using foreign words when English ones do as well, and have no patience with people who call their breakfasts *déjeuners*, and their relations *bêtes*, but *shauri* is a word as impossible to express correctly in English as *harikari.* It is a peculiar African mode of torture, which consists in conveying the smallest possible amount of information in the greatest possible number of words, and when you have got to the end, starting again at the beginning. I am sorry to say it seems to find favour with Europeans who have been long in the country, and some of them become quite as proficient in it as the natives.

Sir Gerald Portal had discovered that anything like serious work was made impossible at Kampala by the prevalence of this custom, and having retired to Ntebbi, a pretty peninsula about twenty miles off, to work in peace, he was so struck with its advantages that he had determined to make it the headquarters of the administration. To this place Macdonald and I went on the 24th of November.

CHAPTER VI

PREPARATIONS FOR WAR

Arrival of the caravan—Sudanese troops—Their "uniform"—Port Alice—Deceptive promise—Kabarega, his words and deeds—A nightmare—Unpleasant rumours—I decide on action—Tall talk—Position of affairs—Mwanga's religious views—Missionary work—Hitting two birds—Return to Kampala—Owen's victory—Surprise of the Waganda—Declaration of war—Choice of a commander-in-chief—Mwanga's little pleasantness—And mine—Afternoon tea—Spire's royal guest—An informal reception—Mwanga's faith—"Excursions and alarms"—The steel boat—The observatory—Kakunguru—Concentration of troops—Preparations complete—Mwanga's promise—Movements of the enemy—Leave Gibb in charge.

MY caravan, with Muxworthy, Gibb, and Thruston, had arrived at Kampala a few days before my departure, and I had at once packed off the last-named to Port Alice, as our headquarter at Ntebbi had been christened by Sir Gerald Portal. I found him hard at work drilling the troops, who struck me as being unexpectedly efficient, although the character of their costumes would have prevented an impartial critic from describing them as "smart." These consisted of pairs

VIEW FROM THE FORT, PORT ALICE

(*To face page* 67)

of calico drawers, pretty equally discoloured (my military eye was gratified at this one item of uniformity), either calico tunics, cut to suit the taste of the wearer, or faded blue jerseys in varying stages of decay; while the heads of the minority were adorned with worn-out "tarbushes," the majority wearing broad-brimmed straw hats of native make, decked with the feathers of the golden-crested crane. The latter were rather picturesque, but unfortunately of every conceivable size and pattern. The troops were armed with "Remington" or "Snider" rifles, both in rather an advanced stage of disrepair.

The station at Port Alice is situated on two hills, connected by a saddle, on the higher and more northern of which are the stores and European quarters, the southern one being occupied by the large, neatly laid out village in which the Sudanese troops and their families live. A fine panoramic view of the surrounding country and the lake, dotted with islands, is thence obtained, and at first sight the position seems a good defensible one, and likely to be healthy. A few days' residence, however, and a closer inspection, shows that the position is surrounded with "dead ground," and would be difficult to defend, except with a large force; while some beautiful stretches of what appears at a distance to be green turf, at the foot of the hill, are in reality shallow arms of the lake, hidden by the growth of rushes, from which, in the early morning, a cold miasmic mist creeps over the hilltop. I soon made up my mind that, both from a military and sanitary point of view, the station would be better at a lower level, and as little had been done beyond the erection of some thatched storehouses and officers' huts, I ordered the discontinuance of further work until I was able to select another site.

Undisturbed by *shauri*-ists, I got through a good deal of useful work during the first few days of my stay at Port Alice, but on the 1st of December I got news which forced me to return at once to Kampala. It was to the effect that Kabarega, king of Unyoro, had sent large armies to make simultaneous attacks on Toru on the west and Usoga on the east. This news was sent me by the Katikiro Apollo. Shortly afterwards two other messengers arrived, one from Mwanga, enclosing a letter in Arabic, which he had just received from Kabarega, and for a translation of which he asked, and another from

Gibb, whom I had left in command of Kampala, bringing to my notice a rumour that Mwanga and Kabarega were going to combine and turn us out of the country.

I happened to be in the middle of an attack of fever when I received these various items of news, so I sent for Macdonald, and, handing him the correspondence, tucked my head again under the blankets, and devoted myself to my shivering fit. When I woke up, after the hot stage, I could not for the life of me make out whether I had had a nightmare, or had really received some news, and it was not until I had seen Macdonald that I was enlightened on this point.

Whatever Mwanga's private sympathies might be, I did not think it likely that he would willingly allow himself to be swallowed by Unyoro for the sake of getting rid of us, nor did I think that his chiefs and people had any dislike to our presence. Nevertheless, Gibb's news was worth careful consideration.

As to my action with regard to Kabarega, I had no doubts. Setting aside all his previous acts of hostility, for which it might or might not be desirable to punish him, I had now to face the plain fact that he was at that moment invading the kingdom of Kasagama, whom Captain Lugard had placed on the throne of Toru, and the province of Usoga, a part of the kingdom of Mwanga, to whom Sir Gerald Portal had promised provisional protection.   Apart from the fact that, were Kabarega's armies to be successful, the two flanks of Uganda proper would be threatened, I felt that I could not allow such acts of open hostility to pass unnoticed, without damaging our prestige as a power whose friendship was worth counting on.   I therefore determined at once to march on Kabarega's capital, and there, if possible, dictate to him terms of peace, which would safeguard us from his aggressions in the future.   I accordingly wrote him a letter, in which, after enumerating his various hostile acts, I announced that I should march at once on his country, and that, unless in the meanwhile he had sent me guarantees for his good conduct in the future, and a substantial indemnity for damage done in the past, I and my army would be across his frontier within twenty-one days of the date of writing.

This was very "tall talk," for my army, of

which I spoke so grandly, consisted of 700 men, distributed as follows :—

Usoga, 100.

Kampala, 200.

Port Alice, 150.

Singo, 250;

with barely one hundred rounds of ammunition per man.

If I could have taken the greater part of these men with me, I should not have had too big a force with which to tackle Kabarega, who was said to have 8000 guns and rifles and 20,000 spearmen ; but with his armies to the right and left of me, I could not leave Usoga and Singo unprotected ; while, in the face of Gibb's news, I should not have been justified in leaving Uganda wholly unguarded, and facing the possibility of finding myself between the two fires of Mwanga and Kabarega.

A more serious matter still, was the religious attitude of the king, a monarch of very varying convictions, who then seemed to be strongly inclined towards Roman Catholicism. Under normal circumstances, it would have been a matter of indifference to anyone but himself in which form of faith he repented of his vices, but under the peculiar conditions of Uganda at that time, it was very desirable to avoid any change in his views. Had he become a Catholic, a large proportion of his subjects would have gone over with him, and consequently, the provinces set aside for Catholics becoming insufficient for them, they would have at once clamoured for more land, a request which would have been vigorously refused by the Protestants.

The Protestants, on the other hand, loving Mwanga but little at the best of times, would probably have tried to dethrone him.

Given two factions, spoiling for a fight, and the withdrawal of the troops, such a state of affairs could only have had one result—a civil war. The first news of this would have obliged me to return from Unyoro at once, closely followed by Kabarega, who, elated with what he would believe to be my weakness, would certainly have pushed on into Uganda, to find that country practically defenceless in the throes of internecine warfare.

In this state of affairs there were obviously only two things to be done: (1) to undertake a little missionary work on my own account, and convince Mwanga of the beauties, spiritual or otherwise, of the Protestant faith; and (2), in the event of my exhortations not having a very permanent effect, to make it as difficult as possible for the Waganda to cut each other's throats.

Now it was clear that the fewer Waganda there were in the country, the fewer throats there would be to cut, and the fewer people to cut them, and the greater the proportionate strength of the small garrison I wished to leave behind; so, having grasped this, I made up my mind to take the fighting population of the country with me, a course which also would have the advantage of giving me a larger army with which to attack Kabarega.

Having settled all this, and issued the necessary orders for collection of food, and instructions to the various officers concerned, I started off for Kampala, where I received a report from Owen, informing me of the complete success of his expedition against Kikukuri.

After a very trying night march, often having to wade chest-deep, he came upon the Wanyoro, whom, after three hours' hard fighting, he completely defeated. As the enemy were chiefly concealed in long grass (or reeds) he had found firing to be of little use, and had taken position after position in a series of bayonet charges. He was accompanied by Lieutenant Villiers (Royal Horse Guards) and M. Decle.

This victory was a great surprise to the Waganda, who, knowing Kikukuri to have a very large force at his disposal, had confidently expected Owen's defeat. That 200 Sudanese should have defeated so many thousand Wanyoro was looked upon as a very marvellous performance, and added greatly to their prestige, and on the strength of this I convened a great meeting of chiefs to announce the declaration of war.

The meeting took place on the 4th of December, and, having read Owen's report, I explained my position with regard to Uganda and Unyoro, and telling the chiefs that I intended to attack Kabarega, called upon the king to assemble his army to co-operate with me. I have frequently been told that this co-operation was the last thing he wanted; but be that as it may, he made no objections, and orders were at once issued for the war-drum to be sounded throughout the land.

This business over, the selection of a commander - in - chief for the Waganda army had to be discussed. Mwanga was averse to his appointment altogether, suggesting that the various chiefs should be under my direct command, but having already had some experience of the conversational powers of the Waganda, I was determined to have direct dealings with one person only, and insisted on a single channel of communication between myself and my allies.

The process of selection was the cause of a good deal of " chaff " on the part of Mwanga, who in turn, with much giggling and poking in the ribs, asked all his most useless favourites whether they would not like a place in the forefront of the battle. His gaiety was temporarily rather damped by my suggesting that there could be no more kingly duty than that of the post under discussion. For a moment his brown skin turned an ashy grey, and the beads of perspiration started out on his forehead, until, seeing, I suppose, a twinkle in my eye, he burst out laughing, and frankly owned that he preferred to be in a safe place. Finally, the honour was conferred on Kakunguru, a member of the royal Wahuma race, who had held a similar post in the Mohammedan war, and to whom the king at once administered the oath of fidelity.

This over, Mwanga's spirits knew no bounds,

and on his hearing that Macdonald and I were going to the front, he, with shrieks of laughter, went through pantomimic representations of all the more unpleasant incidents of a battle. He then insisted on my telling him stories of bloody wars, which I did with so many gruesome details that he expressed himself more delighted than ever that I was going to the front and that he was going to stay behind.

All this while sloppy tea was being handed round in three old battered enamelled iron cups (all we had), which, as soon as they had been emptied by the three most important persons, were filled for the next, a little more water being added to the black kettle in which the brew was concocted. I do not know what the last recipients thought of it, but they, fortunately, were not ill on the spot.

This important business finished, I had conducted the king to the door, and was having a minute's chat with Kakunguru, when I was surprised to see His Majesty going off with a little Swahili imp called Juma, who acted as Spire's assistant. As I supposed he knew his own business better than I could, I did not interfere until I saw him being led to the back of the shed in which Spire had pitched his tent, and caught sight first of a soapy and astonished face and then of a naked white man's bust appearing round the corner to meet him. I then grasped the situation, and rushed to the rescue. It turned out that Spire, who was performing his evening ablutions, and whose knowledge of Swahili was at that time rather limited, had tried to ask Juma which was the king, and that his request for information had been misinterpreted into an order to bring the monarch to him, and that the little wretch had trotted off and boldly dragged Mwanga after him.

Early next morning, having just tumbled out of bed, I was wandering about the fort in my pyjamas, when Mwanga made his appearance all alone, saying that he had an important matter which he wished to discuss with me privately. This turned out to be his unalterable intention to at once embrace the Catholic faith; so, in my rather unofficial costume and on an empty stomach, I had to turn my attention for two hours to this very weighty matter, with the result that he left vowing that he would remain faithful to Protestantism, at all events until my return from the war. I confess that I had some slight doubts on this point, which were strengthened by my receiving in the afternoon a long letter from Monseigneur Hirth, the Roman Catholic bishop, bringing to my notice the king's true conversion to Catholicism, and urging me not to interfere with that liberty of religion which it was the boast of Great Britain to uphold.

Between these announcements came a visit from an important chief, who told me, "on the highest authority," that the king had forbidden the Catholics to join my force, and that when I and the Protestants were safely out of the way, he and the Catholics were going to make things warm all round. Altogether, it was a lively day, and I was glad to get to bed. I see an entry in my diary for next day (December 8th): "No bombs, thunderbolts, or other missiles dropped on me to-day. Kakunguru looked in in the morning and took such a hopeful view of affairs, that I passed the rest of the day awaiting some awful catastrophe, but it did not come off."

During the next few days the fight for the king's soul went on merrily, and this, with preparations for the war and despatches for home, kept me pretty well occupied.

As soon as I had settled to attack Kabarega, I decided to take with me the steel rowing boat which we had on the lake, in case he should take to the islands of the Nile or Albert Lake, and sent word to Mr. Purkiss (an ex-sailor) to come and take charge of her. He arrived on the 9th, having been seriously ill with hæmaturic fever when my message reached him, and even after his arrival at Kampala was hardly fit to travel. He, however, went off to Mununyu (the port of Kampala) on the following day, and on the morning of the 11th marched into Kampala with her, divided into sections, each of which was carried slung on a pole by two men.

Among our minor preparations was a field observatory, made tripod fashion with three long bamboos, and which I hoped would be high enough to enable a man to see over the tall grass; but although it placed a man's feet twelve feet above the ground, we found when we got to Unyoro that it was practically useless, the grass often reaching well above the observer's head.

In all these preparations Macdonald was of the greatest help to me, and Kakunguru saved me an immensity of trouble by the intelligent arrangements which he made for the concentration of his army on the frontier. This was no light task. The frontier district, in which I had decided that the concentration was to take place, was thinly populated, and poorly supplied with food, and would not support for long the force of 16,000 men that Kakunguru hoped to collect; it was therefore necessary that the concentration should be as nearly as possible simultaneous, so as to allow of the army moving on at once to fresh feeding grounds in Unyoro. As troops were being collected from districts as much as two hundred miles apart, separated by foodless tracts, and connected by only the merest apology for roads, this required a considerable amount of organisation, and I cannot speak too highly of the way in which Kakunguru carried it out.

By the 12th all our preparations were complete, and on the evening of that day Thruston marched in with the Port Alice detachment. The king had renewed his promise not to change his religion during my absence, and Monseigneur Hirth had also agreed to let the matter stand over until my return. Satisfactory news kept coming in as to the enrolment of troops, and everything seemed to be progressing favourably.

My chief anxiety now was with regard to the attitude of Kabarega, as to which the most contradictory opinions were expressed on every side.

Some authorities were certain that he would make a determined stand on the Kafu; others that he would defend his capital to the last; others again were sure that he would retire to Mruli and fight with his back to the Nile, or move in the opposite direction to the islands of the Albert Lake. The Budonga and Bugoma forests were also mentioned as convenient districts into which he might retire, and thence carry on a guerilla warfare. As I was anxious to get the war over as soon as possible, I sincerely hoped that he would adopt one of the two first-mentioned courses, but in this, as will be seen, I was destined to be disappointed.

I settled to take with me 400 Sudanese troops, leaving 300 to take care of Uganda; of these 100 were to remain in Usoga, 100 at Kampala, 50 at Port Alice, and 50 in Singo. As I had no troops to spare for a line of communication, I expected to be completely cut off from Uganda, of which I left Gibb in charge, after thoroughly discussing with him the line of action to be taken in the event of any change of religion on Mwanga's part causing disturbances.

CHAPTER VII

THE CONCENTRATION ON THE FRONTIER

Marching-out state—An heroic band—An unappreciative population—Description of country—Waganda road-makers—Slow
progress—Difficulties with the boat—An imposing procession
—The importance of a drummer—A stormy interview—News
from the front—Alternative routes—Decle decides to leave us
—Makwenda's—German regulations—Arrears of pay—Loss
of Spire—We leave Makwenda's—Change of scenery—Herd
of elephants — Change of plans — A Merry Christmas —
Waganda justice—Crossing the frontier—Our allies—Waganda
wars—Kaduma's—The situation—Lack of commissariat—Concentration complete—A field day—Keen soldiers—A council
of war.

ON the 13th of December I marched out of
Kampala, with 200 Sudanese troops, 200
armed porters, 200 unarmed porters, 8 milch cows,
12 donkeys, 1 Maxim gun, and the steel boat.
The Europeans with me were Captain Macdonald,
staff officer; Captain Thruston, commanding the
Sudanese; Lieutenant Arthur, who, on joining
Major Owen, was to command the other Sudanese
wing; Dr. Moffat, medical officer; Mr. Purkiss,
in charge of the steel boat; and Spire, my servant.

The majority of us were not in a very promising condition to start on a campaign. Moffat and I were both suffering severely from jigger sores, and had to limp along bootless and with our feet wrapped in bandages, while he was barely recovered from a bad attack of fever. Purkiss was only just convalescent from his attack of hæmaturic fever, and Spire was in the middle of an attack of malarial fever.

The troops and porters, of course, marched in single file, and the force covered a good deal of ground and made a fairly imposing show, while the band emitted a volume of sound which, considering its small size, was simply marvellous; but in spite of all this we seemed to attract little or no attention. Neither the king, chiefs, nor missionaries came to see us off, and an officer's guard in London causes more excitement than seemed to be felt in the first step of a war, the result of which, if successful, would be the enormously increased importance of Uganda, whose present king had never been able to maintain his suzerainty over Unyoro; while, if unsuccessful, our failure could only result in the eating up of the country by Wanyoro hordes.

The first big stage of our march was to

Makwenda's, the capital of Singo, situated about forty miles due east of Kampala ; but as the rains were barely over, and the direct road crosses the Maanja and its numerous affluents, I decided to take a somewhat longer and more southerly route, on which we should find less water.

This route, like that already described, from the Napoleon Gulf to Kampala, runs along the northern slope of the watershed, and is even more deeply undulated than the other.   The country is almost uninhabited, and entirely given up to reed-like grass, some twelve or fourteen feet high. Through this winds a footpath hardly a foot wide, and leading straight ahead over the highest parts of hills and the bottoms of valleys.

I have never met a people so utterly regardless of physical obstacles or the first principles of road - making as the Waganda.   A little rounded summit (perhaps one hundred yards in diameter) if it happens to be in the direct route, is as conscientiously surmounted as if it were an impediment in an obstacle race, the shirking of which would entail disqualification ; while not one yard will the Waganda road-maker go out of his way to cross the upper, and probably dry portion, of a valley if the deepest and boggiest part happens to lie in the direct line of march.

These constant ups and downs, combined with the narrowness of the path, made the progress of the boat party very arduous and slow. The boat sections were about six feet across, and consequently, being about six times wider than the path, had to be forced through the stiff grass. When going down hill this could be done with comparative ease by advancing in rushes whose impetus carried the reeds before it ; but up hill the sections had to be pressed on by sheer force, a fatiguing mode of procedure, which necessitated halts every few yards to take breath. The result was that Purkiss and his party rarely arrived in camp until two or three hours after we had settled down, and had the further unpleasantness of being caught in the thunderstorm which came on every afternoon.

On the morning of our last march into Makwenda's (December 17th), I got a letter from Owen, saying that he would wait there for my arrival, and then push on to make arrangements at the front ; so, instead of making our usual half-way halt, I went on ahead, accompanied by my servant and flag-bearer.

When about an hour's march from the fort, I came upon the band of the Sudanese regiment drawn up along the roadside. After presenting arms (bandsmen carry rifles in Uganda), they turned to the right and followed me, whacking their drums and tootling on their old cracked bugles at their loudest. I wish I could have seen that procession—it must have been a very funny one. First, a big Sudanese soldier carrying a Union Jack; then a very seedy-looking Englishman in an old karkee coat, dilapidated breeches and gaiters, his feet bandaged in dirty rags, limping along with the help of a walking-stick; then a small Sudanese boy laden with a field-glass, a camp-stool, and a big bunch of bananas; and lastly, the full band of the regiment in single file, swaggering on with that sense of importance which only comes to those whose good stars lead them in the way of hitting drums. We had now got into a populous district, and the inhabitants seemed to be duly impressed with the importance of a person for whom such an imposing pageant had been organised; and, thinking me a man worthy of consideration, plied me with large quantities of bananas and *pombi*. Luckily, Fadl el Mula, my Sudanese boy, seemed able to dispose of an unlimited number of the former; and the latter, although a satisfying, is not a very intoxicating liquid; and on reaching the fort, I was in a sufficiently intelligent state to discuss plans with Owen. Before doing so, however, I had to undergo a rather stormy interview with the Makwenda, who, it seemed, looked upon it as his right, as the frontier chief, to take command of the native army, and imagined that it was owing to my machinations that he had been cut out by Kakunguru. Although I was able to reassure him on this point, I could not induce him to serve under his successful rival, but he promised to send a good strong contingent.

The news from the front was very meagre, and our topographical information even more so. The general opinion seemed to be that Kabarega would hold the Kafu, of which there were two fords, one about 1200 yards wide, in low ground and with bushy banks, the other 800 yards wide, with clear rocky sides. The direct road *via* Ntuti and Kaduma's was said to lead to the former, while the latter was best reached by a more westerly route passing through Fort Grant; this road, however, was described as a very bad one. In spite of this, the advantages of the clear banks and narrower river, seemed to me so great for the force having superiority in firearms, that I unhesitatingly decided on the western route, and ordered Owen to concentrate his force at Fort Grant, and there await our arrival, collecting all possible dry food in the meanwhile. Having settled this and a few details, Owen started off at three in the afternoon, to make the best of his way to Fort Grant.

M. Decle, who had accompanied Owen in the expedition against Kikukuri and back to Makwenda's, stayed behind, unable to make up his mind whether to go to the front with us or not. Having travelled so far across Africa, he was naturally anxious to go a little farther, and see Unyoro, and possibly the Albert Lake; but as private matters urgently required his presence in Europe, he was torn by the conflicting claims of duty and pleasure, and it was not until the morning of my departure that he finally decided in favour of the former.

The fort at Makwenda's is a square stockaded enclosure on the summit of a little hill over-looking a fertile country, and facing Lake Wamaba, or Isolt, as it was rechristened by Captain Lugard. Like most forts that I have

VIEW FROM MAKWENDA'S

(To face page 88)

seen in this part of the world, it was far too big for the garrison which would probably be spared to defend it, but the stockade was a very strong one, and the whole place was in excellent order. As soon as he heard that I was coming, Owen had begun to build a special house for my reception, but unfortunately the mud floor had not had time to dry before I arrived, so I could only admire my palatial residence, and had to put up in the smaller but very comfortable hut which he had occupied.

While I was at Makwenda's, a letter reached me from Captain Langheld, the officer commanding the German stations on the Victoria Lake, informing me that, owing to certain irregularities on the part of Waganda canoemen, he had been obliged to make a regulation that not more than three canoes would be allowed to take goods from German territory unless accompanied by a European. This news was rather startling. Owing to lack of cloth (the coinage of Uganda), the troops were four months in arrears of pay, their clothing was worn out, the Europeans had long been without the boxes of provisions to which they were entitled; and we were, in fact, short of everything. Now a large consignment of the various things we wanted had, I knew, just arrived at the south end of the lake, and I had made arrangements for these to be brought to us by canoes under the charge of a Swahili headman, and was looking forward to finding a good supply stored at Port Alice on my return. Now all this nice little plan was knocked on the head. I was only leaving three Europeans in Uganda—Gibb at Kampala, Wilson in charge of stores at Port Alice, and Grant in Usoga; as none of these could be spared, there was nothing for it but either to go without our stores, and bear the complaints of the troops, or send back one of the few English officers of the expedition. Loath as I was to do this, I did not see any alternative, when Macdonald made the brilliant suggestion that Spire might like to take the job. He was pretty well worn out with fever, and had had quite enough of African marching, and jumped at the offer, so he was at once appointed "Water Transport Officer," and sent back to Port Alice; while I was handed over to the tender mercies of Fadl el Mula, an intelligent little boy, but as mischievous as a monkey, and requiring a steam laundry to keep him clean.

On the 19th we started off again, accompanied for the first hour by Decle, who, having definitely made up his mind not to go on with us, now bitterly repented his decision.

Our road lay through an uninhabited country, over the highlands separating the systems of the Maanja and Kitumbui rivers, and was at first much of the same character as that through which we had passed in the first stage of our march. After two days, however, the landscape became more interesting, the eternal ridges and furrows giving place to higher features, with some originality of character. Masses of rock began to protrude through the monotonous grass slopes, the unwonted sight of an occasional tree gladdened our eyes, and, greatest comfort of all, the grass decreased in height from about fourteen feet to three.

Although the sun was hot by day, the nights became much cooler, and I was very glad to put on a second blanket when I went to bed.

Numerous tracks of elephants were crossed, and I saw one herd of about twenty-five, just out of range on the far side of a river.

Possibly owing to a chill in the night, I managed to get another attack of fever, and although I walked off the shivering fit pretty successfully, found the hot one singularly unpleasant, as we tramped along under the noonday sun.

On the fourth day of our march I got a letter from Kakunguru, dated from Ntuti, the frontier village, saying that our information about the roads was wrong, and that it was the direct, and not the Fort Grant one, which led to the rocky crossing of the Kafu. As he was in a position to get the best information, I could not neglect this news, and had to change all my plans. So I sent off a message to Owen at Fort Grant, telling him to concentrate at Ntuti at once. On the next day we marched into that place, where I found a note from Owen dated December 25, 3 A.M., saying, "What a merry Christmas! We will be in by 10 this evening."

I had hardly settled down in my tent, when I received a visit from Petro, the chief of the place, who wished to lodge a complaint against a Mohammedan Waganda, who, he stated, had forcibly entered his house, and struck him when he tried to turn him out. As the man did not deny the charge, I told Petro that, as he was the chief of the district, and both he and the prisoner were Waganda, he had better settle the case according to Waganda law, and asked him what the usual punishment was for such offences. He promptly replied, " Death." As I had expected to hear at the most twenty lashes, I was rather taken aback, and said that as soldiers were valuable just then, I would try the case myself.

So far we had kept clear of the Waganda army, the detachments of which had followed roads to our right and left, but at this point they had all converged to follow the only road leading thence to Kaduma's, the point of concentration, and the strain of so large a force had proved beyond the slender resources of this poor district, which was now completely denuded of food. We had carried six days' provisions from Makwenda's, the last of which we ate on arrival at Ntuti ; consequently, until we could reach some more favoured land, we should have to go without that useful article.

The water was also extremely scarce, and what little there was practically undrinkable. We had all become pretty well accustomed to bad samples of this beverage, but I do not think the most hardened of us complained at the smallness of the ration of black slime which was issued on that day.

Take it all round, Ntuti did not seem a desirable

place to make a prolonged stay in, so, in spite of the long march which Owen's troops would have, I settled to move on as soon as possible after they arrived.   Having another attack of fever, I went to bed early, and did not see Owen until we all paraded by moonlight at 1.30 next morning.

We crossed the frontier at 6.30 A.M., and made a short halt on the far side of the swamp (this time a real one, and not merely a sluggish river) which divided Uganda from Unyoro. A very unpleasant place it was, bathed in the cold morning mist, and infested with mosquitoes. The water, however, was more plentiful and better than that at Ntuti, and we Europeans took advantage of the halt to refresh ourselves with cups of hot tea.

Between Ntuti and the frontier, the country had been barren and destitute of all life but a few hartebeestes, who must have earned rather a precarious living on the scattered tufts of rushlike grass over which we sleepily stumbled every now and then.   Beyond the swamp, however, the scene began rapidly to change for the better, and we soon found ourselves entering a succession of banana groves, which extended up to and beyond Kaduma's.

As we approached that place, we overtook various detachments of the Waganda army, some still waiting for the sun in the little bee-hive-shaped huts which they had put up for the night's shelter, others already on the march, pushing forward at a steady jog-trot, shouting, brandishing their spears, and seeming far more like a crowd of school children out for a holiday, than the manhood of a nation about to engage in a life and death struggle with its most formidable neighbour. The fact is, war with these people is not a very serious matter, and although I meant business, they were happily unaware of the fact, and probably thought that after a pleasant little jaunt, during which they would, with luck, have a chance of surprising some Wanyoro villagers, and shoving spears through their bodies, they would all return home, the richer by a few goats or head of cattle.

Except in peculiar cases, such as the religious conflicts of Uganda, native wars are little more than cattle-raiding expeditions, in which the loss of life is comparatively slight. The combatants seem to have a very good idea of their relative strengths, and the side which knows itself to be the weaker, after a certain amount of shouting, spear-brandishing, and firing in the air, generally wisely retires before it has placed itself in any serious jeopardy; while, even if it does make a stand, the long grass and inaccuracy of the marksmen's aim prevents even improved modern rifles from being very deadly.

Whether, counting on the loot which they expected to get, they had indulged in a little extravagance, or whether they were impelled by the same instinct which makes us put on our best clothes for a battle, I cannot say, but they were certainly very smartly dressed. Even those who wore bark cloths had got new ones, and the majority had replaced their home-made material by *merikani* (calico), which, although hardly in keeping with our idea that a soldier should be as inconspicuous as possible, looked very well on their brown skins. A savage, however, trusts less to artificial means than to his own powers of stalking if he wants to be unobserved, and as a rule likes to make as much show as possible, with a view to impressing the enemy. For the same reason, while we enjoin strict silence at night, in the vain hope that our whereabouts will be unknown, they like to shout, beat drums, and fire off guns, in the perhaps more reasonable one that the enemy, knowing that they are wide awake, will not try to molest them.

Although their choice of weapons was rather varied,—ranging from a Winchester rifle to a hedging-hook,—the kit of the Waganda at this stage of the campaign was fairly limited and compact, consisting generally of a couple of grass mats, and occasionally an earthenware cooking-pot, and I think the only unusual article of equipment which I noticed was a six months' old baby, which one stalwart spearman invariably carried on his head. As the expedition progressed, however, these simple necessaries were augmented by many strange articles of loot, among which small birds in cages were a prominent feature. Although I had seen Mr. Arthur Roberts in the part of a French soldier with a birdcage attached to his knapsack, I had never expected to command an army in which a large proportion of the troops would be similarly equipped.

Our allies, although picturesque, soon proved themselves to be a great nuisance on the line of march. Their favourite mode of progression seemed to be in a series of short rushes. At one moment a shout and a clatter warned us of the approach of a battalion; at the next, hustled into the bananas, we felt as if we had just been overtaken by a herd of stampeded cattle. A few minutes later, we found our late assailants all seated on the narrow path, which they blocked for some hundred yards. After laboriously wading through their bodies and getting clear of them, a few minutes' peace would be ended by another rush, perhaps complicated by a cross stream of a fresh body starting on a foraging expedition to our right or left. In spite of remonstrances on my part to the chiefs, and on their part to me at the rough treatment which their men sometimes got at the hands of the Sudanese, this sort of thing went on to the end of the campaign, but naturally increased in vigour when the whole Waganda army was collected together, and in unpleasantness when later on it became impregnated with smallpox.

Soon after noon we marched into Kaduma's village, at least so I was told, for no sign of a village was visible, all trace of the original habitations being obliterated in the sea of huts, which stretched as far as the eye could reach. It was not until this moment that I realised the size and peculiarities of my command. The position was this—eight Europeans in command of 400

Sudanese troops, fairly disciplined, poorly armed, and badly supplied with ammunition (we had barely 100 rounds a man), and about fifteen thousand wholly undisciplined savages, of whom about eighty per cent. were armed with spears, fifteen per cent. with guns, and five per cent. with modern rifles, and a large proportion of whom, if rumour was to be trusted, would have hailed with satisfaction the suppression of the white man by Kabarega.

I had, however, complete confidence both in the fidelity and fighting power of the Sudanese, and in the loyalty of Kakunguru and some of the chiefs, and my anxieties on the score of possible treachery or the superior force of the enemy were small compared with those in connection with our food supply. Including women and camp followers, we had about seventeen thousand mouths to feed, and every mouthful of the food they required would have to be furnished by the country we passed through. Judging from what I had seen in Uganda, I had, I confess, grave doubts as to whether this could be done, but Kakunguru was confident that the resources of Unyoro were equal to the strain, "unless," he added, " Kabarega retreats and lays waste the country behind him." Although I thought this was not an unlikely course for him to attempt, I did not look upon it as a very serious matter, as I had little doubt that we could reach him and drive him out of the food district which he would have to reserve for himself before we actually starved to death. People march and fight well when they have to do so for their dinners.

Perhaps a word of explanation may be well here to show why we had no commissariat arrangements. In the first place, I practically had with me the whole able-bodied male population of Uganda, only old men, boys, and women being left behind, and the latter were required to till the ground ; next, as the only beasts of burden were human beings, and as the frontier provinces are very sparsely inhabited and cultivated, food brought from distant districts, some of them a fortnight's march off, would have been all eaten by the carriers on the way ; again, the supply of Uganda consists almost exclusively of bananas, which do not bear carriage well ; and lastly, posts on the line of communication would have had to be garrisoned by Sudanese, whom I could ill spare for such work.

Making our way through the dense crowd of

spearmen who thronged the streets of this mush-room town, we came to Kakunguru's head-quarters, a large and substantial hut in the middle of a neat enclosure, and were welcomed by the Magubbi, as a Waganda general is called, and by Mr. Pilkington of the Church Missionary Society, who had accompanied him, and had already built a church.

Kakunguru told me that the concentration was progressing very satisfactorily, and that he hoped the last detachment would arrive next day.

Some time was then spent in selecting a site for our camp, no easy matter, as the best ground seemed to be already occupied, and the few open spaces available were in an indescribable state of filth. However, we at last settled down in the least objectionable spot, and made ourselves as comfortable as we could.

As Owen and the Fort Grant detachment had had about eighteen hours' nearly continuous marching, I thought that they had done a very fair day's work; but this was the first time that Owen had had the whole of his Sudanese together, and could not resist the temptation to see how his new toy worked; so, as soon as tents were pitched and huts built, he paraded his 415 men, and with

Thruston and Arthur as his wing commanders, and Villiers in charge of the Maxim detachment, started off for a nice little two hours' field-day in the thunderstorm which had just come on.

I must say for a Sudanese soldier that you cannot drill him too much ; he simply revels in it. I do not know that he cares so much for such practical work as was practised that afternoon, extending for the attack from single file, and such like manœuvres, but his thirst for knowledge of more ornamental exercises is quite insatiable. Often on a moonlight night I have been awakened by the rattle of arms, and, looking out of my tent, have seen two privates solemnly putting each other through the manual or bayonet exercises in the midst of the sleeping camp.

While the field-day was going on, I received a deputation of chiefs, each followed by one retainer carrying a chair or camp-stool and another holding an umbrella over his head. Kakunguru and the greater ones established themselves under the shelter of my tent, while the persons of less importance formed a semicircle outside. Then began a form of entertainment which I was forced to put up with on every succeeding afternoon throughout the campaign.

Kakunguru having announced that the subject for discussion that afternoon would be the forcing of the Kafu, each chief in turn explained in great detail his views on the subject, taking the opportunity of introducing his opinion on a variety of matters which did not seem very relevant. This done, I was asked to give my decision on the various schemes proposed, and as I had no intention of letting some fifty persons know, for the possible information of Kabarega, what my plans were, answered on true *shauri* principles, with many words and little meaning. My answer seemed to give general satisfaction, until Kakunguru announced his views on the subject, when the debate was started again from the beginning, and the whole process repeated again and again, until the setting sun reminded my friends that they must be thinking of the more important matter of supper. Then, with many allusions to my extraordinary sagacity, they bade me good-night, and, picking their way carefully over the filthy ground, filed off to their temporary homes.

CHAPTER VIII

CROSSING THE KAFU

First casualty—Advance of the army—Kakunguru—A fine sight
—Obstructionists—Nakatoma—News of Kabarega—The Kafu
river—Led astray—In sight of the enemy—Reconnaissances—
An impracticable crossing—Begin bridging the river—The
Baranwa ferry—The Toru army—A home-like fog—Colds—
Holding the bridge head—An undesirable camping-ground—
Across the Kafu.

ON the morning of the 27th of December
the concentration was completed, and on
the same afternoon our first casualty was brought
into camp, with a bad wound in the chest from
a Wanyoro spear.

Small parties of the enemy were reported to
be hovering about in the neighbourhood, but
only the mildest of skirmishing had been indulged
in.

Our foraging parties had been out for a considerable distance, and as Kakunguru reported
that the food supply of the district was exhausted,
it was evidently time to move on. So on the

morning of the 28th the army as a whole marched off together for the first time.[1]

Kakunguru, who on the previous day in camp had been dressed in Arab costume, now appeared in European clothes, a check shooting jacket and knickerbockers to match, knitted stockings and shooting boots, the whole sur-

[1] Strength as follows :—

Europeans	8	
Native officers	14	
Sudanese non-commissioned officers and men	415	
Waganda great chiefs	15	
„ riflemen	207	
„ musketeers	3,308	
„ spearmen	10,600	
Masai spearmen	11	
Swahili headmen	8	
„ Askaris	25	
„ porters (armed) . . .	209	
Total combatants . .	———	14,820
Swahili porters (unarmed) . . .	56	
Enlisted Lendus	97	
Sudanese followers	100	
Waganda followers	1,000	
Waganda (attached to headquarters) .	20	
Wanyoro chiefs	2	
„ men (bearer company) . .	110	
„ interpreters and guides . .	13	
Servants and interpreters . . .	34	
Artisans	3	
Total non-combatants . .	———	1,435
Grand total		16,255

mounted by a turban. Mounted on the primitive steed of Waganda chiefs, a man, he dashed about the camp in all directions, giving orders and trying to get into some sort of form the huge mob under his command. The other chiefs, too, were full of energy, some dressed in Arab and some in European clothes, but the majority in a medley of the two, but nearly all wearing the leopard-skin apron which is the badge of chieftainship. All were dashing hither and thither either mounted or on their own feet among the crowd of spearmen and riflemen.

It was certainly a wonderful sight, that surging mass of spearmen ; near me full of life and savage exultation, but gradually toning off into a great trembling sheet, whose edges were lost in the morning mist; and as I looked over my command, I felt proud at having been chosen as the successor of men who, without the aid of a single soldier, had placed me in the position of being able to summons this great horde of Central African allies.

Having got our immediate front clear, the Sudanese troops, Maxims, and baggage marched off in single file, following the main track, the Waganda being supposed to follow other paths on their flank.   Probably large numbers of them did so, but a remnant, quite sufficient to be a nuisance, followed the broad and easy road which led to the destruction of the regulars' formation, and indulged in the annoying practices which I have already described.

Our line of march lay through thin bush, which offered no particular obstacles to our progress, and by noon we had finished a ten miles' march, which brought us to the large banana groves of Nakatoma.

Some slight skirmishes took place between the enemy and our scouts, but the former did not seem to be in any force.   One prisoner was taken, who stated that Kabarega was going to make a stand on the Kafu.

The march on the following day was in very dense forest, through the thick undergrowth of which we, with difficulty, pushed our way.   The progress of the boat party was terribly slow, and as, being now in the enemy's country, we could not allow it to lag behind, we were forced to make frequent halts to let it come up with us.   At half-past two, however, we at length reached a clearing large enough for us to camp in, and which had the advantage of being

covered with sweet potatoes ; a pleasant change
of diet after the eternal bananas of Uganda.

The country through which we had been
passing was covered with thorny trees not more
than twenty feet high, but to our front and at a
lower level stretched the belt of heavy timber
through which the Kafu runs. Beyond this we
could see the camp-fires of the enemy, and in
the distance the famous mountain stronghold
of Masaja Mkuru (the big man) and the row
of decapitated cone - shaped hills under which
Kabarega's capital was said to lie.

I at once sent forward a reconnaissance to the
river, which was said to be two miles distant, and
on its return learned that the Kafu was about
twelve hundred yards broad, and choked with
papyrus ; that its banks were lined with considerable margins of bog, overgrown with thick
bush, and that there was no commanding ground
to be found on our side. Then, and not till I
had found it all out for myself, did Kakunguru
come, and with many apologies say that he had
made a mistake, and that the Fort Grant road
was after all the one we should have followed, the
rocky ford which we had been trying to make
for being about a day's march up stream.

THE KAFU RIVER

(To face page 108)

The situation was too serious to be angry about, so I simply told Kakunguru that, as he had led us into this mess, he must make the best of it, and begin bridging the first thing next morning. I, however, made up my own mind that nothing would induce me to attempt the passage at this place if Kabarega showed any signs of seriously contesting it, and at once sent off Thruston with a hundred men to see if he could find any more favourable spot down stream, and ordered Owen to start at daylight next morning with another hundred, to find and report on the Baranwa ford, which we had been trying to hit off. Thruston found nothing much better than the place we were at, and reported the river to be broad and papyrus-choked, with thick forest-lined banks for many miles down stream.

Owen, who did not return until five in the afternoon, and had had a long and difficult cross-country march through thick bush, had succeeded in discovering the Baranwa crossing. He described it as about a thousand yards wide, and choked with papyrus, through which what appeared to be a canoe channel had been cut; its banks were lined with forest, but not so thick as that in our neighbourhood, and there was high rocky ground on both sides of the river. He considered that there was a very good position for the Maxims on our bank.

While reconnoitring this position, he was fired on from the opposite bank, which he then discovered was occupied by a considerable force of the enemy. Further investigation showed that it had camped on our side of the river on the previous night. On his returning the fire, the Wanyoro soon withdrew, and after waiting for some hours, he felt sure that they had moved away altogether.

Kakunguru was convinced, on hearing the news, that this was the rearguard of the army sent to invade Toro, which had been hastily recalled on Kabarega's getting news of our approach. This surmise afterwards proved to be correct. We also heard that the force had suffered severely from hardships and disease, and returned home in a very dilapidated condition, circumstances which accounted for its rather humble behaviour in face of Owen's small party.

On the whole, Owen's news sounded satisfactory, but I continued pushing forward the bridge, as I had now settled, if Kabarega stood his ground, to hold this, the Utema ferry, with the Waganda and one company of Sudanese, and make a night march with the rest of the Sudanese to Baranwa, and get them across in the steel boat, using any canoes we might be able to seize.

Our camp was in a low, damp situation, from which a heavy mist rose morning and evening, and the smoke from thousands of camp-fires, concentrated into a small space, combined with this, and produced the closest imitation of a London fog that it has ever been my misfortune to experience. By eight in the evening we could not even see our neighbours' fires, only a few yards off, and it was not until nine or ten in the morning that the sun began to show himself, poached egg - like, through the veil of smoke. One curious and unpleasant effect of this was an epidemic of what appeared to be severe catarrh. Moffat said it was only irritation of the mucous membrane, but we certainly sneezed and coughed and blew our noses in a way which would have done credit to people suffering from the most ordinary of English colds.

As, shortly before Owen returned, Macdonald had reported that the bridge was about three-quarters of the way across, I ordered Arthur to parade with a company and get to the opposite bank as well as they could, holding the bridge head if they were able to do so. They got down to the water by sunset, and as the bridge had by then been partially completed to within one hundred and fifty yards of the farther shore, they were just able to wade across, up to their necks in water, holding their rifles and ammunition above their heads.

They found the ground for a mile beyond the actual stream so swampy that Arthur considered it unadvisable to camp there, and pushed on to Usamba, where he bivouacked.

Early next morning he sent me a message that he had seen no signs of the enemy, so I at once gave orders for a general move across. Not wishing to be jostled by the Waganda over twelve hundred yards of wobbling fascines, I postponed my own departure till five in the evening, by which hour I hoped that the bridge would be clear. I was, however, disappointed. I think they must have waited for me, for I found a great crowd on the bank, and, after edging my way through it, came to the newly-made road, apparently a beautiful dry avenue cut through the miniature forest of papyrus which hid the water except in our immediate neighbourhood. It was perfectly clear of traffic, and I walked contentedly along it for a couple of hundred yards, when my heart sank as I heard the familiar shout behind me, and my body soon followed its example, for the Waganda were at their old tricks, and before I had time to turn round, a thousand were close packed all round me, and the floating papyrus on which we walked had sunk three feet below the surface. However, this little wetting did not matter, for when we reached what I suppose I must call "land," we had to traverse, sometimes nearly waist deep, · the mile of slush which Arthur had very correctly reported as undesirable for a campaigning ground.

CHAPTER IX

OCCUPATION OF THE CAPITAL

Programme altered — A sharp look-out — Change of scenery —
Wanyoro forethought — Ghostly defences — A misapplied
offering—Enter into the capital—Forestalled—A pleasant site
—We stop to loot—Mail for Europe—Intentions of the army
—Prisoners—News of Kabarega—Plans—Settle to push on.

I HAD calculated on reaching Kabarega's capital on New Year's day, but the stupid mistake about the ford had delayed us twenty-four hours, and on the 1st of January we were still some fifteen miles off.

If we were to have a stand-up fight at all, I now expected it would be outside the capital, and as I did not want to get in late in the afternoon, fagged and perhaps foodless, I sacrificed the accuracy of my programme for more practical considerations, and, making only a ten miles' march, camped on some high ground, from which all the country round the capital was easily visible.

We had seen a good number of Wanyoro on the hills overlooking our line of march throughout the day, but no skirmishing had taken place, nor had the foraging parties come across any force of the enemy. We thought it better, however, to camp in a rather more compact formation than we had hitherto adopted, and to keep a sharp look-out for a night attack.

On the Unyoro side of the Kafu the country undergoes a complete change, much resembling northern Singo; indeed, the two countries seem to be one, severed by the great alluvial valley of the Kafu. Unyoro, however, is far more thickly populated and highly cultivated than its sister in Uganda, and its inhabitants, instead of courting starvation by relying entirely on that favourite food of locusts, the banana, plant large quantities of beans and sweet potatoes, and seem generally to have some idea of laying by for a rainy day.

This habit, usually an advantageous one for them, proved also to be greatly to our profit. Had I been obliged to depend entirely on bananas, I do not know how I should have provisioned the forts which I afterwards left in Unyoro, but, thanks to the nice little stores of beans and grain which we found buried about the country, I had no difficulty in this respect.

We made an early start next morning, and after

crossing a boggy stream, entered the valley in which Kabarega's capital is situated. Following this for a couple of miles, flanked to the west by a high peak and to the east by a lower range of hills, we came to the mouth of a large valley which enters it from the east. On a mound in the centre of this a hundred little curling columns of smoke showed that Kabarega had retired, and, following the usual Wanyoro custom, had taken care that no strangers should burn his capital.

Although he had not personally interfered with our progress, he had employed such means as lay in his power to gain the alliance of any unseen forces who might be persuaded to annoy us, and with this end in view had impaled one of his subjects in our path, and at another point buried in it a ram, whose head was left above ground. The poor brute was alive when we found him, but, in spite of his having been voted to the gods, was, I regret to say, soon turned into mutton, and treated as such.

We came across another curious object just outside the ruined gates of the town, a single hurdle, into the upper bars of which bushes had been interlaced, pointing upward,—just such a one as may be seen any day on a steeplechase course at home,—and unless Kabarega is a votary of that sport, I can only suppose that it had some superstitious significance, but I was never able to get any satisfactory explanation of its uses.

Placed, as I have said, on a mound at the junction of two valleys, and surrounded with picturesque grass and rock-covered hills, Kabarega's capital is a very pleasant place. A nice stream of clear water flows three hundred yards off at the foot of the mound, while to the back rich banana groves extend as far as the eye can reach ; to the front, beyond the stream and over a low cultivated hill, may be seen, on a clear day, the distant blue mountains near Kavalli's, on the farther shores of the Albert Lake.

Every building in the capital had been carefully burnt to the ground, and only a few charred and still smoking poles remained to show the position and great extent of the king's enclosure.

The Waganda were naturally anxious to stop and search for loot ; so, thinking that if Kabarega did not mean to fight us, no amount of hurry on my part would force him to do so, I only marched on for a mile beyond the town, and there encamped for the night.

I had told Gibb to send off a mail on the 18th

of January, by which I hoped to send home despatches reporting my progress up to the capital; but on my explaining to Kakunguru that I wished to open communication with Uganda next morning, he explained that no small party of Waganda would dare to return without a Sudanese escort, and further hinted that most of the members of his army looked upon this as the legitimate end of the campaign, and had probably already made up their minds to return to their homes by the earliest opportunity. This opportunity, he said, would be afforded if I opened the road; in which case I might find that his fifteen thousand men would dwindle in a very short time down to himself and a few chiefs. This view of the feelings of my army was a new revelation to me, and at once decided me to postpone the pleasure which the sight of my handwriting would doubtless cause in England.

One or two prisoners had been taken, and an escaped Waganda slave also came in. The prisoners were, as the interviewers at home say, " very reticent," but the slave was full of information, which proved to be mostly false. He said that, on hearing that we had crossed the Kafu, Kabarega had sent off his women, children, and cattle to Mruli, but had himself waited until the previous morning, when, after setting fire to his town, he had followed them, and was going to make a determined stand in Chope, a district bordering the Nile. The army recently despatched into Usoga had been recalled and was to join him there.

Whether the news was correct or not, it was evident that Kabarega was retiring before us, and, knowing that it was necessary for the peace of Uganda that his power should be broken,—a result which would not be brought about by a mere punitive expedition,—I saw that we must either capture him or drive him out of his kingdom. If it was true that he was making for Chope, the latter alternative would probably be the only one open to me. There were certain difficulties, however, even in the way of arriving at that.

The country between us and Mruli was said to be very barren, and at the present season badly supplied with water, and even Kakunguru, who had unlimited confidence in the foraging powers of his compatriots, was doubtful whether we could get across. I could, of course, send a small force in pursuit of Kabarega, but this would have to be composed of Sudanese, and I should not have liked to send less than four hundred to attack his large army. To do this I must leave the Waganda alone to work their own sweet will, which would probably have led them, after capturing all the women they could lay hands on, to go back to their homes, and possibly while away the time until my return in their favourite pastime of a religious civil war. However, the information as to the country was too meagre to allow of my making any very definite plans, so I determined to push on in one body as far as the food and water supply allowed me.

CHAPTER X

Lendui—In touch of the enemy—Plans for attack—Moved on—
An ambuscade — An energetic chief — Wanyoro ˙roads —
Kabarega—A pedestrian—A little outing—Kibuguzi—In sight
at last—Order of battle—Gone away—Stirring them up—A
substitute for dinner—Change of plans—The plover trick—
A camp fire — A reconnaissance to the front—We retire—
Bujenji—Captive beauties—The Lady Kangao—A pioneer of
civilisation—The captives freed—A diabolical plot—A buck-
hunt and its results.

A SHORT march over a good road, on the
3rd of January, brought us to Lendui,
situated in an elbow of a range of hills, and
overlooking a broad banana-covered plain. I
had intended to push on for another two or three
hours, but as this was such a good food district,
and there was some doubt as to what we should
find ahead, Kakunguru begged me to stop.

At about five o'clock Waganda scouts brought
in word that the enemy were encamped in force
about two hours' march ahead of us, at the foot
of the range of hills. Kakunguru was certain

that we should be attacked, but the position was a very favourable one to us, and I did not agree with him. I, however, at once sent forward a reconnaissance under Owen to find out the enemy's real strength and position, and carefully note the road to it, with a view to our making a night, or, rather, early morning attack. I hoped, by following the road to within about a mile of the camp, and then striking off it slightly to the left over the hills, to find myself at daybreak in a position commanding the camp and cutting off Kabarega's line of retreat.

I proposed to execute this movement with the Sudanese troops, leaving the Waganda to rush up at daybreak and complete the rout, taking a cross-country route, which cut off the big bend made by the high road under the mountains.

This, like a good many other nice little plans I made, was knocked on the head by the news which Owen brought back at eight that evening. He had pushed on into the enemy's camp, which he found deserted, but the fires still smoking. The enemy had evidently cleared out on hearing of our approach. He was further confident, from the small size of the camp, that the force reported near was not Kabarega's army, but only a rearguard.

As Macdonald, who was making a survey of our route, was anxious to get into the hills to obtain a better view of the country, I let him go ahead next morning with the advanced guard, consisting of fifty Sudanese. On reaching a little saddle near Kisibagwa, he was suddenly attacked in some force by a body of Wanyoro ambuscaded in the high grass, but although they fired at a range of about ten yards, they did not succeed in doing him any damage. He soon managed to drive them out of their ambush, and pursued them closely through thick grass and bush up a hill about three hundred feet high, and over its summit, whence he had a good view of their retreat. He estimated their numbers at 200, and from the sound of the bullets believed that they were nearly all armed with rifles. He killed one and wounded three, having no casualties himself.

This does not seem a very great result for half an hour's fighting at close quarters, but it must be borne in mind that in this class of work the combatants rarely see each other, and that, although the Wanyoro waste a great deal of ammunition in random shooting, our troops were trained never to fire unless they could see their man plainly, and that seeing a man, even with better troops than they were, is not synonymous with hitting him.

We afterwards heard that this ambuscade was under the command of a chief, who, taunting his companions with their cowardice, had volunteered to check our advance if Kabarega would give him 200 picked men armed with rifles. His request was granted, and his defeat was said to have had a very demoralising effect on the Wanyoro army. I have said that I was told all this, but I think I should add that what I was told was very rarely true.

The Waganda also had a skirmish, in which they killed five of the enemy and lost one of their own number.

Kabarega is not, I believe, a wholly estimable character, but I must say for him that he kept his roads in a far better condition than my friend and ally Mwanga. In Uganda it is almost impossible to ride anywhere, but there would have been no difficulty in driving a carriage along any part of this road, which was a good width, and kept clear of weeds, while every stream was carefully bridged.

In peace time it is said that roads about to be used by Kabarega are always strewn with clean grass; but I suppose on this occasion his royal progress was rather too hurried to allow of proper preparations being made, for we saw no signs of any such luxury. He seems to be an energetic old man, and always walks on his own feet, instead of being carried on the shoulders of a man, as was the custom with the kings and chiefs of Uganda before we introduced horses. I remember asking one of his subjects whether I had put him to much inconvenience by turning him out of his capital and causing him to wander about the country, and I was assured that, on the contrary, I had conferred a great favour on him, as he found the sedentary life in his capital most irksome, and was delighted at being given the opportunity for such a little outing as I had provided for him.

The end of the day's march brought us to Kibuguzi, still at the foot of the range of hills which we had on our left all day, and situated in a rather nasty bush country, in which it was difficult to find a good camping-ground. However, by burning the bush, we secured ourselves a fair field of fire.

In the afternoon Macdonald and Owen climbed up the hills to our left, and got a good view of the country ahead of us, and clearly made out a camp about eight miles to the north-west, which from its size they were certain was that of Kabarega's whole army. They described it to me, with the help of a sketch, as being at the foot of the centre one of three hills connected by saddles' running transversely to our line of advance, and rising out of a densely wooded plain.

We were now on the outskirts of the Budonga forest, in which many of the prophets of Uganda had predicted that Kabarega would make his stand; and the reliable information that his whole army was really halted within reach of us made it seem probable that their forecast had been correct. Kabarega's camp was off the main track, and the country between it and us seemed very difficult, so I did not think it advisable to risk a night march, nor did there seem much prospect of carrying out any flank movement by day, when all our manœuvres would be visible from the hills behind the enemy's position. I therefore determined to make a direct attack, trusting to our superiority to break him up, and to the Waganda spearmen to pursue him.

On the following morning we were off at daylight, and after crossing the range of hills, found ourselves overlooking the plain on the far side of which lay our hitherto elusive adversary.

As this was the last point at which I had any hopes of seeing either my own troops or the enemy for some time to come, I told the former off into the formation in which I proposed to advance. This was in echelon from the centre, the Sudanese and Maxims occupying the central position, the Waganda musketeers the ground to their flanks, slightly thrown back, and the Waganda spearmen the extreme flanks. All were in single file, each column being sufficiently separated from the others to allow of its extending to its front. A thousand Waganda spearmen preceded us by about a mile.

Our progress was very slow, we were following no path, and each column had to force its way independently through high and very dense grass and thick thorny scrub, while the ground, which had appeared to be a plain when viewed from a height, proved to be decidedly undulating, and here and there intersected by deep ravines clothed with the densest of tropical vegetation.

Thanks to the distinctive drum sounds of the

various chiefs, we kept a far better line than I should have expected, although a good deal of closing towards the centre took place. At noon a low bush-covered ridge was approached, the summit of which was seen to be lined with Wanyoro riflemen; but, after opening a heavy but comparatively ineffective fire on our advanced spearmen, they retired, and the main body gained the ridge without opposition.

From this place we again caught sight of the three hills of Bitiberi on which we were marching, but we were unable to make out the enemy's camp, nor could we see whether the hills themselves were occupied. Another two hours' marching, however, brought us to their foot, and showed us that Kabarega or his generals had again thought discretion the better part of valour. No sign of the enemy was to be seen, and after another hour over exceptionally tiring ground, we gained the summit of the central hill without opposition. On this Villiers was just setting up the Maxim when I arrived, and under Owen's orders was on the point of firing it. I was, I confess, completely pumped, and only just managed to do the last fifty yards at a feeble run, and make it understood that I did not wish the firing to begin until I had found out what it was all about.

Our position commanded a fine view over the Budonga forest, which stretched as far as the eye could reach to the northward. A little over two thousand yards off many columns of smoke showed the position of the enemy's camp, but the huts were hidden in the trees. It was at this that Owen was going to fire, saying that he wanted to stir them up, but it struck me that we had done about enough of that already, and that I would much sooner let them have a quiet night's rest, from which they might wake up fresh and cheerful, ready for a fight on the morrow; but I had no great hopes that they would do this: they had abandoned a very strong position for an indifferent one, and if they had meant fighting at all, would almost certainly have held the ground which we then occupied. Although they were just within range of our Maxims, they were separated from us by a deep ravine and a belt of what appeared to be very dense forest, and I estimated that it would take us at least two hours to reach them. It was by this time about half-past three in the afternoon, and after the very tiring day the troops had had, I did not feel

9

inclined to attempt an attack which would probably only end in disappointment, so treated my own men with the same consideration which I had shown to the enemy, and gave them a quiet afternoon.

We were now in a country utterly destitute of food, and I was told that no more would be procurable in the direction we were taking, until we reached the province of Magungu, some fifty miles distant. Kakunguru also casually mentioned, in the course of the inevitable afternoon *shauri*, that his men had eaten nothing since breakfast, and had brought no supplies with them. I asked him what he proposed to do, and he said he would let them sleep. Although this plan offered an excellent temporary substitute for dinner, I hardly supposed that they could be induced to walk in their sleep to the Victoria Nile, and failing that, it would be necessary to devise some means for their subsistence.

I had now no doubt that Kabarega had been delaying our march by a series of rearguard actions, and that he, with his large herds of cattle, had retired into the depths of the Budonga forest, either intending to push through to the food district of Magungu, to turn eastward and join his ivory, which was said to have been sent to Mruli, or merely to stay where he was and enjoy the spectacle of my army dying of starvation.

Whatever plan Kabarega might have in his mind, it was pretty certain that, if he did not want to fight, we should not catch him up by following such a proverbially slow process as a stern chase. It was also certain that his present road led directly away from Mruli, and it struck me as possible that he might be playing the old plover's trick of leading us away from his nest, and that if we turned back and went straight for that, he might either follow us and risk a fight for the sake of his ivory, or, thinking that, having got that, we should depart in peace to Uganda, he might return to his capital; when, by making a dash with a small force, we might possibly catch him.

I accordingly announced to the Waganda chiefs that, having failed to catch Kabarega, the next best thing was to secure his ivory, and that I intended to turn back next day and march straight for Mruli. These sentiments were very highly approved of by my audience, who had, I fear, long entertained the idea that wandering about

after Kabarega, while his ivory was lying some-
where ready to be seized, was a shameful waste
of time.

Having got rid of my chiefs, I was congratu-
lating myself that the day's work was at last over,
when I was roused by a shout, and, looking out
of my tent, saw that the long grass about fifty
yards in front of it was on fire. All hands soon
turned out with sticks to beat down the flames,
but a strong breeze.was blowing, and the vegetation was thoroughly dry, and it was not until the
whole of the Sudanese huts had been destroyed,
that we were able to get it under. Our tents
had a very near shave, and the Maxims had
to be hurriedly packed up and carried to the
rear. The troops had had such a hard day's
work, that I was very sorry for them having to
go out and collect fresh boughs and grass, with
which to build their temporary habitations. However, it was they who had started the fire through
carelessness, and I suppose it served them right.
I must say they were wonderfully cheerful about
it, and seemed to look upon the whole thing as
rather a good joke.

At sunrise next morning, the fires of a large
camp some ten miles to our north-west showed

that Kabarega had moved on during the night. However, I thought it better to make sure that he had not left anyone behind, so sent Thruston and one hundred men to reconnoitre to the front, while we retraced our footsteps of the day before. The enemy's camp proved to be even more difficult of access than I had anticipated. It took Thruston and his party nearly three hours to reach it, and it was late in the afternoon before he rejoined us at our halting-place, Kitongi, about five miles to the north-east of the point whence Macdonald and Owen got sight of Bitiberi.

The first part of the march being over our tracks of the day before, the grass was well beaten down, and our progress fairly easy; but after about three hours we veered off to the left, and, striking across country towards the main road, got into very difficult ground, which delayed the boat party considerably.

Small parties of Wanyoro were seen, and two Waganda were brought in, both having rather severe bullet wounds. The district in which we halted was a comparatively poor one, but just supplied us with food for the night.

The next day we followed the high road connecting Kabarega's present capital with Masindi (a former one) as far as Bujenji, whence the road to Mruli branches off. The district was very fertile, and seemed capable of supporting us for several days. On arriving there, I at once sent off a large reconnoitring party of Waganda towards Mruli, with the double object of leading Kabarega to suppose that we were going that way, and finding out what the food supply on the road really was. I was anxious to know this, as, although I did not intend to go there at once, I thought it possible that I might return to Uganda by that road.

Taking advantage of the halt we had to make while the reconnoitring party were away, I had a parade of the ladies who had been captured or come in to us during the course of the operations. There were about one hundred and fifty of them in all, of whom forty were Wanyoro, and the remainder Waganda, whom Kabarega's raiding parties had at various times seized as slaves. I dealt with the latter first, asking each in turn whether she wished to stay with the Wanyoro, or return to her own people. Only two chose to stay, so, putting them aside, I started on the rather delicate task of deciding who was to take care of the remainder. The younger and stronger

BUJENJI

(To face page 134)

ones seemed to have a quite remarkable number of uncles, cousins, and brothers in camp, who all declared that they were the only fit and proper persons to take charge of them until they were handed over to their husbands or fathers. Being unable to decide myself on the relative claims of their many would-be protectors, I left the matter in the ladies' own hands, and, placing the men in a row, told each to point out to me the warrior whom she considered the most suitable. Perhaps the relations of the older ones were mostly dead, or had not come to the war; at anyrate, they were very scarce or retiring, and I had some difficulty in securing care-takers for these doubtless worthy, but somewhat unprepossessing matrons. However, in course of time, I got them all provided for, except one poor old hag, who looked like a balloon with the gas out, and who was not recognised even by a great-grandson; so I handed her over to the Kangao, who, as a deacon and a married man, I felt sure could be entrusted with her, without any risk of scandal; for the Lady Kangao accompanied her husband throughout the expedition. She was a cheery little person, clothed in the brightest of handkerchiefs. The one round her waist was decorated with a vivid representation of the orb of day, which had a most exhilarating effect as she tramped ahead of us in the gloomy forest. She was kind enough to take a great interest in me, and sent me sticks of vanilla which she found in the woods, saying they would make my breath smell sweet.

Having disposed of the Waganda, I next turned my attention to the Wanyoro beauties. They did not seem to have been selected with any great care, and were not at all the kind that I should have taken the trouble to capture had it been my habit to go in for such practices. A good many claimants, however, came forward for their hands and hearts, which they seemed perfectly willing to transfer to their captors; but, in spite of all appearances to the contrary, I could not forget that I was a pioneer of civilisation, and that as such it behoved me to conduct war on the most approved philanthropic principles. I therefore informed my audience that it was Kabarega, and not his people, with whom I was at war, and bade the ladies return to their homes, and tell their relations that they need have no fear as long as they did not fight us. I added that if, instead of running away and leaving us empty *shambas*, from which we could only help ourselves, they would come in and bring food, they would be rewarded for their trouble. After some little demur, they said they would deliver my message, and were marched out of camp, I have no doubt thinking that I was trying to make them instruments for a diabolical plot to catch and destroy the population of Unyoro. That anybody, even a white man, should want to pay for food when he could get it for nothing, was a depth of folly far beyond the comprehension of their simple understandings.

Although we were pioneers of civilisation, we did not always behave as such. That same afternoon, an unwary buck ran through our camp. In an instant the whole army was up and giving chase, and almost before I had time to realise what was happening, it was being torn limb from limb.

That faithful friend of man, the foxhound, is not always as scrupulously altruistic as one would wish, when the body of his quarry is thrown to him by the huntsman; but compared with that of my Waganda followers, as seen on that afternoon, his conduct can only be described as courtly. They, not content with using on their neighbours

the teeth, which I had always understood were
the only weapons allowed by the rules of the game,
took advantage of their descent from anthropoid
apes, and used such instruments of offence as
hands, feet, sticks, and stones, even borrowing
from the armoury of man, in their frantic efforts
to secure a mouthful of raw flesh, or the portion
of a bowel.

The sight, instructive while it lasted, was
soon over, and within a minute after the buck's
appearance, those nearest the scene of action
were strolling quietly back to their huts, covered
with gashes, blood, and bruises.

CHAPTER XI

THE INVESTMENT OF THE FOREST

Mruli road impassable—A blow to the chiefs—Unpleasant alterna-
tives—Decide to hem in Kabarega—Kabarega's return—
Attempt to waylay him—An over-zealous chief—Owen's pic-
nic—Return to the capital—Plan of investment—Sudanese
troops at Wadelai—Sites for forts—Masaja Mkuro—A painful
shauri—Vacillation—Smallpox—The Kangao's four hundred
—Loss of ammunition—Expected opposition—A skirmish—
Kitanwa.

ON the 9th of January the reconnoitring party returned, reporting that they had been as far as Kisugu on the Mruli road, that up to that place the food and water supply had been moderate, but that beyond it the country was said to be wholly desert. This was a great blow to the Waganda chiefs, who were intent on getting hold of Kabarega's ivory, and they assembled for the afternoon's *shauri* with very long faces and woebegone manners.

Kakunguru opened the meeting by announcing the state of affairs, and his companions were so dejected that they asked my advice without any one of them attempting to give his own. I said that we had got into this mess entirely owing to the badness of their information; that here we were in a country adjoining their own, and one which hundreds of their compatriots had visited, and yet so little trouble would they take to find out anything about it, that first they had led me to the very worst ferry on the Kafu, and next, but for my insisting on sending a reconnaissance forward, would have led me blindly into a trap in which we should have all starved to death. "Now," I asked, "what do you propose to do? Will you go back to your king empty-handed and say, 'Kabarega is too clever for us; we are unable to bring you anything'?"

They replied that they certainly did not want to go back to the king empty-handed, but confessed that they were at their wits' end, that I was their father, their protector, and their guide, and a very wise man, and they only asked to be allowed to place themselves in my hands. "Then," I said, "if that is so, I will tell you what we will do. We will keep Kabarega in the forest where he now is, and cut off his supplies of food, so that his army will either have to die of want, or will leave him one by one. While we are doing that, I will send a few men to a place I know of over the lake, where I hear that some of their brothers are waiting, and I will bring these brothers over, and we will leave them to guard Kabarega's country. By that time the rain will have begun to fall, there will be water on the road, and, peace having been established, we can send a small party across to Mruli to collect the ivory."

This plan, which entailed a considerable sojourn in Unyoro, did not particularly please them, but they did not like to go back empty-handed, and had owned themselves beaten, so were forced to consent to it. It was therefore settled that we should retrace our steps on the morrow and take up such positions as I might settle on.

Our return, however, was delayed by news which we got that morning. An escaped Waganda came with what appeared to be positive information that Kabarega, on hearing of our retreat, had also retraced his steps, and was then making his way to his capital; later news from our own scouts confirmed this. I at once settled to try to cut him off, and gave Owen orders to start at daylight the next morning with the whole of the

Sudanese troops and our Maxim (the only one that would go off), and make for the Kisabagwa hills, bivouac there without fires, and early on the second morning try to surprise Kabarega. Owen explained, as was very true, that his men could not move as fast as the Waganda or Wanyoro, and begged for a few of the former to use in case pursuit was necessary. I did not much like employing undisciplined Waganda for a delicate operation such as that on which he was starting, but as he was going to conduct it, and not I, I thought it best to let him have his own way. As it turned out, it was unlucky that I did so, as they caused the expedition to fail, although not exactly in the way that I had feared.

Hearing that an attack was to be made on the enemy, an energetic but indiscreet young Waganda chief collected his men, and slipping off in the middle of the night, came upon the advanced guard of Kabarega's force a few miles to the west of Kibuguzi. The usual ridiculous sort of spear-brandishing and shouting performance went on for some time, and then the enemy, thinking that the Waganda were in superior numbers, retired and informed the main body that we were advancing on the capital in

MAPALA (*showing remains of Kabarega's Capital*)

(*To face page* 143)

force. Kabarega, of course, headed back, and returned to his forest.

Owen, with Thruston, Villiers, and Arthur, after a forced march to Kisabagwa, proceeded to climb up the hills, and after spending a very uncomfortable night and day on them, discovered what had happened, and climbed down again in a very bad temper with everybody in general, and the Waganda in particular. It was a piece of bad luck, as Kabarega, completely deceived by our eastward movement, had disbanded his army, and was returning to his capital with only a thousand men.

We—that is, the main body of the Waganda, Macdonald, Purkiss, Moffat, and I—strolled quietly towards the capital, where we arrived at about the same time as Owen on the 13th.

We camped on a hill facing the deserted town on the west side of the valley.

Our failing to catch Kabarega, of course, left us in exactly the same position as that which we had discussed at Bujenji, and I intended to act generally on the lines that I had there indicated to the chiefs. It was clear that we were not likely to defeat Kabarega in open fight, and in the absence of cavalry or mounted infantry it was very unlikely that we should be able to run him down; but for the peace of Uganda I considered it absolutely necessary that his power should be permanently broken, and this, as far as I could see, could only be done by the occupation of his country. I had, however, only seven hundred regular troops at my command, and the problem was how to best distribute them so as to look after some fifty thousand square miles of savage country, of which about half was actively hostile.

After cogitating over this for some time, I came to the conclusion that it could not be done effectually, but that the best makeshift was to cut Unyoro in half by a chain of forts thrown across the neck between the Kafu river and the Albert Lake, and try to come to terms with the chiefs of southern Unyoro. As Kasigama of Toru had already made a treaty with the officials of the Company, and Rikwiamba, one of the southern Unyoro chiefs, was on our side, this seemed feasible. If this plan succeeded, it would have the effect of confining Kabarega within the small north-eastern portion of his kingdom, bounded by the Kafu, the Victoria Nile, and the Albert Lake. Its success seemed chiefly to depend on our power of convincing these people of Kabarega's inability to resist us; failing this, it was hardly to be expected that the southern Wanyoro would throw in their lot with us while they were separated from him by so slight a barrier as our chain of detached forts.

My first thought, therefore, was the belittlement of Kabarega. Situated as he was in the foodless Budonga forest, it was certain that before long he would soon eat up any supplies that he had with him, and be forced to come out to collect food. Now my tame locusts had eaten up all the supplies to the east of the line between his capital and Masindi; the country to the north-east of that, in the direction of Fovira on the Victoria Nile, was reported to be very barren; consequently the only food available for him was to the north, in the Magungu province and to the south-west, so that if I could occupy those two districts, I should be able to starve him out. As, however, I proposed to make a chain of forts from Kibiro on the Albert Lake to the Kafu, I did not want to eat up all the food on that line, while to the south of it was the Bugoma forest, as destitute of food as that of Budonga. The district to the north of Kisabagwa was reported by Owen to be very rich, and in that I determined to quarter the

10

Waganda army, occupying Kibiro and its neighbourhood with half the Sudanese, and sending the other half along the lake shores to Magungu, where I hoped their presence would prevent the utilisation of that province by Kabarega.

I have said that this arrangement was only a makeshift, but it was one which might be expanded into something really useful, if I could only manage to increase my regular army by some three or four hundred men.

Now I knew that the whole of Emin Pasha's force had not been taken over by Captain Lugard, and that Fadl el Mula Bey's battalion was still at large, and had been last heard of at Wadelai. Therefore, taking advantage of our proximity to that place, which was only thirty-five miles north of the mouth of the Victoria Nile, I proposed to send a detachment of the Magungu force down stream in search of the Sudanese wanderers, under charge of an officer who would have instructions to enlist them.

As the neighbourhood of the capital seemed the proper place for the headquarters of the force to be left in Unyoro, I spent the afternoon of our arrival and the following day in thoroughly exploring the ground, with a view to selecting a good site for a fort. I, who had done most of my active soldiering in Egypt, had a fancy for level ground with a good clear field of fire, but Macdonald, who had seen his active service on the north-west frontier of India, loved commanding positions, in the search for which he nearly walked me off my legs, over every grass-covered mountain in the neighbourhood.

We obtained some fine views of the country from various peaks, but came across no position in which I should have cared to find myself shut up with a hundred men and a very limited supply of ammunition. The hilltops were too far from the water and too large to be easily defended by a small force; while the valleys were all too narrow and commanded by hills at too close a range; there were none of the positions that I like, the ones in which the enemy must have a good long run in the open before they can reach the fort. The hill which we were encamped on seemed the best, but was far from perfect, so, as I did not intend to build the fort until my return from Kibiro, I postponed a decision until I had time to look about a little farther afield.

Owen, who shared Macdonald's love of heights, and to whom it was positive pain to spend twenty-four hours without a twenty miles' march, begged hard to be allowed to make a reconnaissance to Masaja Mkuro, which he was certain was an ideal position for a fort, and one from which, he assured me, heliographic communication could be established with Uganda. My information and personal observation led me to believe that it was a decapitated cone, without water at the top, on which a small garrison might easily be reduced by thirst; and that, having no signallers, facilities for heliographic communication, although theoretically desirable, were practically unimportant. Further, that the expedition would take three days, would probably waste some men and ammunition, and that, even if it were desirable, it might well be postponed until our return; so poor Owen had to undergo the martyrdom of sleeping in the same place for three consecutive nights.

On the 13th we all moved off together to Kitoba, the point at which the Waganda were to branch off to the north to take up their position on the outskirts of the forest. On the march, at about four miles from the capital, we crossed the Hoima river, a running stream thirty feet broad, on the farther side of which was what appeared to be an ideal site for a fort. This, however, did not save me from being trotted up all the hills round Kitoba, which we found to have the usual disadvantages of distance from water and big rounded tops.

That afternoon's *shauri* was an exceptionally long and painful one, as the whole line of conduct of the Waganda during our separation had to be discussed; but everything seemed to be settled at last, and the chiefs made to understand that they were to constantly patrol the edges of the forest, and be ready to drive Kabarega back at any point at which he might show himself, and to confine their foraging operations to the north and east, leaving the food supply on my line of forts untouched.

Vowing that they would not fail in the smallest matter to follow my orders, they all withdrew; and I gave a sigh of relief; for the question of the disposal of the Waganda had always been a difficult one. They did not at all relish the idea of being left without the support of the Sudanese, and I knew that it would take all my persuasive powers to make them do so. It soon proved that my fears had not been groundless, for, just as I was going to bed, the whole band trooped back again, and announced through Kakunguru that they could not possibly go to Kisabagwa, but were willing to stay where they were, instead of coming to Kibiro with me as they would have wished. As it was absolutely impossible that they should be allowed to stay where they were to eat up all the food, and as, if I put their backs up, they were perfectly capable of packing up their traps and marching to Uganda, there was nothing for it but to go through the whole argument again. After about two hours' talk, they for the second time departed with the same protestations that they had before made, but leaving me very doubtful whether I should not have a repetition of the performance next morning.

I used to think that the king was an exceptionally vacillating person, but later experience convinced me that in this respect he differs but little from his subjects. They all seem to be held in the power of the last strong man that they have come in contact with. I have no doubt that in the afternoon they had been thoroughly persuaded by my arguments; then, as they sat over their camp-fires in the evening, some chief had held forth, and carried them away with him ; then they had been persuaded by me again, and probably, before the next day was finished, had all, in their hearts, gone over to the man in possession, but luckily I had been able to allude to some personal considerations which kept them from acting on the advice of my rival.

To rule these people one should be in constant touch with them, which is unfortunately very difficult under existing conditions in Uganda, where the Commissioner's many duties take up much of the time which he would otherwise devote to the pleasure of daily and nightly *shauris.*

A good many cases of smallpox had by this time broken out in the Waganda army, and I strongly urged on the chiefs the necessity of isolating them,—advice which was wholly disregarded.

Apart from the rest of the Waganda, a force of four hundred men under command of the Kangao had from the first been attached to headquarters, and entrusted with the duties of collecting intelligence and providing food for the regulars. These, I decided, were still to remain with me, and act as messengers between my headquarters and Kakunguru's camp.

A great loss of ammunition had been going on lately among the armed porters. These men carried ten rounds of Snider ammunition each, which was counted by an officer every night. The pouches were not of a very good pattern, and it was possible that a round might occasionally be lost by accident; but since we had been joined by the Waganda, it had been noticed that hardly a day passed without several men in each section being two or three rounds short at the evening inspection. This sudden increase of loss naturally led to the suspicion that the Waganda had something to do with it, but nothing could be proved, and we could only tell the Swahilis that the value of the cartridges would be mulcted from their pay. They are not paid, however, until their return to the coast, and the prospect of so distant a punishment had no more deterrent effect on them than that of the Day of Judgment.

At Kitoba, however, clear proof was forthcoming against a Swahili who had been caught in the act of selling his ammunition to a Waganda. The buyer, unfortunately, escaped; but as it was now certain that the Waganda did buy ammunition from our porters, I sent for Kakunguru, and explained to him clearly that I should shoot the very next man caught doing so. Macdonald wanted me to shoot the porter at once, but I thought that, as we were on the point of parting from the Waganda, it was not a favourable time for making an example, and contented myself with assembling the Swahilis, and telling them I was determined to stop a practice which endangered the safety of the whole force, and that I would do so if I had to shoot the whole of them. I then had punishment administered to the offender, and from that day forward not another round of ammunition was lost.

From the capital to Kitoba, the country had been one mass of banana groves, sweet potato and bean fields, but soon after leaving next morning, we entered a thick bush country destitute of cultivation. The road, however, was broad and good, and even the boat was able to keep fairly well up with us.

Before leaving, I had been told by Kakunguru that his scouts had been as far as Kitanwa, and reported that the enemy was in force in the neighbourhood, and intended to contest our advance to the salt mines of Kibiro. As these mines are one of Kabarega's chief sources of wealth, I thought it not unlikely that this news might be correct, and especially that, when the Wanyoro saw only the small Sudanese force with which we were advancing, they might at last make a stand.

After marching for about an hour we heard firing on our right, which soon increased in volume, and it was evident that a sharp skirmish · was taking place, but owing to the thickness of the bush we could see nothing, and for the same reason were unable to get out of the long single file in which we were advancing. I rigged up the field observatory once or twice, but it was not high enough to let us see over the bush and grass, and there was nothing to be done but march steadily on with our eyes and ears open.

It was rather tantalising work being so near the enemy, who were evidently making a stand, and being utterly unable to get at them, nor could we tell whether they were engaged with the Kangao's four hundred who were scouting for us, or with the main body of the Waganda. As the firing gradually seemed to die away to our right rear, I thought it probable that it was with the former, in which case our occupation of Kitanwa would probably be uncontested.

Having by mistake taken a wrong road,—that leading to Magungu,—we had to retrace our steps for some distance, and then got into a very narrow bypath, along which our progress became slow.

A little before three we left the bush, and after crossing a valley with a sluggish, boggy stream, ascended a slight ridge, and found ourselves among the banana groves of Kitanwa.

CHAPTER XII

THE OCCUPATION OF KIBIRO

Hopes of peace—A prisoner wanted—The governor of Kibiro—
Macdonald's reconnaissance—Capture of Kibiro—A barren
district—Baboons—View of the Albert Lake—Incendiaries—
Water, water all around—A desolate scene—Food difficulties
—Value of Kibiro—Difficulties of supply—A man-hunt—A
grain store—The descent to the Lake—A mummy—The boat
afloat — Description of Kibiro — A foraging expedition —
Arthur's naval action—Preparations for the Magungu expedition—The dummy Maxim—Navigability of the Victoria Nile.

THE Wanyoro had so clearly shown their
unwillingness to fight us, that I thought
it possible they might now be induced to make
peace if I could only get into communication
with them. So far we had wholly failed to do
this. A few insignificant and stupid prisoners
had been captured and released, promising to
take peaceful messages to their friends, but it is
doubtful if these were ever delivered, and even
more doubtful if they were listened to even if
they were.

What I wanted was some influential person,

who, convinced of our good intentions, could be sent to discuss the matter with his fellow chiefs. Report said that just such a man was to be found at Kibiro, an important town, owing to its salt industry, and ruled by a governor who had not taken any active part in the operations against us. I knew that to the suspicious savage mind any invitation to come in and have a chat would have been worse than useless—indeed, I do not think I could have persuaded any one to give the message; but if I could only manage to take him prisoner, I felt sure that I could make use of him. Therefore, as soon as the troops had had a short rest after our arrival at Kitanwa, I sent Macdonald forward with a small party to spy out the land, and report on the possibilities of a night surprise on Kibiro.

He returned soon after sunset, and reported that, after marching for about three and a half miles over a barren, rocky country, he had come to the edge of the escarpment falling into the Albert Lake. From this place he got a good view of the town, which he described as a large collection of the usual beehive-shaped huts, disposed on a plain between the foot of the escarpment and the lake; after examining it carefully through his glasses, he was sure that it was still fully occupied.

On receiving this news, I ordered Owen to parade a company at once, capture the place, and take as many prisoners as possible. He got off at ten with Arthur and a hundred men. Hearing no more of him, I started at five next morning with Purkiss and his boat, which I was very glad at last to have a chance of putting on her natural element.

Half a mile's march took us out of the cultivated land, and we found ourselves in a district of bare black rocks. Here and there a little soil had collected, clothed with short tufts of burnt-up grass or occasional stunted trees. Our road followed the summit of a ridge, the left side of which was deeply scored with gorges losing themselves in their turnings among the mountains; while its right sloped gradually down to a valley running parallel to it, from the farther side of which rose a range of rugged hills. A few columns of smoke on the farther side of these seemed to indicate the presence of inhabitants and consequently cultivation, but we saw nothing more human than the troops of big baboons who sat on the rocks and complacently watched our

progress with hardly more interest than the inhabitants of Uganda had shown when the soon to be
victorious army had marched out of their capital.

We had been walking on for about an hour,
watching the wall of rock which cut the sky in
front of us, when I noticed that it had suddenly
become lower, that is, that there appeared to be
more sky, and was wondering on the cause of
this strange phenomenon, when a little sparkle
near the horizon showed me that I was looking
on the Albert Lake, whose farther shore and the
distant Lur-land hills were lost in the haze, and
were thus blended into one with the clouds. A
few more paces opened out a narrow strip of yellow
sand between the water and the edge of the cliff,
and, stepping off the road on to a little knoll, I
saw what, alas! was no longer the town of Kibiro
lying beneath me. Whether some lingering Wanyoro had stayed behind for the pleasure of burning the town under the conqueror's eyes, or
whether it was the work of some mischievous
Sudanese, was never found out; but shortly after
he entered it, Owen noticed that some huts were
in flames, and within half an hour the whole place
was burnt down.

This news was given in a note from Owen

handed to me while I was watching the ruined town. He said that as he descended the hill, he could see the people flocking out in the moonlight, in such a hurry that they had not time to follow their usual practice of setting the place on fire, but that when he reached the plain it was deserted.

I was disappointed that no prisoners had been taken, and very much annoyed at the burning of the town. However, as far as we were concerned, no great harm was done, as the grain stores were all buried, and during our stay at Kibiro we were able to unearth a large supply of food.

Owen, in his note, had called Kibiro a picturesque spot. I should rather have described it as desolate. Beneath us lay a great stretch of barren shingle, out of which the charred timbers of the wrecked village stood up in gaunt patches. To the right, a torrent, springing out of the rocks, had worn a broad bed in the soft undersoil, leaving a mass of salt-encrusted pinnacles where some harder formation had resisted its action. In the distance these resembled the ruins of some old-world marble city, in strange contrast to the flimsy embers of the Wanyoro village.

Apparently forgetful that he was camped on

the head waters of the Nile, Owen closed his report with an urgent appeal for fresh water to be sent down to him. I replied that as his company was not a strong one, I hoped the Albert would suffice for his stay there. After a good look round, I sent Purkiss on to Kibiro with the boat, ordering him to put it together as quickly as possible, and myself returned to Kitanwa.

From the value of its salt mines it was evidently desirable to hold Kibiro as long as we were obliged to keep troops in Unyoro, and as it was necessary to have the boat on the lake, it also made a convenient spot for a harbour.

It was not, however, a very satisfactory place for a post, as, although the position was from a tactical point of view excellent, and the fresh water was more plentiful than Owen imagined, the district produced no food whatever, and as far as I could see, all supplies for the garrison would have to be brought from Kitanwa ; so, before definitely deciding on the sites for the forts I intended to build, I wished to thoroughly clear up the question of where the nearest points of supply were, and if it were possible to find any food-producing locality nearer to the lake than

Kitanwa, or, better still, one which would actually command the Kibiro plain.

The country to the left of the Kitanwa-Kibiro road was obviously hopeless, so, after a short rest, I started off with Macdonald and half a dozen Sudanese to explore the range of hills to the right, behind which I had seen fires in the morning. We found it to be rather less barren than the ridge on which the road runs, being covered to a great extent with coarse grass, but only occasional small patches of cultivation were seen. As the valley, fairly broad and easy at its upper end, where we had crossed it, approached the lake, it became steeper and more rugged, until it opened into the Kibiro plain in a rocky and impassable gorge, completely cutting off the hills on which we were from the harbour. Consequently, even if the small amount of cultivation on them had been sufficient for the wants of the garrison, the post would have been no nearer to Kibiro, in point of time, than if it were at Kitanwa. I therefore decided to build our fort at the latter place.

On our return journey we spied some Wanyoro peering at us from behind the rocks, and at once sent the Sudanese in pursuit. A most exciting chase ensued, which ended in the soldiers securing one captive, a man of about fifty years old, who from his appearance seemed to be a well-to-do person.

Shortly afterwards I came upon a group of huts, near which I discovered a large grain store, which our prisoner told us was Kabarega's own property, and that as such the people had not dared to empty it. On returning to camp, I sent a guard to look after it during the night, and despatched a party next morning to transfer its contents to Kitanwa. It proved to contain sufficient grain to supply the garrison for six months.

Next morning I started off again for Kibiro with Macdonald, and was followed later by Thruston with a company and a half of Sudanese. Villiers and Moffat were left at Kitanwa, to begin building the fort on a site which Macdonald had selected.

After passing the point from which I had seen Kibiro on the day before, we began the descent of the rocky escarpment, which was so steep that even the Wanyoro had been forced to make a zigzag path down it.

As we reached one of the lower bends, I noticed what appeared to be a man drinking at a little gully about fifty yards ahead of us, but on getting nearer it proved to be a dried-up corpse squatting on its hams, and with its right hand held out scooped up within six inches of its mouth, as if in the act of drinking. It had a bullet wound between the shoulders. Whether the man had been shot in the act of drinking, or after being shot had made his way to the stream, and died just as he reached the water, it was impossible to say; but in either case it was curious that he should not have fallen over as he died. The state of preservation of the body was also remarkable. I have seen plenty of corpses on old battlefields in Egypt, dried up to skeletons covered with parchment-like skin, through which the bones clearly showed, but in this case the flesh had shrunk but little, and seemed as if it had been subjected to some mummifying process. I also missed the " Bombay Duck "-like smell peculiar to corpses in this stage.

I found Owen comfortably encamped on the sandy beach which runs down to the lake, and his men scattered about the plain busily searching for loot. Purkiss was still hard at work on the boat, the putting together of which proved a tough job. The sections had been much strained during the march, and considerable force was required to make them fit together; the screw bolts, too, had got very rusty, and required a good deal of cleaning before they could be got into their places. However, she was afloat, although leaking badly, and Purkiss hoped, with the help of tow and red lead, to have her fit for work in the course of a few hours.

Having inspected the boat, I set to work to examine the position, so as to be able to start fort-building as soon as possible. We were on a shingly plain about a thousand yards broad, extending from the lake to the foot of the escarpment, which rises about fifteen hundred feet nearly sheer from its edge, curling outwards to the north and south so as to inclose Kibiro in an amphitheatre of rocks. From a deep gorge in this escarpment sprang a small stream, which, gradually widening as it traversed the softer ground of the plain, had cut a channel from fifty to one hundred and fifty yards wide, and with banks some twenty feet high. The mouth of the channel had been silted up by the action of the waves, thus forming a miniature lagoon connected with the lake by a bar. A row of scrub-covered dunes, alternating with deep depressions, lined the banks of the watercourse, and very scanty patches of grass sprang up here and there among the shingle.

As there might be some difficulty in feeding the garrison, I wished to make it as small as possible, and decided that it should consist of an officer and twenty-five men; but with so small a force to defend it, it was necessary that the fort should be very strong. I determined to place it in a triangle formed by the lake shore and the little lagoon, thus protecting its front and right flank by water, while, as Macdonald pointed out, we might gain the same protection to the rear by turning the stream into one of the depressions and filling that up. A fort there situated would have a fine field of fire on all sides except to its left rear, where the watercourse and the dunes would afford some cover to our enemy; but, by placing a little look-out post of six men on one of the higher mounds about three hundred yards off, I thought I should be able to prevent any surprise from that quarter.

Soon after I got into camp, Bilal Effendi, the native officer in command of one of the Sudanese companies, reported a large herd of goats on the shore to the south of us, and asked leave to go in pursuit. Thinking it better to have a European in charge, I asked Arthur to take command of the party. After following the herd and their guardians for about six miles over the rugged ground at the foot of the hills, he had suddenly come upon a large body of armed Wanyoro collected in a sandy bay from which he was cut off by some precipitous rocks. A number of canoes were floating in the bay. Seeing that he could not get at them, he thought it best to retrace his steps and renew the attack by water. The day was intensely hot down in this hole, and when he got back at two, he was completely pumped, but full of ardour and anxious to have another try.

By the time he returned, the boat had been caulked up and was fit for use, but as I was going to send her off to Magungu next morning, I was rather loath to let her run any risk in a mere goat-chase; but I wanted to give the troops the treat of some meat, and Arthur was sure, from the appearance of the Wanyoro, that they were not mere villagers, but an armed force, either intending to break through our line to join Kabarega or to attack our camp. After exacting from him the most solemn promises to be back by nine that evening at the latest, and to run no risks with the boat, I let him start, accompanied by Bilal Effendi and eight Sudanese. He returned punctually at the latest hour I had mentioned, and reported that he had had a very successful and exciting afternoon's work.

After sailing south for an hour and a half, he had come upon the bay in which he had seen the Wanyoro, and found it still occupied. The enemy, about three hundred strong, at once opened a brisk fire, which was returned from the boat as she pushed on, until the shallow water prevented her farther progress. Then Bilal Effendi and six Sudanese jumped overboard, and, wading ashore, covered by the fire of the two men Arthur kept with him in the boat, succeeded in cutting out the canoes, and driving the enemy into the hills.

Arthur described the agility with which the Wanyoro bounded up the precipices as perfectly marvellous; he said he would not have believed that any human being could have got over such ground at all. Taking the canoes in tow, and sending off the captured goats in charge of four men, by a path which he discovered, he returned himself to camp.

The canoes were heavy, clumsily made "dug-outs," but proved very useful to us after the steel boat had left. The expedition was also useful by giving confidence to the Sudanese, and showing them their immense superiority over the Wanyoro.

Arthur, like all the officers, except Owen, Thruston, and Purkiss, the three lucky ones selected for the Wadelai expedition, had been rather low at the thought of being left behind while exploration and possible excitement were going on to the front; but I think his afternoon in a baking sun, seated in the particularly cramped and narrow stern-sheets of the *James Martin*, made him realise that the beds of those employed in the naval part of the expedition would not be wholly of roses.

While Arthur was fighting his battle, Owen and I were discussing the plans of the Wadelai expedition. I settled that he was to take Thruston and two hundred men with him, and march along the lake shore to the old Egyptian fort at Magungu, where he was to establish himself until he had either thoroughly defeated any of Kabarega's troops who might be in the neighbourhood, or convinced himself that none of the enemy were in the province.

Having done this, he was to cross the Victoria

Nile with his whole force, and march down the bank of the White Nile to Wadelai, where he would probably find some Sudanese troops under Fadl el Mula Bey. He was to enlist as many of these as possible, and return with them to Magungu. Whether he left a temporary garrison or not at that place was to depend on the number of recruits he might be able to collect. If he got less than one hundred, he was to content himself with making another demonstration against Kabarega from the south, and then bring his whole force back to Kibiro. He was to make a treaty of friendship with the Sheikh of Wadelai, and get all the information he could as to the movements of the Dervishes to the north. He was to be accompanied by the steel boat, under command of Purkiss, and was to keep touch with her as far as possible, always taking care that she and his force halted together at night. Although he begged very hard for it, I had to refuse him the Maxim which worked, and he had to put up with the dummy, which, however, looked very imposing in the bows of the boat.

I had promised the Waganda that they should not be kept at Kisabagwa for more than a month, and thought it probable that they would take French leave if I kept them beyond that time. Although they were not of very much use when it came to real fighting, their numbers impressed the Wanyoro, who, I thought, would probably make a descent on us as soon as the Waganda withdrew. That they would do so as soon as the forts were finished I sincerely hoped; but in the absence of the Magungu expedition I should only have two hundred men, which, although amply sufficient for Kitanwa and Kibiro, would not have been enough, without forts, to guard the whole line from the latter place to the Kafu; while if, on the withdrawal of the Waganda, I left it unguarded, Kabarega would be able to break through into southern Unyoro and upset all my plans. I therefore told Owen that he must be back at Kibiro, whatever happened, within twenty-eight days.

Owen's orders were explained to Purkiss, who was further instructed to collect all possible information about the character of the winds, currents, obstacles to navigation, etc., as well as to the number of canoes and boats available, and what boat-building operations, if any, were carried on. He was also told if possible to push up the

Victoria Nile and find out if it was navigable as far as the Murchison Falls, and, if he could, collect information as to its navigability between them and the Karuma Falls. I was anxious for information on this point, as at that time I had some hopes of establishing water communication with Unyoro direct from the Victoria Lake, but Grant's explorations later on proved this route to be impracticable.

CHAPTER XIII

LIFE AT KIBIRO

Departure of expedition—Making ourselves snug—The salt mines —Mode of collection—Mwanga's perquisites—News from Owen—An unwelcome gift—A good march—Building the fort—The waterworks—Indefatigable fishermen—An alarm —The effects of echo—The harbour—Refugees—Jigger sores —Medicinal springs—A canoe race—A lubberly crew— Naval architecture—Pleasures of Kibiro—Some disadvantages —Swahili cooks—Fires on the hills—A pitched battle— Narrow escape of Kabarega—He leaves his kingdom—A big haul—Return of the boat—Cautious mariners.

THE land portion of the Wadelai force marched off at daylight on the 20th of January, but some slight alteration was still wanted to the boat, and she did not sail until nine. The wind was light and not very favourable, and it was not until nearly noon that we finally lost sight of her, and felt that the Wadelai expedition had really started.

Having got rid of it, we set to work to make the little garrison of fifty men with which I was left as snug as possible. We began by cutting down the scrub on the dunes, which impeded our fire, and, dragging it near the camp, built it into a rough zereba, having one end on the lake and the other on the lagoon. While the men were doing this, Macdonald and I, with strings and foot-rules, were laying out the foundations of the fort and look-out post, choosing a course for the channel by which we hoped to fill up the depression, and discussing the best way to keep open the bar, and so utilise the lagoon as a harbour for the boat.

In the afternoon we followed the stream to its source, and investigated the salt works. I had imagined, on first seeing the place, that the stream was a salt one, which was spread out over the ground to evaporate, but on following it to its source at the foot of the gorge which I have already mentioned, I found that it was a boiling sulphur spring flowing out of a small cavern in the rock, and did not taste in the least salt. That substance was therefore evidently contained in the ground, out of which it was dissolved by the hot water.

The stream, which is a very small one, about eighteen inches wide and three deep at its source, is reinforced by two or three minor springs, and is carefully led in raised channels along the dry river bed, and let off here and there by little sluices into the evaporating tanks at the sides. Having collected the rough salt and earth from these pans, the Wanyoro give it a second washing to dissolve it, and then filter the brine through large porous pots, many hundreds of which are placed in niches in the steep banks. The filtered brine is then re-evaporated in large earthen pans. As the channels and pans are all built on the river bed, down which a heavy torrent must roll from the hills in the wet season, I imagine that all this work is washed away in the rains and has to be rebuilt every year.

Before the departure of the Waganda, Mwanga had impressed on them the desirability of bringing him back a good tribute of salt, which is worth a pound a load at Kampala; he had modestly mentioned two thousand loads as the quantity he would like. Before parting with me, Kakunguru had mentioned this, and had asked leave to send men to collect salt. I had made no objection to this, and, the day after our arrival, about four hundred Waganda had turned up to carry away the first instalment of the king's share of the spoils. The finished salt, stored in

the huts, had, however, all been collected by the
Sudanese, and the searchers looked very glum
when they discovered that, instead of being able
to profit by the work of the Wanyoro they would
have to do some themselves, and spent the day
talking over the matter.　On the following day
another party came, with the same result, and there
the matter ended, and poor Mwanga never got a
single basketful.

At two o'clock next morning I was roused by
my orderly bringing a note from Owen, dated
from Butiaba, a place about fifteen miles off,
saying that he had captured four hundred sheep
and goats, and asking me to send for them.　I did
not quite see why he had not sent them himself,
and, short of men as I was, did not much like
parting with the escort which would be required
for them.　However, I could not afford to sacri-
fice so much food, so I stirred up Bilal Effendi,
and told him to get a party ready to go back
with the messengers.　These men were making
a good march ; fifteen miles out and back, and
out again, and then probably another fifteen miles
as soon as they joined Owen, would make sixty
miles in all, not bad for about thirty hours.

The next day we began the fort, a square

enclosure, with mud walls seven feet high and three feet thick, and with towers at two corners for flank-defence. We could not get on very fast with it; as, to prevent the mud walls bulging, it was necessary to let each layer dry before we began the next; we therefore put only two men on to build, giving them half the remainder to mix and carry mud, and set the other half to work at the water channel. They were not very clever at this job, and had endless mishaps, but, after four days' hard work, had the satisfaction of seeing a fine stream tumbling into the hole. The absorption of the dry ground, however, and evaporating power of the sun were extraordinary, and although a good stream was running in for the sixteen days I was at Kibiro, the water was not up to a man's waist when I left.

The Sudanese were most indefatigable fishers, and in the matter of patience could have given points to any old gentleman that I have ever seen on the Thames. The moment work was over, they began to line the lake shores, or put out to sea in our three canoes, and, armed with bits of stick with strings dangling at the ends, would solemnly sit there until they were seen no more in the darkness. I do not know whether they fished all night, but

they were certainly always hard at work when, at
the earliest streak of dawn, I looked out of my tent
door.

At sunset we were startled by what sounded
like six volleys in rapid succession to the north.
We were all convinced that they were not single
shots, and a good deal of speculation was indulged
in as to what was happening. It was very improb-
able that Owen's force should have been driven
back by any body of the enemy that he was likely
to meet, and it therefore seemed almost certain
that the escort for the goats had got into
difficulties. Bilal Effendi, who shared this view,
was very anxious to go out to their assistance, but
I thought that if the escort of twenty men had
met any force strong enough to defeat them, I
should only be running the risk of getting cut up
in detail if I further divided the thirty men who
were left with me, so, not without some anxiety, I
awaited events.

At eight o'clock the party, with its large herd,
arrived safely, and stated that they had fired
no volleys, but only a few single shots at some
spearmen who had threatened them. I suppose
the echo from the hills had been responsible for
our scare. This news was a great relief, as,

apart from the safety of the men, I had not at all relished the idea of losing a hundred and twenty rounds of our small store of ammunition.

Our waterworks finished, we set to work on the harbour. The former had been nice paddling sort of work, such as I had not enjoyed since the days when I built mud castles with a wooden spade ; but when I began to tackle the harbour, my sense of my own importance increased greatly, and I felt that I was engaged (I admit on a smallish scale) in one of those fights of man against nature which have been the glory of our century. I have mentioned that the mass of water with which I had to deal was about eighteen inches wide by three deep, and it will therefore be understood that our engineering operations were on no very gigantic scale ; but I am sure that Macdonald and I felt as deep a sense of our responsibility as the engineers who had to solve the same problem at the famous Durban bar. We had one advantage over them, however, in that we could try experiments, and even indulge in failures, without being called over the coals by an indignant town council for wasting its hard-earned millions.

Our first operation consisted of simple dredging, which seemed to produce most satisfactory results, and I went to bed after our first day's work, happily convinced that our labours were completed, and that this Kibiro harbour would remain for all time a silent witness to the simple aborigines of the white man's skill.

These rose-coloured dreams were, however, somewhat dulled when, on inspecting the works early next morning, I noticed that the bar had quietly resumed its shape and position of the day before, and that the only change in the aspect of affairs was that a canoe which on the previous morning had been outside and unable to get in, was now inside and unable to get out. I think I expressed my views in accurate if somewhat colloquial English to Macdonald by remarking that water was "rum stuff." However, we got the better of it in the long run, and by means of various breakwaters and embankments persuaded the stream to scour out the sand, and prevented the waves from filling it up again.

After a few days, Wanyoro men and women began to drop in, saying they preferred the chance of having their heads cut off by us to dying of starvation in the forest. They gave a very satisfactory (to us) account of Kabarega's condition, and said that his troops were gradually leaving him to seek districts where there was something to eat.

One woman came in accompanied by a little boy with the worst case of jigger sores I ever saw. He had lost all his toes, the stumps of which were still raw and ulcerous, and the poor little wretch had to crawl about on his hands and knees with his feet lifted off the ground.

We were pretty free from these pests at Kibiro; but Moffat, who came down the hill to visit us occasionally, said that they were exceptionally bad at Kitanwa, and that an alarming number of the troops and porters were disabled by them. He was very pleased at the discovery of the hot sulphur springs, and kindly sent down all his itch patients, who were pretty plentiful, to have a course of baths; he said it saved his sulphur ointment, which was running short.

One morning early some excitement was caused by the sight of three large canoes coming from the northward, following the curve of the bay which lay to our right. At first we thought that they were going to land there, but they paddled steadily on, and, rounding the little promontory between it and our camp, passed within a couple of hundred yards in front of us.

After trying our best to induce them to come in, without effect, Macdonald started off in chase in one of our captured canoes ; but he might as well have tried to overtake an express train on a garden roller. His canoe was very heavy and clumsy, and was manned by the most lubberly crew it was ever my misfortune to see. After hopelessly wobbling about for a quarter of an hour, they had the satisfaction of seeing the object of their chase disappear over the western sky-line while they were still hardly half a mile from land.

Two days afterwards the canoes returned from the south heavily laden with provisions, evidently intended for the force in the Budonga forest. Emboldened by our helplessness at sea, they came close in shore and had a little chat with us, but could not be induced to land. We could, of course, have easily sunk them had we wished, but I thought it more important to prove our friendliness to the population than deprive Kabarega of a few loads of rations.

I had hoped to take advantage of my enforced stay at Kibiro to make a trip to the western shore of the lake and find out the feeling of the people on that side. Kavalli, at whose place

Stanley had stopped, was, I knew, friendly, but the remainder of the chiefs were nominally under Kabarega, and I was anxious to know their real feeling towards him.

I had thought of choosing a calm evening and paddling across in one of our captured dug-outs, steering by the light of the fires we always saw on the opposite shore, but the utter failure of Macdonald's crew as mariners convinced me that this attempt was not likely to be a success, so I thought of trying to turn two of the canoes into a sailing boat, or rather raft, joining them together by a platform and stepping a mast in the middle. Our carpenter assured me, however, that he was thoroughly up in building the class of outrigger canoes common at Zanzibar, and that if I would leave the matter in his hands, he would make me exactly what I wanted. I unfortunately consented, and after wasting a week, he produced a thing with two enormous water-logged beams held out from the sides by other huge pieces of timber, which simply refused to move through the water. As a door for the fort had still to be made, which would take up all the carpenter's time until we left, I had to give up the attempt, to the great satisfaction of Macdonald and Arthur, who were good enough to say that they wished to enjoy the pleasure of my society for a few years longer.

I suppose that, take it all round, Kibiro would generally be described as about as " God-forsaken a hole " as could well be imagined. It was hot, stuffy, deserted, and glaring, and the heat thrown off the cliffs made it even hotter by night than by day, when at all events there was generally a sea breeze ; but I confess I liked it. Perhaps it was partly the satisfaction, after five months' tramping, of being able to go to bed with the knowledge that I should not have to get up at four next morning and march. The presence of water was also pleasant ; my tent was pitched on the beach within five yards of the lake, and it was nice to sit in it by day and see the waves breaking almost on to one's tent-pegs, and to lie at night, when the land breeze had dropped, and fall asleep listening to the ripple of the water.

Then I was fully occupied all day with our various " public works " without being tired by long tedious marches with my eyes fixed on my toes to see what I was going to stumble over next. And last, but not least, there were no Waganda, and consequently no *shauris*.

However, it was not all joy; one night a squall came off the cliffs and blew down all our tents; on another we were invaded by a plague of flying ants, which swarmed so thickly round our lantern that we had to blow out the candle and dine in darkness and happy ignorance of the proportion of ant and goat contained in each mouthful we lifted on our forks.

As I have mentioned the subject of food, I think I ought to say a word about the Swahili cook. To begin with, he is not a cook at all, but merely a person who has just enough intelligence to enable him to place raw food on the top of a fire. I suppose that in prehistoric times there must have been one original real cook, for every successive meat-warmer admits on cross-examination that he has never actually cooked before, but that he has been for a long time a "cook's boy,"—that is, a porter whose duty it is to carry the pots and fetch water.

I had started from the coast with a ruffian who claimed to be a real cook, and drew wages as such, but I soon made him exchange the kettle which he habitually carried on his head for a bale of cloth, and took on an ordinary porter. He, again, was exchanged later on for an ex-cook's boy; and I found, after I had gained a little experience, that the best plan was to change as soon as I had begun to grow tired of any one particular method of making goat nastier than nature intended it to be. I must say for them that, although their repertoire was always the same,—*minchi*, *stewi*, and *roasti*,—the strange and appalling flavours which they managed to impart to these apparently simple dishes varied considerably with the manner of manipulation of the artists.

During the whole of our stay at Kibiro large fires were seen nightly on the hills to the north and south of us, and rumours were constantly flying about as to intended attacks on our camp; once or twice, too, we had authoritative messages from Kakunguru that an attack in force was imminent. I did not, however, place much credence in these reports, as, although our force was small, our position was an excellent one, and it seemed to me much more likely that if he attacked at all, Kabarega would try to hit two birds with one stone, and, by possessing himself of Kitanwa, obtain a good food district for his own use, and at the same time cut off our supplies; but he did neither of these things, and left both forts severely alone.

We, however, did not reciprocate this forbearance. On the 28th of January I had a letter from Kakunguru, saying he had received certain information that Kabarega with his whole force had come out of the forest and was encamped about ten miles to the north-east of us, and suggesting a combined attack. I thought it better to devote all our energies to finishing the forts, and told him to move out himself with his Waganda and try to surprise the enemy.

He started next day with about a quarter of his force, bivouacked a few miles to the west of Bitiberi, and next day quite unexpectedly marched into the middle of the Wanyoro. He was in single file, and it took him a long time to close up his rear; but the enemy were equally unprepared, and a sharp skirmish began between the two advanced parties, gradually developing into a pitched battle, in which the whole of the two forces was engaged. Finally, the Waganda got the best of it, and put the Wanyoro to complete flight, in which Kabarega, running across a bit of open ground from one clump to another, was so hard pressed that he had to drop his favourite rifle, and would almost certainly have been killed, had there been anyone in the Waganda army who could shoot straight. Straight shooting, however, does not seem to be a very common accomplishment in this part of the world, to judge by Kakunguru's statement that the opposing forces were firing hard at each other for three hours at close quarters, and that, as far as he knew, only three casualties occurred.

The results of the action were, however, very important, for after his defeat Kabarega disbanded his force, and with a few personal followers made his way across the Nile into the Wakedi country, of which his mother was a native, and where he was consequently well received. The Waganda also had the satisfaction of capturing three thousand goats, sixty head of cattle, forty guns, ten tusks of ivory, and a great quantity of ammunition, besides recovering five hundred of their countrywomen held as slaves by Kabarega.

On the evening of the 31st of January great excitement was caused by the appearance on the northern horizon of the steel boat. That Owen and his force could have reached Wadelai and sent the boat back in the nine days that had passed since his departure seemed almost impossible, yet that was the only explanation we could think of, if things were going well, and we would none of us allow ourselves to imagine the possibility of a disaster.

We were kept a long time in suspense, for the lake was dead calm, and it was some time after we had finished our dinner before my orderly came to the tent and announced that the boat was near. Then, armed with lanterns, we trooped off to the harbour, and, peering into the darkness, shouted in English, Arabic, and Kiswahili. No answer came back, and for five minutes I thought we had been called out by a false alarm, when a dim black object glided into sight, and was almost instantly lost against a clump of rushes about fifty yards from the shore. Then came a question in Arabic, "Who are you?" and then, "Tell us the names of some of the people here." On this information being conveyed, the boat slid out of the rushes and was soon alongside the pier. "We have had such a rough time of it," said Purkiss, "that we did not like to come in too close until we were sure that you were friends." He certainly looked as if he had had a rough time of it, so, without asking him any more questions, I marched him off to the tent, and after giving him a good tot of whisky, without too much water, regaled him on the remains of the leg of goat which was left from our dinner; after which he told us his story.

CHAPTER XIV

THE MAGUNGU EXPEDITION

Tyawai—Katulla Island—Mpata—Separation of the parties—
Stopped by the *sudd*—False information—Back to Mpata—
A prearranged signal—Treachery—A Sudanese hero—The
last ration—Return to Kibiro—Owen's return—A pleasant
surprise—A sudden attack—Steadiness of the troops—Sling-
ing arms—Arrival at Magungu—Searching for the boat—
In danger from friends—Attack on the fort—An unsatisfactory
raft—Return to headquarters.

AFTER leaving Kibiro on the 20th, Purkiss
had caught up the land force near Butiaba,
just in time to point out and assist in the capture
of the goats which had caused me so much
anxiety; and, anchoring close under the Tyawai
promontory, had slept in Owen's camp. On the
next day, owing to shallow water and weeds near
the shore, he was unable to join the main body;
while on the day after, a strong on-shore gale
springing up, he thought it advisable to stand out
to sea, only putting in when the wind dropped
towards evening. He lay for the night under
the lee of Katulla Island, staying in the boat,

as he did not care for the many strange bedfellows of the crocodile tribe who would have
shared the beach with him.

On the 23rd the land column, of which he got
considerably ahead, appeared in sight, and on his
putting in to meet it, he found it warmly engaged
with the enemy. The fight over, he exchanged
two sound men for a couple wounded in the
action, and put out to an island near Mpata
Point, where he anchored for the night, as on
this squally lake he did not like staying on a lee
shore. This precaution was justified by a heavy
gale springing up in the small hours of the morning, and obliging him to leave his anchorage and
put out to sea.

On his return he found that Owen's force had
marched off and was out of sight, so, having
orders to join the main body at Magungu if for
any reason they became separated, he tried to
make his way to that place, but found the mouth
of the Victoria Nile choked with *sudd*, in which
the boat got jammed. After searching all day
for a channel, he was forced to put back in the
evening to his old anchorage.

On the 25th a gale forced the boat to take
shelter under the western shore of the lake, and

she passed the night near Boki's village, where the crew were able to land for a short time to cook food.

Being told by the natives that a force under command of white men was marching down the White Nile a few miles ahead, Purkiss thought that Owen had succeeded in crossing the Victoria Nile and was marching for Wadelai. On the next day, therefore, he dropped down for ten miles to a point near Iyara's, where the river became very narrow and the current strong; when, seeing no signs of the other party, he put back, sleeping for the night off the village. On the next day he returned to the northern mouth of the Victoria Nile, which he thoroughly explored, without, however, succeeding in finding any channel through the *sudd*. In the evening he returned to Mpata, in the hopes that Owen might have sent back a party with a message for him. Being disappointed in this, he again stood over to the west shore, and when a few miles north of Boki's, felt that his doubts and difficulties were at last over, for on the right bank of the Nile, a few miles down stream, were three distinct columns of smoke, the signal by which Owen had arranged that he was to make his whereabouts known in case of separation. Purkiss had now no doubt that the land force had at last succeeded in crossing from Magungu, and, having cut across the corner, were marching direct for the Katungo ferry.

As these fires were only seen late in the evening, Purkiss waited until the following morning before getting under way, when he dropped down to Iyara's village, and landed to have a chat with his old friend, and see what information could be obtained.

Having been received in a particularly friendly way during his first visit, he landed unarmed, and attended only by two Sudanese. Crossing the eighty yards or so of foreshore, he mounted the high bank which screened the village from view, and was making for the chief's hut, accompanied by two or three natives who seemed to be very friendly, when suddenly one of them rushed up from behind, and, snatching the rifle out of the hands of one of the escort, ran off with it. At the same moment the inhabitants, whom Purkiss noticed were keeping out of sight in rather a suspicious manner, rushed out of the huts and commenced firing on the little party. Finding himself unarmed and accompanied by only one armed man,

Purkiss thought it best to beat a retreat to the boat, which the high Nile bank screened from view; but Farajullah Moru, the man who was still armed, thought otherwise, and, loading his rifle, stood his ground and blazed away, keeping the population in check until Purkiss had returned from the boat with reinforcements.

An Englishman would probably have looked upon himself as a hero after such a performance, and expected to be treated as such, but Farajullah took it quite as part of an ordinary day's work, and would probably have gone through it again an indefinite number of times for the sake of being let off a night's "sentry go."

Having got his party safely back into the boat, Purkiss made his way up stream, but the river was narrow, the current strong, and the boat slow, and the natives who had become openly hostile, kept up a brisk fire from the banks, which were high enough to afford them complete shelter. Luckily their aim was very bad, and they did no damage beyond giving the crew a very unpleasant pull of an hour and a half before they got into clear water. On reaching the lake, however, a strong southerly wind was met, which forced Purkiss to anchor for the night.

On the next day (January 30th) the party sailed across to the old anchorage at Mpata, where they cooked their last mouthful of food; and, being prevented by lack of rations from continuing his search for Owen, Purkiss put the boat's head southwards and made for Kibiro. Head winds and calms, however, made their progress very slow, and as I have already told, they did not reach us until late in the evening of the next day. Having been on short rations for a considerable time, on none at all for the last thirty-six hours, and having had to sleep in the cramped little boat for nine nights in succession, it was not to be wondered at that they were all pretty well done up.

Fearing that something must have gone wrong with Owen, I at once ordered sufficient flour for ten days to be ground, and told Macdonald and Purkiss to start off in the boat next morning with a new crew to carefully search the mouth of the Nile, and, if they failed to discover anything there, to push on to Wadelai. In the middle of the night, however, I got a note from Owen beginning " This is enough to make one's hair turn grey," and explaining that, as the boat had never turned up at Magungu, he feared she must have gone to the bottom, and that, being unable to cross the Nile without her help, he was on his way back. This was bad news for Macdonald, who had been in high spirits at the prospect of his trip.

At noon next day (February 1st), Owen and his party arrived, and were much surprised to see the boat safely afloat in the harbour.

On leaving Kibiro on the 20th, Owen had marched to Butiaba, where, as already explained, he had made the capture of goats. The next day's march took him to Lukwaya, and the following one to Kisamba, and on the 23rd he reached the mouth of the Victoria Nile at Mpata.

Here the boat was sighted near Katulla Island, and while Owen was trying to attract Purkiss' attention, and the men were scattered in all directions collecting materials for building their huts, a large force of the enemy who had been ambuscaded in the long grass suddenly burst on them and opened a heavy fire. In an instant the Sudanese closed in, and before the enemy had time to do any damage, were firing steady volleys, under Thruston's command. These soon put the Wanyoro to flight, and the affair, which with worse troops and officers might have had a disastrous ending, turned into a complete success.

Excellent as the conduct of all concerned was, however, this success was chiefly due to the habit of the Sudanese of always sticking to their rifles and ammunition; whether out for a stroll, doing "fatigue duty," or fishing in the lake, their ammunition belts were always strapped round their waists and their rifles slung over their shoulders. I wish English soldiers, when campaigning, could be taught the same habit.

On the next afternoon the force reached Magungu, where Owen found the old Egyptian fort still standing, but in a rather dilapidated condition.

On the following morning, the boat being still missing, Owen sent a party back to Mpata to look for her, and on their returning without any news, went there himself on the day after with half a company. He had to cut his way through the reeds and wade for three hours to reach the extreme point, whence he hoped to obtain a clear view of the lake. He also lighted signal fires as arranged. Seeing no signs of the boat, he returned to Magungu, where he arrived at sunset, only to find himself cut off from the

MAGUNGU

(To face page 198)

remainder of his troops by a force of the enemy with whom Thruston was actively engaged. As he was in the direct line of Thruston's fire, he retired a few hundred yards, with a view to making a flank movement, when the enemy suddenly began to move off, and soon disappeared to the southward in the fast-growing darkness.

Thruston stated that at about half-past five his position had been suddenly attacked by about two thousand Wanyoro, but that he was well prepared for them, and they had not given him much trouble.

After these two thwarted attacks, the force was not further molested, and, as we afterwards heard, the enemy withdrew from the Magungu district and rejoined Kabarega in the forest. He, thus deprived of his supplies in the north, was forced to make the attempt to break out southwards, which ended in his defeat by Kakunguru.

Owen had managed to get hold of one small dug-out canoe, and in this sent a few men across to the opposite bank, to try to conciliate the Shulis who inhabited that district. They were greeted with a volley of arrows, and much uncomplimentary language ; so, despairing of getting more canoes, he proceeded to make a raft, but the wood in the neighbourhood was so heavy, that, when finished, she refused to fulfil the principal use of such a craft, that of keeping her passengers on the top of the water.

Three days were spent in this attempt, and on its failure, Owen, bearing in mind his orders to be back at Kibiro, whatever happened, within twenty-eight days, thought it best to return at once and report to me.

CHAPTER XV

THE WADELAI EXPEDITION

New plans—Owen's orders—A fresh start—Down the Nile—A warm reception—An awkward position—Running the gauntlet —Unappreciated oratory—Meeting with friends—Wadelai— Reception by Sheikh Ali—Emin's fort—Destruction of ivory— Approach of the Dervishes—A hard pull—Mahaji—Unanswerable arguments—Return.

AS Owen had fulfilled his mission of driving the enemy out of Magungu, I had now no need to think of that province, and the only thing to settle was the best way of collecting the troops, and information I hoped would be found at Wadelai.   Had I had unlimited time, I should certainly have started the expedition again as originally constituted, but twelve days out of the twenty-eight had slipped away, and I could hardly hope that the force would get to Wadelai and back in the remaining sixteen. There seemed the less chance of this as, from Purkiss' information about the *sudd*,[1] it was

[1] Captain Thruston afterwards discovered a passage through this *sudd*.

evident that the force would have to be ferried across the wide mouth of the Victoria Nile at Mpata, an operation which would probably take four days each way. I therefore determined that the expedition should be made entirely by water, and told Owen to be in readiness to sail with Purkiss and twenty men at daybreak on the following morning.

He had orders to make friends with the Sheikh of Wadelai and Fadl el Mula Bey, if the latter was there, and to enlist as many Sudanese troops as he could, up to three hundred, telling them to march down to the point opposite Mpata, where we would send the boat to ferry them across. He was further told never to land without a good escort, to keep as near his boat as possible, and on no account to sleep on shore. Owing to the hostility of the tribes as discovered by Purkiss, I thought it better that they should make the passage of the narrows by night.

On the following morning (February 2nd), Owen sailed, with Purkiss, twenty men, and ten days' rations. I purposely gave him a limited supply of the latter, as I wished to make sure of his being back in time.

They slept that night under Katulla Island,

and on the following afternoon made their way across to the northern mouth of the Victoria Nile, beginning to drop down the river after sunset. At daybreak next morning they found themselves at the southern end of the large "flash" to the south of Wadelai.[1] On their presence being discovered, large crowds soon collected on the banks and opened fire. The numerous floating islands in the "flash" allowed the party to keep under cover from this pretty easily, until its northern end was reached, when the river suddenly became very narrow, and the boat, floating in mid-stream, was within easy range of both banks.

The situation was now very awkward. The stream was running a good three miles an hour, while three and a half miles an hour was the utmost that could be got out of the boat. Judging by the reception accorded him by the riverain population, it seemed very unlikely that Owen would succeed in making friends with the Sheikh of Wadelai, and in that case he would have to make his way up stream again, at a rate of something under half a mile an hour,

---

[1] Although Wadelai and Ayara's are shown on the maps as towns, and are generally spoken of as such, they are really districts extending for some miles up and down the river.

running the gauntlet of twenty-five miles of fire. He determined, however, to push on, and, very wisely refrained from returning the natives' fire, making his interpreter, Tom Nubi, stand up and explain to the people the friendly intentions of the party. At first Tom Nubi's oratorical efforts were greeted with those missiles of lead, wood, and poisoned iron which these children of nature substitute for our more civilised methods of hinting at a speaker's unpopularity; but gradually words won the day, the firing ceased, and questions began to be asked from the banks. By this time Ali's[1] village was in sight on the east bank, and a canoe, manned by three natives, was seen to put out from the western shore. After some parleying and hesitation they came alongside, and explained that they had been interpreters to the Sudanese troops under Fadl el Mula Bey, who had departed many months ago, and joined a party of Dervishes which had visited the place. They promised to persuade the Sheikh to come and meet Owen, which he eventually did, but not until he had kept the latter waiting in the boat until five in the after-

[1] Ali is the name of the present Sheikh ; the village derived the name by which it is known in Europe from his father, Wad Ali (the son of Ali).

WADELAI

(To face page 205)

noon. Even then he would not come down to the water, so Owen had to go about two hundred yards inland to meet him. He however, seemed perfectly friendly, and expressed a wish that his place might again be chosen as the site of a military station, which he said brought trade into the neighbourhood. By the time the interview was over, it was too late to do any more business, so Owen pushed the boat off into mid-stream, and passed the night there.

On the following morning Sheikh Ali sent word that he was too ill to grant an interview, so Owen had to put up with his Vakil, with whom he did some useful business, enlisting fifty of the inhabitants to protect our flag, and giving them a month's pay in advance. He then dropped down to Emin's old fort on the left bank, where he planted the British flag. He described it as being in good preservation and in a commanding position on the river bank, but said that the country in its vicinity was destitute of supplies. A great mass of charred ivory, the remains of Emin's parting bonfire, was lying about.

As he had settled in the morning not to start till sunset, he spent the rest of the day in the fort, collecting information about the country and the general situation. He was told that the population from the north and north-east were running into Wadelai before an advancing force of Dervishes, and as he passed Ali's village on his way up stream, the Sheikh sent a message to say that he had just heard that the Dervishes were close at hand.

Twenty-four hours' hard rowing, during which they had no adventures, brought the party to the outflow of the Nile, whence they coasted up the western shore of the lake to Mahaji Saghir, touching at various villages, where they were received with varying degrees of distrust and hostility. At Mahaji Kabir, however, they managed to get into conversation with the chief, who very clearly and reasonably explained the situation by saying, that, having originally been Kabarega's subjects, his people had made friends with the Egyptians, and allowed them to build a fort at their place. When the Egyptians had gone, Kabarega had come over and destroyed their country and killed the people for being unfaithful to him. " If I make friends with you," said the chief, "how do I know that you will not go away like the other white men, and leave me to be eaten up again by Kabarega. When Kabarega is dead, then will I be your friend, but not before."

Having to be satisfied with this reasonable but rather unsatisfactory reply, Owen turned the boat's head eastward, and reached Kibiro on the 10th of February, without having any further adventures, beyond being nearly swamped by a herd of hippopotami.

CHAPTER XVI

THE CHAIN OF FORTS

Return to Kitanwa—A magnificent structure—A giant flagstaff—
Return to Kitoba—*Pros* and *cons*—Hoima—Site for a fort—
A deceptive lawn—Description of fort—Bark cloth trees—We
open communications—The Waganda again—Spread of small-
pox—Owen's return—The precious boat—Owen departs for
Toro—Macdonald and the ladies—An attack and a stampede
—Utema—Searching for a ferry—A rough march—Baranwa
—A papyrus river—Macdonald to the rescue—I make myself
a nuisance—Unpleasant neighbours—Thurston's command—
A false alarm—A polite message—Retrospect.

I STAYED at Kibiro for three days after
Owen's departure, finishing off all the works,
and on the 6th of February marched up the hill
again to Kitanwa, leaving our fort in charge of
Bilal Effendi and twenty-five men.

During my absence Villiers had done wonders
at Kitanwa, where he had constructed a sort of
mediæval castle, capable of defying all the armies
of Africa. It struck me as rather too big for the
garrison of seventy-five men which it was intended
to hold, but it was so strong that that did not

matter, as I was quite certain no enemy would ever get inside it.

Everything was being done on a magnificent scale there. As I was writing in my tent, on the afternoon of my arrival, I heard the voices of a concourse of men singing in the neighbourhood, and, looking out, saw a hundred Swahilis struggling under a huge tree, which I was told was to make the flagstaff. With a halt every few paces, it crept along very slowly, but got into the fort next day. As long as I was there, the united efforts of all hands were insufficient to make it stand upright. I never heard whether it was eventually secured or had to give place to a less pretentious bit of timber.

After waiting a day, to let Villiers put a few finishing touches to his work, we all marched off to Kitoba, except the garrison of the place and Moffat, whom I left in temporary command, with orders to let me know at once if Owen failed to turn up on the 12th. As by that date the food of the boat party would have run out, I should know, if they failed to appear, that some misfortune had happened to them, and should have to take steps accordingly.

Kitoba possessed the advantage of being a

14

spot whence communication by signal could be established with Kitanwa and the capital, and although we had not any regular signallers, it would have been convenient to have set up communication between them by fires or other means, in case of one of the forts being attacked. On the other hand, I could not have put less than twenty men into the fort, and on the whole I thought it better to concentrate my force as much as possible, and trust to keeping up communication by constant patrols.

On the following day we marched to the Hoima river, the place which I had selected on my way up as suitable for a fort. Seeing a stretch of nice, smooth, short turf, that reminded me of an English lawn, I at once ordered my tent to be pitched on it, but was disappointed to find the tent-pegs could not be persuaded to go more than an inch into the ground. We were on a gentle slope of solid, flat rock, only just covered with a thin layer of soil. I afterwards found out that short grass only grows in this part of the world under these conditions, and that with only a foot of soil on the rock it will grow above a man's head.

Having settled down, we set to work to select

a site for the fort, and finally chose one on a very slight rise, about four hundred yards from the river, and surrounded by a fine open plain, on which hardly a mouse could creep unobserved. As this was to be the headquarters of the Unyoro force, I settled to give it a garrison of two hundred men, a force large enough to allow Thruston, whom I was leaving in command, to make any expedition that might be necessary, and still leave a sufficient garrison to protect the post. The fort had therefore to be made fairly elastic, that is to say, big enough to hold the full garrison, with their wives and families, whom I had promised should be sent up to them, and at the same time capable of being defended by fifty men, or less, if Thruston took the bulk of his troops away on an expedition.

After consulting with Macdonald, I decided to make a large open stockade of bark-cloth trees, for the accommodation of the troops and their families, defended at its two opposite corners by strong mud forts, small enough to be held if necessary by thirty men.

As we had made a short march, I at once set all hands to work to cut and collect branches of bark-cloth trees, to make the stockade and form the skeleton on which the mud walls were built.

This wood has the advantage of growing when stuck into the ground, and consequently stockades made of it, instead of rotting, become yearly stronger; even when used as the framework of a mud wall it does not die, but sprouts out at the top. By using this wooden support, we were able to build the walls of the little forts a good deal thinner than was the case at Kibiro, and the work went ahead at a great pace.

Not so the despatches and letters which I was trying to write. Having fairly started this post, I felt that I could now do without the Waganda, and might therefore safely open the road. I therefore settled to send off Arthur and fifty men to take down mails and bring back some cloth and other stores which I hoped were awaiting us on the frontier, and accordingly set to work on my correspondence. I had not counted on the Waganda, however, who, being now within reach, trooped down on us, and wasted interminable hours of my time.

They were very pleased to hear that I was at last ready for a move, for the smallpox had spread to an alarming extent among them, and as Kakunguru said, "If we stayed here much longer, there would be none of us left." So great was their number of sick, that, in spite of their desire to get hold of Kabarega's ivory at Mruli, the chiefs did not think it could be done now, and suggested that we should all go back to Uganda by the shortest road, and make a fresh expedition later on. As Kabarega had fled across the Nile, I did not see that I should do much good by wandering about the country any longer, and therefore willingly assented to their proposal. It was agreed that they should begin moving homewards as soon as possible. They had to wait for a few days for a column of 2000 guns which Kakunguru had sent, under the Catholic chief Lwekula, to look after a hostile force said to be collecting in the Bugoma forest.

On the 11th of February I got a note from Owen, written from Kitanwa on the previous day, telling me of his safe return and successful trip. This was a great relief. The expedition had been a trifle risky, and during the whole time of its absence I had been on tenterhooks, fearing that something might happen to my precious boat, which was our only means of obtaining information from the north. Without it a Dervish army might get across the Nile before we could hear a word of their approach ; with its help Thruston would always be in a position to get early news, and, if he was sharp about it, cut up in detail any force that had to cross over to Magungu.

On the following day Owen himself turned up, and after a day's rest began to long (and make his longings felt) to be on the move again, but I could not spare any men from the works, and he had for five whole days to find some other outlet for his energies. On the 18th, however, I sent him off, accompanied by Villiers, thirty-eight Sudanese, and forty-seven Swahilis, with orders to restore confidence in Toru, establish a post on the Albert Edward Lake, and form the confederacy of friendly southern Unyoro chiefs which I have before mentioned.

In the meanwhile, Arthur had returned with his loads of cloth, the fort was finished, and the Waganda camp had been accidentally burned down, with the loss of three lives, so everybody was ready for a move. On the following day, Macdonald, Arthur, Purkiss, and I, with seventy-four Sudanese and the Kangao's Waganda, marched off, leaving Thruston and Moffat behind—the former, however, was to join us temporarily at the fort I proposed to build on the Kafu.

As we passed the neighbourhood of the

Waganda camp near Kabarega's capital, I sent Macdonald to make arrangements about the prisoners, and see that no Wanyoro women were carried off. He had a hard day's work, which I could fully appreciate after my small experience in such matters, having to deal with 1683 captives of the gentler sex, all of whom and all of whose captors had decided and volubly expressed ideas on the question of their future. He ended in restoring 507 Waganda ladies to their friends and relations, and liberating 1174 Wanyoro.

Having done this, he was just starting to rejoin me, when a message was brought into camp that a Wanyoro army under Ireyta, Kabarega's principal general, was marching towards the capital, and had camped the night before at Kibona.

Macdonald at once ordered Kakunguru to turn out his men, which he said was done with admirable promptitude, and at four in the afternoon a Waganda force of 2500 guns started to the eastward. The manner in which they turned out was the only admirable part of their performance, for, on meeting the Wanyoro at eight o'clock the next morning, the force with one accord turned tail and ran away, leaving Kakunguru with only three or four chiefs and a hundred guns. Fortunately, the Wanyoro were as much impressed by the Waganda as my allies had been by them, and also executed a rapid movement to the rear. Macdonald, however, did not know this when he joined us at ten that evening, so, only having heard the first part of the story, I sent off a message to Thruston, telling him to reinforce Kakunguru at once.

Next day we moved on to Utema, our old halting-place on the Unyoro side of the Kafu. Thence we made some vain searches for a good site for a fort; but the ground near the river was a mass of swamp and forest, so I decided to move on to the Baranwa crossing, which Owen had reported on favourably during our upward march.

The journey was a very hard and unpleasant one, by hunters' tracks through thick forest, and over numerous swampy tributaries of the Kafu. Although we did not see any of them, there must have been a good many Wanyoro hanging about, as they managed to cut off and kill five of the crowd of sick Waganda who were with us. We had been troubled a good deal in this way throughout the campaign. Even when almost within touch of Kabarega's army, the main body had been left severely alone, and it was often difficult to realise, when we were marching through an apparently deserted country, that numbers of the enemy were concealed in the long grass within a few yards of us. Yet that this was the case was proved by the fact that stragglers, even within a few hundred yards of the column, were almost invariably killed.

The country near Baranwa did not seem much more promising than that through which we had been passing all day, being all clothed in dense bush. After I had nearly despaired of finding a good place, I caught a glimpse of a grass-covered knoll among the tree-tops, and, climbing up it, found myself on a tongue-shaped hill, abrupt on three sides and sloping easily down to the river on the fourth. Here I at once made up my mind to build the fort, and, sending for the troops and porters, ordered the camp to be pitched on its summit. It was not quite a perfect situation, but by cutting down a good deal of bush, I hoped to get a sufficient field of fire; and at all events water was easily accessible. It also commanded the ferry, an important matter if the Wanyoro should ever attempt to dispute the passage of our convoys.

As it turned out afterwards, it was the only

one of our forts which was attacked, and its small garrison were able to hold their own without any difficulty.

Looking down from the hill, we seemed to be surveying a pretty grass-covered meadow at the edge of a wooded park, so impossible was it to realise that the smooth mass of green below us was a broad river overgrown with papyrus. Yet, as Macdonald afterwards tested in a most practical way, any one stepping into that forest of rushes would have to sink through some ten or twelve feet of running water before he reached solid ground. When, a day or two later, he was watching the Waganda making a bridge, one of them slipped off and disappeared into the water. Macdonald at once jumped in after him, but after two attempts was unable to find the body, which had undoubtedly been carried down stream and jammed between the strong V-like stems of the papyrus; he was taken out thoroughly exhausted, and ought to think it lucky that he did not share the fate of the man he tried to rescue.

While I was waiting for the camp to be pitched, I discovered that Baranwa was the home of a large and particularly voracious tribe of mosquitoes. These tormentors had occasionally visited us at night, but on the whole I should say that Unyoro was but little troubled by them. I fancy they must all have collected at Baranwa, where they bit me impartially night and day, in spite of the various evil-smelling ointments with which I smeared myself, and which made my human companions shy of even coming as far as the door of my tent.

Baranwa had the further disadvantage of being within about eight miles of the famous Masaja Mkuru, which Owen had been so anxious to occupy, and whose lower slopes contained a considerable Wanyoro settlement. These people amused themselves during our stay by cutting off stragglers and small foraging parties; and besides the men actually killed, we had some bad cases of wounds to doctor as best we could.

On the next day we devoted all our energies to clearing the bush, and, that done, began building the fort, an irregular enclosure, with mud walls, capable of holding fifty men.

On the 23rd, Thruston marched in with a hundred men; he had come by a direct road from Hoima, thus avoiding the bad march which we had had from Utema. He had been fired at a little on the way, but had seen no force of the enemy. I had a long talk with him over the prospects of his new command. His force was small (350 men) and his supply of ammunition unpleasantly limited (about fifty rounds per man), but his men were good and his forts strong and well supplied with food, and if he kept his eyes open and patrolled constantly, I saw no reason why he should come to grief. Events showed that I was fully justified in this assumption, for he always proved himself far more than equal to any force that Kabarega could muster against him. Thinking also that he might some day be seized with a desire to visit that historically interesting, but otherwise unattractive spot, Wadelai, I gave him strict orders to confine his naval explorations to the Albert Lake. I thought the boat had run quite enough risks for the present.

On the 25th the bridge and fort being finished, and the cleared bush all turned into a zereba, Thruston returned to Hoima with fifty men, leaving the remainder of his hundred as a garrison. He had just had news that Kitanwa had been attacked, and a message from the native officer in command, begging for leave to abandon the post. He was naturally anxious to see for himself how things were going on, and I sent by him a polite message to the officer in charge, informing that person that if he did carry out his wish, he would very shortly find himself strung up to a tree.

I afterwards had a letter from Thruston, telling me that the whole thing was a scare, caused by a few Wanyoro firing guns in the neighbourhood, and that he was sending the officer in command down under escort to be dealt with by me. Showing the white feather is such a very rare crime among the Sudanese, that I did not think it necessary to make an example, so merely told him that digging potatoes and not soldiering seemed to be his trade, and kicked him out of the service.

We were now on the eve of leaving Unyoro, and I naturally looked back over the ground we had covered, and wondered whether the expedition had been a success; on the whole I thought it had. It is true that we had neither captured Kabarega, as I had hoped, but hardly expected, nor made peace with him, nor had I got the extra troops that I wanted;[1] but we had hustled Kabarega all over and out of his kingdom and jammed his followers into the small northern

[1] As a result of the expedition, Thruston afterwards got these.

part of it. We were bringing back to Uganda, as a visible sign of our success, the six hundred Waganda women we had rescued from slavery.

Our boat on the Albert would enable us to watch the outflow of the Nile, and get the earliest information of any Dervish advance from the north, and our chain of forts closed the only route by which Kabarega could seriously threaten Uganda. I felt pretty sure that if this only held, I should in time force him to give in for mere want of ammunition. I must explain that he had long been carrying on the lucrative trade of middleman, importing guns and ammunition, which he exchanged with the tribes to the north for ivory and slaves, and with these bought more guns and ammunition. Thus, by stopping the supply of arms, I should not only impoverish him, but take away his means of carrying on war.

CHAPTER XVII

THE RETURN TO UGANDA

BEFORE daylight on the 26th of February
we crossed the Kafu, and, eaten up by
mosquitoes, did a fifteen miles' march through an
open forest country.   One or two stragglers were
killed by wandering Wanyoro on the road, but
no opposition was offered to us.

A long march next day took us to Ntuti, where
the Waganda, hitherto so anxious to return to
their homes, began to regret the flesh-pots of
Unyoro; for a flight of locusts, immediately following the advance of the army, had destroyed
what little food the latter had left, and there
was literally nothing to eat in the district.   We

were told that the whole road to Makwenda's was too destitute even to supply the few porters we were taking back with us. We killed an ox for them, and I decided to move on next day, and divide into two parties, Arthur and myself going by a westward route past Fort Grant, while Macdonald and Purkiss followed that through Bulamwezi, on which I wanted a report, as I thought it might be found suitable for making a waggon road.

In the evening, Mr. Forster, who had been in charge of Singo, came in for orders. I had arranged that he was to march my escort back to Unyoro and take charge of the monthly convoy to and from that country. He stated that, during our absence, he had had a few skirmishes with the Wanyoro in the neighbourhood of Fort Grant, but no casualties.

On the following morning, Arthur and I marched off in a westerly direction, and soon entered a wooded, mountainous country, abounding in running streams, pretty cascades, and fine views over a succession of valleys and mountains, but exceedingly trying to walk over. We halted for lunch by a natural arbour in the forest, near a rocky burn, where we thoroughly enjoyed a cup of tea and a tin of biscuits, which, being so near the end of our journey, we thought we might safely broach. We could not afford to waste very much time in this enticing spot, and soon began toiling up the seemingly endless hill on which Fort Grant is situated.

I suppose that when æstheticism and military necessities clash, the former must be expected to go to the wall, but I must say it struck me that, considering the beauty of the country which lay all around, some spot might have been chosen a little less hideous than that in which the fort was placed. It was in the middle of the turtle-backed, treeless *veldt* which formed the top of the mountain we had been toiling up, and whose upper edges just cut off the view on all sides. A walk of half a mile in any direction brought us to the edge of a fine panorama over rocky gorges, sheltered valleys, and bold peaks, but from the fort itself nothing was to be seen but dull dried grass. I admit that from a defensive point of view the situation was excellent, and, after all, it had been made more for the use of soldiers than artists.

It also had the advantage of possessing a glorious climate, and although, the chain of forts having been established across Unyoro, it was no longer necessary from a military point of view, and I had consequently settled to abandon it, I made up my mind that, as soon as I could get a road made, I would make a health station there.

Four thousand feet, the average level of Uganda above the sea, is just too low for the health of Europeans on the Equator, but the extra two thousand feet of this district made an enormous difference, and I see no reason why the highlands of Singo should not be perfectly suitable for European colonisation.

As I had settled to abandon the place, there was a good deal to be done in making an inventory of stores, etc., at which Arthur had a good grind on the following day.

A ten hours' march on the 2nd, over grassy uplands, brought us to the edge of a steep crater-like depression, down which we scrambled for fifteen hundred feet into a prosperous little village nestling in banana groves.

Soon after our arrival it began to rain, and kept it up all night, and was still doing so when we started next morning; so, after six hours' drenching, during which the slippery roads made our progress very slow, I halted by a roadside puddle and camped for the night.

Two more marches through a very sparsely inhabited country, scored in all directions with the tracks of elephants, brought us to Kisongola, on an arm of Makwenda's lake. Through this we had to wade on the following morning, stumbling over papyrus roots and sticking in black mud, for a good hour and a half, but as it was then towards the end of the dry season, the water, which during the rains is chest deep, did not come much above our knees. An hour's march on the farther side of this gave us time to get dry, and landed us at Makwenda's, where I found the fort in very good order, under the command of Lieutenant Suliman Effendi.

After a day's halt, we started off again, taking this time the northern and more direct road to Kampala, which necessitated crossing the Maanja river.

Like another and more universally trodden one, these Uganda roads are paved with good intentions. I found that during my absence the Makwenda had expended a great amount of labour in doing no possible good. He had widened the path from a few inches to over a hundred feet, but the narrow track is just as good for porters as a wide one, and as he had followed the line of the original path over hill and dale, the gradients of the new road were just as impracticable for carts as the old one. He had begun a beautiful bridge over the Maanja too, but unfortunately he had not finished it, and probably never will; so that, although one could have driven a coach and four over about three-quarters of the width of the river, it was as much as we could do to drag our donkeys across the remaining fourth.

One of the great difficulties to continuous road-making in Uganda, under the present system, is the law which makes each proprietor responsible only for that portion which passes through his own property; much on the same principle as that on which we make householders sweep the snow from in front of their own doorsteps, and with much the same results. An uninhabited house at home causes an accumulation of snow on the pavement, and an uninhabited district in Uganda means uncleared tracks and unbridged rivers, which render the cared-for parts of the road often inaccessible even for donkeys.

Three days' pretty hard marching took us to

Kampala, where, in spite of the smallness of our party, we were received with a good deal more enthusiasm than had been shown as we marched out.

Half an hour afterwards, Macdonald and Purkiss marched in, and reported very favourably on the Bulamwezi road, which avoided all the hills.

On the 17th, Owen turned up from Toru, where his mission had been completely successful. He had reinstated Kasigama as king of Toru, Usangoro, and Kitakwenda, and with the help of Rakwiamba, chief of Mwengi, and Kagigri, chief of Chaku, had formed a confederacy of friendly chiefs, subject to Kasigama, and had left small garrisons of seven and fifteen men respectively in Kasigama's capital and Usongoro, on the Albert Edward Lake. He reported that considerable loss of life had taken place in consequence of Kabarega's invasion of the country, but that our counter-invasion had happily caused the recall of the army before it could reach the capital.

It may seem that these twenty-one men whom Owen left with Kasigama would not afford the country any great protection against invasions of Wanyoro, and that if it was not sufficiently strong to defend itself and Kasigama, such a small force, cut off from all assistance, was only a source of weakness. I, however, looked upon our chain of forts from the Kafu to the Albert as strong enough to prevent any invasion from the north-east, and left these men simply as symbols of our friendship, and as a nucleus round which the tribesmen might collect to repel any inroad of Manyuema from the west.

As I have already explained, my measures in this region were purely defensive, and taken with a view to avoiding any possible threat on our west flank; but the reports of Owen and other Europeans who have since visited Toru and the neighbourhood of Ruenzori convince me that the country is well worth holding for its own sake. Salt and ivory will certainly enable it to keep its head above water for some years to come, while the Ruenzori region only requires to be connected with the Victoria Lake by a road to make it a very promising field for colonisation.

With Owen's return the Unyoro expedition may be said to have come to a close, and Owen, Villiers, and Arthur, who had only been left behind by Portal on the understanding that they were to leave on my arrival, began to turn their thoughts homewards. Macdonald, also, had long been due in India. If I had let them all go at once, I should only have had seven Europeans left, of whom only two, Gibb and Thruston, were soldiers; so I had to harden my heart, and only give Owen and Macdonald leave to go right away, sending Villiers a stage on the homeward journey to take charge of Kavirondo; while to poor Arthur I confided the very troublesome task of marching up to Unyoro again with the families of the troops left there.

Owen and Macdonald were to have started together, but I had to keep the latter for a few days to go into the question of stores, etc., for which I was making out an indent for him to take home. As I think I have already hinted, to keep Owen waiting for a few days is a course very apt to disturb the general peace of the community; so, after giving him his usual twelve hours' rest, I let him start off; with a heavy heart at losing such a cheery companion and dashing soldier, but perhaps with a slightly incredulous smile as I heard him assure Macdonald that he would wait for him at Kikuyu.

CHAPTER XVIII

PARADE AND POLICY

Mwanga's behaviour—A mistaken idea—Collection of troops—
"God Save the Queen" — Mwanga's mount — A brilliant
inspection—Over ambitious—A sham fight—A divorce case—
A great and happy king—Little drawbacks—The salt convoy
—Heirs to the throne—Succession changed—An unwelcome
nephew—A matter of the affections.

HAVING got rid of all the business consequent on the expedition, and despatched
a catalogue of my various wants to the coast, I
set to work to see what had been going on
during my absence. Gibb, who had managed
affairs admirably while I was away, said that
everything in Uganda proper had been very
quiet, but that some of the Usoga chiefs had
been giving trouble. Mwanga was also reported
to have made some remarks before his chiefs
hardly consistent with his alleged friendship
with us. I did not attach very much importance to these reports, which are the usual
precursors of a change of religious views on his

part. As, however, I had only marched back with about twenty sick men, a general idea had got abroad that I had left all my troops in Unyoro, and I thought it better to dispel this at once; so, taking advantage of the Mohammedan feast at the end of Ramadan, I made arrangements for a big parade, and sent orders for troops to be collected from Singo and Usoga.

I believe this was the first purely show parade that had ever been held in Uganda, and the men thoroughly enjoyed preparing for it; so, to our great discomfort did the band. Although their ideas of harmony were crude, and their instruments antediluvian, their zeal was surprising, and during the few hours in which they were not playing at the head of the troops, they were practising "God save the Queen" to the windward of my hut in a manner which, I confess, was a severe strain on my loyalty.

At last the great day came off. As the king's pony was lame, I lent him mine, and, waiting for him outside the parade - ground, we rode on together with a fair amount of dignity until the troops presented arms, a manœuvre which my steed seemed to think required a reply on his part. I do not know exactly how he began, as I was looking away; but the second act of his performance was a wild gallop through the crowd, during which he was closely pursued by Mwanga's umbrella-bearer, and warmly embraced round the neck by his Majesty.

When the party had been led back, we proceeded to inspect the line, which, as Gibb had previously spent several hours in shoving each soldier into his place, presented a very respectable appearance. Then came the manual, bayonet, and firing exercises, the latter with blank cartridge, which was highly appreciated by the population. If we had only been content to stop there, the review would have been a great success, but unfortunately we were ambitious. I had, I am thankful to say, yielded to Gibb's strongly expressed opinion that a march past could only end in disaster, but had insisted on an "advance in review order." For about six paces this went beautifully, then the flanks gradually crept forward, and the line assumed the shape of the Turkish emblem, its concavity becoming more and more accentuated, until the strain on the centre was too great, and it broke itself into two bodies resolutely marching to meet each other and win or die. At this stage of the proceeding Gibb's stentorian "Halt!" was heard above the discord of the band, and the king remarked that the Europeans were very clever; so I told him that the review and sham fight were over, and invited him to adjourn to the fort and help me try a divorce case.

Mwanga was delighted with his morning's work and the prominent part he had been allowed to take in the proceedings, and his appearance as he left the parade-ground was a great contrast to that which he had presented as, perspiring and dejected-looking, he rode on to it, apparently under the impression that his last hour had come. He was now all smiles and jokes, and interrupted the proceedings of the court with cheerful but irrelevant remarks even more than was his wont. I took advantage of his happy frame of mind to impress on him that, thanks to me, he was now the greatest king in all the part of Africa which he knew. Mtesa, I said, had been acknowledged by all to be the most powerful king of the lake region, and had even put Kabarega on his throne; but of late years people had begun to whisper that Kabarega was more than equal to his master. They could now say this no more, and if any one asked who was the biggest man between Kavirondo and the country of the Lendus, there could be only one answer—"Mwanga, king of Uganda, and friend of the English." I think, as usual, he was impressed with these, the words of the last speaker, and said he would never cease to show his gratitude to me ; but I am afraid the impression did not last long, and that, before many hours were over, he was reminded that, however satisfactory his foreign relations might be, he was unpleasantly tied down in the much more important matters, to him, of domestic legislation and indulgence in the freaks of his rather unconventional fancies.

I also, as I thought, showed my friendliness to Mwanga and his people by making him a very handsome offer about the Toru salt. This commodity was worth twenty rupees a load at Kampala, and as, by Owen's agreement with Kasigama, the products of the salt lake were handed over to us, I thought it as well to get some advantage out of them, and at the same time give popular employment to the Waganda. I therefore proposed that Mwanga should furnish our monthly convoy to Toru, receiving in payment one load of salt for each load of stores delivered there.

After bargaining for a few extra loads for himself, the king agreed to this proposal, and, as the arrangement was an exceedingly favourable one for him, I imagined that the matter was settled. I had forgotten that employment is never popular with the Waganda. When the time for the first convoy to start came round, and I asked why the porters had not turned up, I was told that I had not given enough notice; so, as I could not wait for them, I had to take Swahilis off other work and send them instead. On the second occasion I was told that the Waganda would not go without an escort, so I again had to send Swahilis. The third time the Waganda came, but twice as many of them as we wanted, and said that they could only take half loads. I explained to them that they would only be given half loads of salt, but this did not prevent a large contingent joining the party after it had left Port Alice, whose leader assured the officer commanding at the Salt Lake that he had my permission to bring back as many full loads of salt as he had people.

This claim was of course disallowed, and after that the Katikiro confessed that his people did not like the work.   If he had said that they did not like any work, he would have been nearer the mark.

In spite of their distaste for all forms of labour, I must say that the desire of the Waganda to obtain calico is so great that we had no difficulty in getting local labour in exchange for that article, although once a man had got as much as he wanted for the present, nothing would induce him to appear again at the works until his new garment was worn out.

It was, however, a great innovation getting them to work at all.   Before the luxuries of civilisation had been put in their way, the Waganda men never voluntarily did any work at all, the unmarried youths living with their friends, and never taking possession of a *shamba* until they had secured a wife or wives to till it.

I was next obliged to take a step of some importance.   Mwanga has three nephews, one a Mohammedan and two Catholics, all of whom were by Waganda law eligible to succeed him, but who were all out of the country.   The two Catholic boys had been taken for safe keeping to German territory, during one of the religious wars, by Monseigneur Hirth, who, in spite of promises to the contrary, still refused to return them; while another period of throat-slitting for the love of God had resulted in the deportation of little Ramazan, the third nephew.

Now, when a king dies or is kicked out by his subjects, it is generally the custom among uncivilised people for each party to select a candidate for the throne and fight for him, and it struck me that if for any cause Uganda should be suddenly deprived of Mwanga's rule, the two little Catholic boys, who were beyond the control of the administration, might be made the centre of intrigues dangerous to the peace of the country, and I did not feel inclined to let my own or my successor's hand be forced in this matter. I accordingly assembled a meeting of great chiefs, and, having put the matter before them, it was agreed, on my recommendation, that the two boys should be excluded from the succession.

This action had met with Mwanga's entire approval; barbaric potentates do not like heirs to the throne to be too handy to step into their shoes, and he was greatly relieved to feel himself secure from this source of danger; but his satisfaction was somewhat diminished when he learned that I was sending to the coast for young Ramazan. On the top of this came a decision of mine on a personal matter which was very unpleasant to him, being concerned not only with what he considered his right to take possession of any person or thing in his kingdom, but also with his affections.

CHAPTER XIX

LIFE AT PORT ALICE

Return to Port Alice—Try to get comfortable—Site for the Resid-
ency—A surfeit of perfection—Three enemies to comfort—
Choice of site—The view—Road-making—Primitive ideas—
Distribution of work—Waste of timber—Brick - making—
Waganda reed-work—Danger of fire—Death of Purkiss—A
kabanda—Comparisons—French and English—Insect life—
A flight of locusts—Defeated—Waganda carelessness—A
matter of discipline—Witchcraft—A wise precaution.

HAVING finished these weightier matters, I
moved on to Port Alice, where I set to
work to make myself and other people as comfortable as our rather destitute circumstances in
the way of tools would permit. There I found
Wilson, who had been in charge of the station
during the Unyoro expedition, and Purkiss, who
on his return had again been attacked by hæmaturic fever; he was, however, nearly recovered,
and had made good progress with a cart which
he was building.

I had made up my mind, during my first
visit to Port Alice, to build my own house near

16

the lake, and at once began to carefully examine the country before selecting a site, taking advantage of my explorations to make a map of the neighbourhood.

I soon found that the only difficulty lay in the number of nearly equally perfect sites at my disposal, all nestling in grand virgin forest, and all affording lovely peeps of the lake.

As from a picturesque point of view there seemed to be nothing to choose between them, and as all authorities agreed that their proximity to the lake made them equally unhealthy, I had nothing to do in making my choice but select the one which seemed to afford most protection from the three chief enemies of comfort in this part of the world, Waganda tom-toms, wind, and mosquitoes. After many careful experiments, I choose a rocky bluff on the shores of a little bay to the east of the Ntebbi peninsula, facing Damba, Komi, and Nzazi Islands, screened from the prevailing wind by a wooded promontory, and from all human habitations by a dense belt of forest, in which, however, a natural clearing of some fifty acres was caused by an outcrop of rock. Over this sufficient earth had not collected to allow of the growth of trees, or even that favourite haunt of the mosquito, long grass, but it was covered by alternate patches of lawn-like turf and bracken. Between the clearing and the edge of the bluff was a belt of forest about a hundred yards wide, and in this I planted the pegs which marked the corners of the future Residency.

At first we merely cleared away the trees actually on the site of the house, then a few of the less shapely ones were removed, and then, after many careful trials, one by one those that stood in the way of any pretty peep.

When all was done, I found myself looking from my verandah, first on to a terraced flower-garden, then a natural lawn, dotted with rocks, bracken, and wild-flowers, which reached to the edge of the bluff; this in its turn, overhanging a narrow belt of trees and creepers, dropped some eighty feet on to the sandy beach which fringed the little bay.

To the right and left the sides of the bluff merged into forest-clothed ravines, through which winding paths gave one the chance of a stroll in deliciously cool shade, even in the hottest part of the day.

It was, however, several months before the

place got into such civilised shape; and before I could even begin the house, I had to make it accessible to the cart, which Purkiss had by this time finished. The first step towards doing this was to get it off the top of the hill on which it had been built, and consequently the first stage of my house-building was the making of a road down from the fort, an operation which nearly exhausted all Purkiss' and my stock of patience. Nothing would induce the Waganda labourers to see that a flat road could be made on a sloping hillside. Their first idea was simply to clear the turf off the top and throw it far away. Then, having explained to them that they were to build it up on the lower side of the road, they piled it up into a ridge there, and dug out the upper side, so as to make the roadway slope the reverse way to the hill, a proceeding which caused it to be all washed away by the first thunderstorm. However, we got it done fairly well at last, and then had pretty plain sailing to the edge of the forest, cutting through which, with our few and very indifferent tools, proved a tough job.

As soon as the cart could get to the house, we set to work in earnest, dividing the workmen into three parties, the Waganda to cut reeds and small wood for roofing, the Lendus to make bricks, and the Swahilis to cut trees and split boards in the forest. Owing to our lack of a pit-saw, this last was a very tedious and wasteful process. A tree was first split in half with wedges, and each of the halves then pared down with adzes into boards, so that two boards not only used up a whole tree, but generally took four men about a week to get out. The bricks we made in triple moulds, and found that the Lendus took to the work very well, and soon got to turn out about five hundred a day. We burnt them in kilns made of themselves—that is to say, we simply made a big stack of about ten thousand at a time, with seven flues running through it. Of course the outer bricks were not baked, but they were put aside and used for the next burning.

As I was anxious to get away from the fort as soon as possible, I settled to build my own study, which I could also use as a sleeping-room at first, in Waganda fashion, of reeds. This style of building only requires a skeleton of poles, across which sticks are lashed horizontally as a framework on to which the upright reeds forming the walls are laced. The work goes quickly, and is very neat, and has the further advantage of giving ample ventilation without any draught; but the reeds have the disadvantage of being very inflammable. To Waganda, who have practically no household possessions, this is not a very important matter; but Europeans, who know that they cannot replace any little comforts or treasures under six months, generally fight rather shy of native-built houses. When the rest of the house was finished, I built brick walls outside the original reed-work room, leaving the reeds inside as a decorative lining.

After we had been at work for about a week, Purkiss was attacked by hæmaturic fever for the third time, and, seeing that there was no hope of his being able to stand the climate, I sent him off to the coast as soon as he was able to move. I had a very cheery letter from him from Kikuyu, saying that he was quite recovered, and was looking forward to his return to Uganda after a rest at home; but the next mail brought the sad news of his death at Kibwezi, from a fourth and fatal attack of his complaint. From every point of view he was a very great loss—a charming companion, a thoroughly reliable assistant, excellent at managing natives, and a man who could turn his hand to anything, and always do it well.

While my house was building, I was living in a structure known as a *kabanda*, although shed is shorter and just as descriptive. In its beginnings it was merely an outer awning of thatch put over a tent whenever the traveller stopped long enough in one place to make it worth his while to give himself extra shelter from the sun ; but it gradually grew into a much more pretentious edifice, if one can properly call a place pretentious at which any self-respecting English cow would turn up her nose.

The one which formed the temporary head-quarters of Her Majesty's representative in Uganda was a hut forty feet long by twenty broad, with thatched walls and roof, the latter sloping down to within about three feet of the ground. The tent which was used as a bedroom was pitched near the farther end, the space behind it being utilised as a bath and dressing-room, while the front part of the shed, lighted by an opening which served as door and window, did duty as dining-room, sitting-room, audience chamber, and hall of justice.

Having had the pleasure of staying at Antananarivo with M. le Myre de Vilers when he was Resident - General in Madagascar, I could not help comparing our relative positions. His headquarters and mine were approached by very similar roads, or, more correctly, were equally unapproachable, owing to similar absence of roads, although of course the forest track which connects the Madagascar capital with the coast was hardly a sixth of the length of mine; but, like mine, all his necessities and luxuries had to be carried up on porters' heads. Yet he was living in a two - storeyed, tile-roofed house, with glass windows, polished mahogany panelled doors, and rooms painted, decorated, carpeted, and furnished in the very best Parisian style, with pictures on the walls and a grand piano in the corner of the *salon*. I was living in a windowless hovel, with bare earth for a floor and a few old biscuit-boxes for a table. From a spectacular point of view there was no doubt that my friend had considerably the best of it; but, looking at it from another aspect, the advantage was as certainly on my side. He, with half a company of *Infanterie de Marine*, had not the power even to make the Hova Queen bridge the swamp which surrounds the capital. Diplomacy might occasionally enable him to get his own way in unimportant matters, but in greater ones there was no middle course between accepting the will of the astute old Prime Minister and Prince Consort or calling in the aid of a French army. I had not a single English soldier, but I had some seven hundred bull-dog Sudanese. The king of Uganda, if a little inclined to be tricky, was thoroughly obedient, the chiefs had already shown their willingness to accept any laws I thought it desirable to make, and fifteen thousand of the people had just volunteered to help me fight a neighbouring state. I do not want to hint that these differences in our positions were in any way due to the ability or otherwise of either of us or our predecessors, but the double contrast is, I think, worth noting.

During my rides to and from the fort to my house, and in my map-making wanderings, I found the insect life of this district a most interesting study ; the changes it underwent were marvellous. At one time every tree and bank would be covered with clusters of bright black and yellow caterpillars; on another these would be replaced by emerald-green ones ; while a third would produce nothing but purple ones with yellow spots. Then the whole country, including my room, would be covered with nasty little washed-out green things, that crawled impartially into my bed, my pyjamas, and my boots; then came a plague of horrid hopping things, a sort of cross between a spider and a grasshopper, which seemed very fond of human society. Of course the jigger was always with us; he goes on for ever, with a fine contempt for seasons. The locust, too, seems to be pretty free from fancies as to weather; we had seen some very big swarms during the Unyoro expedition, while the dry season lasted, and now, in the wet weather, we were treated to a monster army. I thought at first that the hills on the farther side of the gulf were on fire, then, what seemed to be a smoke - cloud swept across the lake, hiding the water, and a quarter of an hour later darkness and a whirring sound told me that the enemy was upon us. Next day every banana leaf on the peninsula was gone, and nothing but bare uncomfortable - looking stems were to be seen in the groves; but nobody seemed to care, and not a Waganda took the trouble to walk out and try to save his crops. I told Ereya, the sub-chief of the place, that he and his people deserved to starve, but he only smiled pleasantly, and said very likely I was right.

During this plague I found that my shed had one very decided disadvantage in addition to its more obvious ones. As evening came on, the locusts seemed to regard its grass walls as most suitable resting-places for the night. It happened that I was out until after sunset, and did not discover the invasion of my premises that had been going on until I came in and lit the candle, which the locusts, mistaking for the rising sun, took as a signal for renewed activity ; but they probably thought they had had a rather short night, and might enjoy another forty winks, for it was not until I sat down to dinner that they thoroughly woke up, and began taking flying leaps at the white tablecloth and plate of tomato soup, which seemed to have a special attraction for them. The worst of it was, that, buried as they were in the grass walls, it was impossible to get the lazier ones out, and as, after turning my whole establishment on to them for half an hour, I found the bombardment going on as briskly as ever, I gave it up as a bad job, and simply went to bed and put the light out.

Although the Waganda would do nothing to

save their crops, the native captain in charge very wisely turned out the troops to protect our own patch of cultivation, and out of this arose a rather knotty point of military discipline. It appeared that when the flight came some twenty soldiers were working in our fields, but that, as it happened to be dinner-time, they had gone away as usual, and left the crops to take care of themselves; whereupon the captain gave them each three days' confinement to barracks. This sentence they considered unjust, and appealed to me, saying that they had never been specially ordered to drive away locusts. I told them that soldiers were men who were employed by the Government to protect its property, that if that property happened to be a kingdom invaded by other soldiers, it was their business to fight for it, and if it happened to be a cornfield invaded by locusts, they must shout and wave sticks for it. They seemed to be quite satisfied with my decision. When they have a grievance, they like to have a good talk about it. I must say they are capital fellows, and the only thing about them that ever gave me any trouble was their inveterate habit of dying when they were bewitched. A strong healthy-looking man would come to me one day, and with a most correct salute, report to me that Bakhit Madi or Farajullah Shilluk had bewitched him because he had refused to give him a piece of fish, or let him marry his daughter, and that unless I had the man killed at once, the spell would certainly take effect. No amount of argument on my part would have any effect on him, and next morning my old friend Bilal Effendi, from Kibiro, who had been promoted to staff officer at headquarters, would come with a long face and report his death. The odd part of it was, that post-mortem examination always proved that the victim had absolutely nothing the matter with him.

The Sudanese never took the law into their own hands, but the Lendus did once. They got hold of two women accused of witchcraft and made them drink the poison which they had scraped off one of their arrows. One died and the other did not, and this was of course taken as conclusive proof of the guilt of the one who had succumbed to the ordeal. I thought that possibly the woman who had died might have had a sore in her mouth, but a careful examination proved that this was not so, and I can only suppose that the one who escaped must have taken the precaution of spitting the stuff out again. The case was rather a difficult one to settle, as the ordeal had taken place in the Lendu camp; there were no independent witnesses present, and the Lendus swore with one accord that the women had taken the poison voluntarily.

As I have mentioned the Lendus once or twice, perhaps I ought to say a word about who they are. When the Sudanese troops were left to their own devices by Emin, at Wadelai, they whiled away their time by making war on the nearest tribe, which happened to be that of the Lendus, and having destroyed the villages and crops, and annexed the flocks and herds, proceeded to utilise the people as slaves. When the troops left, the Lendus, not caring to go back to their devastated country, elected to follow their conquerors, and, headed by their king, trooped after them to their new homes in Uganda.

I had the honour of being counted among his majesty's friends, and saw a good deal of him while the road-making and building operations were going on. He was a humpbacked dwarf of singularly unprepossessing appearance, but a cheery and intelligent little man, and took a great interest in all my improvements. He generally took up a position on an ant hill while the work was going on, and issued orders to his people with great vigour in the wholly unpronounceable language which they spoke. Like all his subjects, he was quite naked, with the exception of tufts of grass slung fore and aft from a string round his waist.

The Lendus are, of course, a very low tribe, possessing the minimum of intelligence, and are quite useless as soldiers, but they are sober, industrious, and cleanly, qualities in which the more civilised Swahilis are sadly lacking, and only the last of which can be put to the credit of the Waganda. They were consequently rarely ill, suffered but little from jigger sores, and were always available for any work they might be wanted for. I often wished that I had more of them, but if nature is allowed to take her course, I have every reason to hope that my successors will have no cause for complaint in that respect.

CHAPTER XX

THE MRULI EXPEDITION

Affairs in Unyoro—Fear of Kabarega—Kabarega's return to Mruli
—Determine to stir him up—Gibb to command—His health—
His orders—Bulamwezi—The old Egyptian fort—Means of
crossing the river—A complete surprise—The Waganda look
after themselves—Kabarega returns—Effect on the Wanyoro
An unlucky start — Grant's expedition — A hard time —
—Waganda ideas of discipline—Two new posts—Hardships—
Bad for rheumatism—Gibb's breakdown—The doctor takes
his place—Departure of Gibb and Arthur.

VERY satisfactory reports had been coming in
from Thruston as to the state of affairs in
that part of Unyoro which we actually occupied.
The people were settling down round our forts,
and quite a large colony had established itself at
Kitanwa, under the leadership of a powerful chief.
The inhabitants of Kibiro had returned to their
homes, and were working the salt, of which they
gave us the royalty formerly taken by the king;
but the districts between the range of our protection and the country actually occupied by Kabarega
were deserted, the inhabitants fearing to incur

suspicion of sympathy with us if they settled down in our neighbourhood. From inquiries which he had made among the friendly Wanyoro, Thruston was convinced that the bulk of the population would be only too glad to settle down peaceably under our rule if they were once relieved from the fear of Kabarega's vengeance, and that unless they were enabled to do so, a famine would certainly result, from the large districts which were being thrown out of cultivation.

As I had received information that Kabarega had recrossed the Nile and settled at his old capital near Mruli, I determined to make another attempt to capture him, or, at all events, further weaken his prestige by again driving him out of his kingdom, and by capturing the store of guns and ivory which he was said to have collected on Mruli Island. I therefore called together a council of chiefs, and, reminding them of my promise to help them to get the ivory at Mruli, asked if they were prepared to start on a fresh expedition. They all said they were anxious to do so, and after the usual amount of discussion it was agreed that they were to assemble their troops at the Kangao's capital in Bulamwezi on the 20th of April. They were

17

to be accompanied by two hundred Sudanese troops.

As Thruston was in command of Unyoro, Gibb and Arthur were the only two military officers I had left. The former was very anxious to command the expedition, and as Arthur had had about enough knocking about, I gave it to Gibb, although he was so crippled by rheumatism that, except on the occasion of our grand parade, he had not been outside the fort for months. Indeed in the early morning he could hardly walk at all. He said he could be carried in a hammock, and although I felt that his taking part in the expedition would probably permanently injure his health, I was very glad to be able to place the command in the hands of so good a soldier. I gave him Mr. Grant as his second in command, telling that officer to march direct from Lubwa's and meet him in Bulamwezi.

I explained to Gibb that the object of his expedition was not a fresh invasion of Unyoro, but rather an attempt to either kill or capture Kabarega, or, failing that, to weaken his power by driving him out of his kingdom or taking his treasure. I gave him orders not to allow the Sudanese troops to proceed more than a day's march beyond the Kafu; and as I was anxious to conciliate the Wakedi, with whom Kabarega had friendly relations, I instructed him on no account to fight with them, or allow his troops to cross the Nile into their country. After occupying Mruli, I directed him to obtain all possible information as to the navigability of the Nile between that place and the Victoria Lake, and to finish his expedition by a military promenade through Usoga, whose chiefs, I thought, would be all the better for a little ocular demonstration of our power. He was also directed to establish two small forts, one near the northern frontier of Bulamwezi as a protection against possible Wanyoro raids, and the other at Namionjua, where the Nile is crossed by an important ferry, which was reported to be much used by the trading caravans taking arms and ammunition to Unyoro.

On the 12th of April, Gibb was carried out of Kampala in his hammock at the head of 150 Sudanese troops. He was joined at Chuanguzi in Bulamwezi by Mr. Grant and 50 Sudanese from Usoga, and at Nabutaka by the Makwenda commanding the Waganda contingent, with 102 riflemen, 909 musketeers and

4244 spearmen, 5255 in all. He described the country through which he had passed as being very hilly, but traversed by a good road. After leaving Nabutaka, however, a densely wooded country was entered, which extended for two days' march beyond the frontiers of Bulamwezi. From this point the country became flat and swampy, but no great difficulties were encountered, and on the 4th of May the force unexpectedly came upon the site of the old Egyptian fort at Mruli, situated near the junction of the Kafu and Victoria Nile rivers, but the actual point of confluence was lost in a great mass of islands.

Owing to the dense growth of papyrus lining the banks for a depth of a hundred and fifty yards, the river was found to be unapproachable near the site of the fort, and the camp was moved for about a mile and a half to a spot whence a channel had been cut through the reeds.

As hardly any opposition had been encountered so far, it was probable that the Wanyoro, if they intended to make a stand at all, would do so either on the opposite bank or on the islands, which were supposed to hold Kabarega's treasury and arsenal. Grant therefore reconnoitred the position from the top of a tree, and made out one large island, on the shore of which a great number of canoes were drawn up.

I had given Gibb our Berthon boat, and had also arranged with the Waganda that they were to take with them three canoes, in pieces, to be sewn together on arrival at the Kafu. Of course this little flotilla was insufficient to ferry across any body of men in face of opposition, but I had hoped that it would enable Gibb to capture more canoes for that purpose. Acting on this idea, he made arrangements for surprising the island as soon as the canoes were ready, and before daylight on the 7th, embarked on his cutting-out expedition.

Sending Grant up stream in one canoe, and his interpreter, Francis, in another down stream, to cut off any canoes trying to escape, he put off himself in the Berthon boat, manned by five Sudanese, and accompanied by a canoe with three more, direct for the island. Although the river was a thousand yards broad, and he took some time pushing his way through the *sudd*, the Wanyoro seemed to have been entirely unaware that he had any means of crossing the water, so that they were taken completely by surprise, and after a very moderate opposition he was able to effect a landing and capture all the canoes. Although there were a great number of these, only thirteen were found to be fit for immediate use.

Gibb at once sent all the seaworthy canoes back to his camp to bring on the rest of his force. The Waganda, however, thought that taking part in an organised attack was very poor fun, while there was a chance of independent looting, so, quietly taking possession of them, proceeded to scatter in all directions on their own private business, leaving Gibb and his eight men in possession of the island. Of course, if there had been anything to capture on it, they would have spoiled all chance of success, but, as a matter of fact, there was very little. Kabarega, who had long before got wind of the expedition,[1] had moved off with all his cattle and valuables to Chope, and ever since the beginning of my expedition had kept his ivory in the Wakedi country; it seemed doubtful, too, whether his so-called arsenal existed at all. Nevertheless, a thorough search was made of the islands on the next and following days, and, although about

[1] I had a letter from Thruston, written a few days after Gibb's departure from Kampala, saying that he had heard of the expedition from Unyoro sources.

a hundred sheep and goats were captured, nothing of any value was found.

Although the expedition had been a failure in so far that Kabarega had neither been killed nor captured nor his treasure taken, its effects were very satisfactory, as it caused him to leave his kingdom and cross the Nile a second time, and thus helped to reduce his prestige. Reports from Thruston stated that the fact of our having been able to reach Mruli and the islands, which the Wanyoro looked upon as inaccessible, had produced a profound impression in the country.

Having finished the first phase of his expedition, Gibb set to work to accomplish the second, that is, the establishment of the forts, the exploration of the Nile, and the march through Usoga. Wishing to protect his front while he was choosing the site for the forts, he gave the Makwenda orders to remain at Mruli with the Waganda till they received permission to retire. He then sent off Grant with forty Sudanese in ten canoes to work up stream, joining the main body every night at places which were agreed upon.

Grant had an unlucky start, for while he was ferrying across some Wanyoro prisoners whom he was going to liberate on the Unyoro bank of the river, the canoe containing them began to sink, and three of the Sudanese escort, losing their heads, jumped overboard and were drowned.

Having landed all the prisoners, Grant proceeded up stream, battling for three days against a very strong current and frequent attacks of hostile canoes; and found it impossible to effect a landing owing to the dense growth of papyrus which lined the river banks. He once saw a rocket which Gibb sent up as a signal, but although this gave him the satisfaction of knowing that the main body were near, it was not of much practical use to him, neither giving him the food of which he and his men were by this time in urgent need nor affording protection from the Wanyoro fleet which dogged his steps. He, however, pushed on until a barrier of reeds in Lake Kioga definitely stopped his further progress, when, pretty well worn out from want of sleep and food and the strain of constant ambushes from among the reeds, he turned the head of his flotilla towards Mruli, where he expected to find provisions and shelter in the Waganda camp.

The party was very heavily attacked during the return journey, and, longing for food and rest as all were, it is perhaps better to leave to the imagination the remarks which were made when, on arriving at their starting-point, they found the Waganda camp deserted.

Finding no food, there was nothing for it but to push on. Luckily they had arrived early in the day, and by half-past nine in the evening came upon the Waganda halted for the night on their homeward march. It turned out that, not caring about Mruli, our allies had simply left it, making up their minds to return to Kampala, and without taking the trouble to let Gibb know, had proceeded to carry out their intention. Gibb told me afterwards that he had found the Makwenda anxious to carry out any orders given to him, but quite powerless to control the small chiefs and men of his undisciplined horde.

Grant then joined the main body near Namionjua, receiving orders to proceed to that place and hold it while Gibb selected a site for his fort to the north of Bulamwezi. The place chosen was Banda, and having completed the fort, Gibb left in it a garrison of eighteen men, and rejoined Grant. Although he met with no opposition from the enemy, his march was a very trying one, the country being intersected by many large papyrus-choked rivers, more particularly the Sezibwa and Lusenki, the latter of which took fifteen hours to cross, wading shoulder deep.

As the rainy season was in full swing, the expedition does not seem to have been a very suitable one for a person suffering from acute rheumatism.

Unfortunately, neither Gibb nor Grant could sketch, and the expedition brought back no information, other than verbal, on the topography of this little known district.

After building a fort at Namionjua, in which a garrison of ten men was left, the expedition crossed the Nile into Usoga, and made easy marches through that country to Lubwa's, halting at the headquarters of the various chiefs, hearing their grievances, and generally trying to set up a little order in that neglected country.

On the 28th of June, Gibb returned to Kampala so utterly crippled by the hardships of his expedition, that I determined to send him home by the first opportunity. Luckily, two new officers had arrived on the 14th, Major Cunningham and Doctor Ansorge. I asked the latter to give me a medical opinion on the state of

Gibb's health, telling him that if he found him unfit to stay in Uganda, I should have to ask him to take his place as Commandant at Kampala. On his reporting that Gibb was utterly unfit to remain, I put him in charge of that post.

On the 13th of August, Gibb started for the coast, accompanied by Arthur, who was also fairly worn out, and whom I had not the heart to keep any longer; so that, in spite of the new arrivals, I was not any better off for officers than I had been since the detachment left after the Unyoro expedition.

CHAPTER XXI

AFFAIRS IN UNYORO

Trespassers—"Berti Pasha"—Attacked by Dervishes—Exchange
of flags—The force brought over—Followers—Attacks on convoys—Masaja Mkuro—A cascade of stones—A difficult ascent
—A gallant charge—Wanyoro agility—Change of feeling—
Wadelai again—The Semiliki river—Kabarega asserts himself
—And gets defeated—The butcher's bill—Mahaji Saghir—
Post to the westward—Hostility of Uma—A forced march—A
wakeful cow—Surprise of Kabarega—Fireworks—An offer of
peace—Thruston resigns his command.

IN the meanwhile Thruston had not been idle in
Unyoro. Hearing early in March that a
force of Sudanese, under a European, was
encamped on the western shore of the Albert
Lake, he embarked at Kibiro in the steel boat,
and arrived on the 23rd of March at Mahaji
Saghir, where he found a company of Sudanese
troops flying the Congo Free State flag. The
native officer[1] in command stated that they had
been sent by "Berti Pasha" (Captain Baert) from

[1] There were no Europeans with them. The white man reported
by the natives was probably an Egyptian clerk who had accompanied the force.

Wandi to establish a fort on the Nile. They had originally been 400 strong, under command of Fadl el Mula Bey, but the advanced party, which was accompanied by their colonel, had fallen in with the Dervishes, and been completely exterminated by them. The other remaining company was said to be encamped in the hills two days off. They were accompanied by a huge crowd of followers. As the district they were then in was (on the latest information we had) within the British sphere of influence, Thruston explained to them he could not permit them to fly a foreign flag, and presented them with an English one instead, which was duly received by a guard of honour and much saluting. He also told the officer in command that, if required to do so, he would have to bring his men to the eastern shore of the lake. In reporting the matter to me, he said that the force was wholly unprovided with money or trading goods, and was living entirely on plunder, and asked for instructions as to its disposal. I did not receive the report until the 8th of May, but at once sent off a special mail with an answer, telling Thruston that the presence of such a force, living under such conditions, was not permissible within our sphere of influence. I ordered him to withdraw them at once to the east shore of the lake, and eventually send them to Uganda.

On receiving my orders, he returned to Mahaji Saghir, accompanied by Mr Forster, and marched the force down to the Kitonga ferry on the White Nile, and thence to the Victoria Nile, which he crossed at Magungu. This operation was only rendered possible by the help of Amara, a friendly Wanyoro chief, who pointed out to him a passage through the *sudd* by which the steel boat was enabled to ascend to the neighbourhood of the fort. As it was, the crossing of the two ferries were tedious and difficult undertakings, the Sudanese, women, children, and slaves, numbering hardly less than ten thousand. Fortunately, a great number of the latter deserted before the second ferry was reached, and probably not more than five thousand persons marched into Unyoro.

In the meanwhile, the Wanyoro, of whom a large hostile force was collected round Masaja Mkuro, had taken to attacking our monthly convoys, so on his return Thruston determined to put a stop to this nuisance, and, marching out on the 20th of May with a company of Sudanese and the chief Amara's friendly Wanyoro, reached

MASAJA MKURO

(*To face page* 270)

the foot of the mountain soon after mid-day. He found it to be surrounded by a considerable village, which was, however, deserted, and saw a large standing camp at the top, held by a great body of the enemy, partially screened by a rough parapet of stones. The mountain, whose sides were in many places perpendicular, and everywhere excessively steep, rose about a thousand feet sheer out of the plain, and was ascended by two zigzag footpaths.

Leaving the friendly Wanyoro and fifty Sudanese to guard the foot of the mountain and cut off the retreat of the enemy, Thruston with the remaining fifty began slowly to creep up the side. From first to last they were almost entirely in view of the defenders, who poured upon them a continuous cascade of rocks and stones. Luckily, these were of a friable material, and got considerably broken up in their descent, and although everybody got a good deal knocked about, not many serious casualties occurred. As the summit was neared, the ascent got so steep that the men were no longer able to walk upright, but took to their hands and knees; and at the same moment the Wanyoro, discarding their more familiar weapons of defence, took to the—in their hands

—far less deadly implements of modern warfare. A downhill shot is a difficult one for the best of marksmen, and Wanyoro may, I think, fairly be classed among the worst, and although a hail of lead passed, perhaps unpleasantly close, over the assailants' heads, no damage was done.

Always bearing in mind the smallness of his store of ammunition, and thinking that blown men would not have much chance of hitting the sea of heads just bobbing above the parapet, Thruston very wisely refrained from returning this fusillade, and after giving his men a good rest within a few yards of the top, sounded the charge, when, with a loud cheer, the gallant fifty rushed the parapet, and put the defenders to what, if they had had any, would have been the point of the bayonet; unfortunately, they had not, and the butt ends of the rifles had to take the place of that useful weapon.

The Wanyoro, however, who had never dreamt that their hitherto impregnable stronghold could be carried, were far too disconcerted to notice these little details of equipment, and with one accord rushed across the plateau, making the descent of their fastness in a manner more creditable to their agility than their courage.

Having disposed of Masaja Mkuro, Thruston next turned his thoughts towards Wadelai. Knowing of what vital importance she would be to us for reconnoitring purposes, if we were ever attacked from the north, I was rather loath to let the boat run the risk of a second voyage down the Nile; but Thruston and Moffat had between them made treaties with all the chiefs on the western shore of the Albert Lake, as far as Boki's, and the former reported a very marked change of feeling towards us on the part of the Lurs, I therefore thought it as well that he should visit the scene of Owen's labours, and see what was going on there.

Starting on the 13th of June for Kibiro, and touching at Mahaji Saghir, Thruston dropped down to Wadelai, finding the inhabitants both there and on the way very friendly. He described it as "a God-forsaken hole," and left next day, calling on his way up stream at Iyara's village and recovering from that chief the rifle which had been stolen from Purkiss' escort. Before returning to Kibiro, he visited the south end of the lake, and explored for a few miles the mouth of the Semiliki river, which connects the Albert and Albert Edward lakes. It was about forty yards wide, and of considerable depth, but the current was too strong to be stemmed by his rather clumsy boat and indifferent crew.

He said that this end of the lake was very shallow, and was evidently being silted up by the large quantities of mud and *sudd* brought down in the rainy season. The latter formed a mass of floating islands, through which the river had forced a passage, its course being marked by a strong current extending several miles into the lake.

Although this trip brings me up to the date at which I left events in Uganda, for the sake of convenience I shall go ahead a little and sketch Thruston's adventures up to the date of his and my departure for the coast.

So far we had chiefly taken the initiative, but early in August Kabarega seemed to think that he would like to have another turn. Accordingly on the eighteenth of that month he despatched his eldest son, Majasi, and his principal general Ireyta, with all his available followers, to Mapala, giving them orders to collect a force with which to attack our fort at Hoima. This concentration of troops was effected without Thruston's suspicions being roused, and the first intimation he had of a probable attack was caused by the sight, on the 26th, of a crowd of Wanyoro overlooking our fort from Mapala hill. He at once sent out a reconnaissance, which reported three large camps near Kabarega's old capital. On the morning of the next day a party was sent to keep touch with the enemy, and Thruston made arrangements for a night march, with the object of surprising the Wanyoro on the morning of the 28th. The scouts, however, returned at about nine, and reported that the enemy had struck camp and was marching to attack the fort.

Thruston at once fell in the troops, and, leaving Moffat, with half a company, the Swahilis, and sick, in charge of the fort, marched out, in less than half an hour, with a hundred and fifty Sudanese, Amara's friendly Wanyoro, and a small colony of Waganda Mohammedans who had settled near the fort.

The enemy's riflemen were drawn up on the near side of a little ravine, partly concealed in the long grass. Behind them on the farther side was an immense crowd of spearmen, while Mapala and the neighbouring hills were covered by many groups, evidently waiting to see what turn events would take before committing themselves too definitely to action. Majasi, mounted on a man's shoulders, was being carried up and down the line encouraging his men.

Fire was not opened until the opposing forces were within a hundred yards of each other. It was then warmly kept up by both sides, the enemy making a good stand for some time, but, owing to the inferiority of their shooting, being gradually forced over the stream, on the farther side of which they formed up.

Leaving a company to attract the attention of the enemy, Thruston led his remaining fifty Sudanese some distance up stream, and, crossing the ravine with them, took the Wanyoro in flank, completely doubling them up, while simultaneously the company which he had left made a front attack. Even then the majority of the tribesmen would not own themselves beaten, but collected in groups in the long grass, from which they only turned out after a considerable amount of opposition. At length, seeing that the day was lost, they broke up and scattered in all directions over the hills.

In this class of warfare it is always very difficult to estimate either the number of the enemy or their killed, while the former calculation is further complicated by the doubt as to who should be counted as a combatant. Counting the potential combatants, *i.e.* the onlookers who would be converted by a victory for their side into active enemies, the numbers in this case might fairly be put at tens of thousands, but Thruston modestly confined his estimate to the number of riflemen, which, on the statement of a Sudanese deserter who had been one of Emin's men, he reckoned at 750. He claimed that of these he killed 200. Among the onlookers were considerable contingents of Waganda, Manya-mezi, and Manyuema; a force of Langus had also accompanied the reconnaissance of the previous day, but, not liking the look of our fort and the grassless plain in front of it, had retired before the fight.

Our loss was eight wounded and our expenditure of ammunition 3000 rounds. This was by far the most important fight we had had since we crossed the Unyoro frontier in January, and I hoped that the lesson would be a sufficiently severe one to make Kabarega feel inclined for peace; but I felt sure that any overtures on our part would only make him think that our losses had been more severe than he had imagined. I therefore determined, on getting the report of the engagement, that I must give him another lesson, and sent Thruston orders to attack him at the earliest possible opportunity, and, after thoroughly beating him, to offer him terms of peace. As the report was only sent to Uganda by the ordinary monthly convoy leaving the frontier on the first of each month, it did not reach me until the 8th of September, and my answer was not handed to Thruston until the 3rd of November, In the meanwhile other events were taking place in Unyoro which require noticing.

Feeling that I ought to have some look-out down the Nile, to give us warning of any possible hostile movement from the north, I had ordered Thruston to establish a small post at Mahaji Saghir, opposite Mpata Point. This he did, and made a treaty with Tukwenda, the chief of the place ; who, in consequence of his friendship for us, thus became an object for hostility on the part of Uma, one of Kabarega's adherents, on the west side of the lake.

Events having occurred which made it desirable to move our post on the western shore of

MAHAJI KABIR

(To face page 279)

the Albert Lake more to the south, I gave Thruston orders to change his fort from Mahaji Saghir to Mahaji Kabir. As, however, he knew that our withdrawal from the latter place would certainly leave Tukwenda at the mercy of Uma, he thought it necessary to break the power of that chief before leaving. On the 11th of October, therefore, he sailed from Kibiro to Mahaji Saghir and thence proceeded, with the garrison and 150 of Tukwenda's followers, to march by land through Uma's country to Mahaji Kabir, which was reached after a few days' march without any serious opposition, the enemy being chiefly armed with bows and arrows and indifferent "trade" guns. Uma's village was destroyed on the way.

While in charge of the monthly convoy to the frontier in October, Mr. Forster fell into a Wanyoro ambush, and was somewhat severely pressed, losing two Swahilis and one Sudanese killed and three Sudanese wounded. He said that the enemy seemed to have at least one fairly good shot among them, as his cook and donkey, who were marching close by him, were killed, while a tusk of ivory which was being carried by the porter immediately in front of him was hit by a bullet, the splinters striking his face. The marksman was evidently just good enough shot to hit the white man's neighbourhood, and I should think that his performances must have had the effect of making Forster's society somewhat undesired by his black companions in succeeding convoys.

Forster learned from a prisoner that the party which had attacked him was a detachment of a large force sent to make another demonstration against us by Kabarega, who was furious at the failure of the last expedition, and who appears to have made it rather hot for his generals.

On receiving this news, Thruston at once marched out with all available troops and made a reconnaissance in force to Bitiberi, where he found traces of a large camp. A Waganda refugee afterwards stated that the force which had attacked the convoy consisted of 220 riflemen.

This convoy on its return brought Thruston my orders to attack Kabarega, and on the 3rd of November he started with 237 Sudanese to make a forced march to Machudi, to which Kabarega had returned after his exile in the Wakedi country. This place, about ten miles to the west of the Victoria Nile, is seventy-eight miles from Hoima, and the force covered this distance in three marches, arriving at Kabarega's headquarters at two in the morning. Not a soul was stirring as the force defiled through the silent streets, barely lighted by the setting moon. Elated at the almost unhoped-for surprise which they had managed to effect, they were full of hope that they would succeed in finding and surrounding Kabarega's house before an alarm was given. This hope was not destined to be fulfilled. First the keen senses of an insomnious cow caused her to give a note of warning to her fellows, who passed on the signal until it reached the ears of a lazy watch-dog. He, remembering his lapse of duty, made up for his past silence by a piercing yelp that soon woke his master, who rushed, gun in hand, into the very arms of the midnight marauders, and before he could be stopped, a report from his weapon had roused the whole community. In an instant they were rushing out of the huts, firing wildly into the darkness, and urging the women to run for their lives. This advice was probably superfluous, and for some minutes a fine representation of pandemonium let loose was afforded for the edification of Thruston and his band ; they, however, all intent on Kabarega, pressed steadily on through the mob of shrieking women, squalling babies, yelping curs, and fusillading men, and, within two minutes of the first alarm being given, had reached and surrounded the royal enclosure, unfortunately just too late, for on the first note of danger, his wily majesty, hurriedly throwing a blanket over his shoulders, had jumped out of bed and fled into the darkness.

Thruston afterwards heard that Kabarega had been warned of his approach by his general Ireyta, but, refusing to believe that our men could cover so great a distance in the time, had thought himself perfectly safe, at all events for another night, and had not taken any precautions. "Never despise your enemy" is not a bad military maxim for any soldier to remember, and it is one which Kabarega will probably particularly lay to heart.

In the meanwhile, Sheikh Amara and his merry men, who had accompanied the expedition, thought the time had come for them to have a little fun. Whirling in the air some smouldering embers, they soon had a nice collection of torches. With these they proceeded to set the town on fire, and were soon rewarded for their trouble by the joy of hearing the powder magazine explode, and the sound of that amusing cracker-like popping which results from placing a few thousand cartridges on a bonfire. Probably a great amount of valuable property was destroyed, but Thruston and his troops succeeded in saving over three hundred head of cattle, two thousand rupees' worth of cloth, and all Kabarega's household goods, including his trebly consecrated insignia of royalty, the famous brass and iron sceptre and copper spear, which Sheikh Amara asserted he valued almost more than his kingdom. In his house was also found a photograph of Casati, which Thruston sent me to forward to the relations of that gallant officer of Gordon.

Thruston stayed all the next day at Machudi, to give Kabarega a chance of fighting, should he wish to do so, but supposing, from the absence of all signs of hostility, that for the present the king had no warlike inclinations, he affixed to the door of his house a letter in Arabic, offering him terms of peace. He then retraced his steps to Hoima.

During Thruston's return march he was almost continually harassed by ambushes, and lost two men killed and four wounded, and had himself a near shave, a bullet passing through his left breast pocket and just cutting his skin.

Worn out by almost incessant marching, and the mental strain of his difficult command, he handed over the charge of Unyoro to Cunningham in the beginning of January, and returned to England for a well-earned rest.

CHAPTER XXII

THE ANKOLI EXPEDITION

The new troops—Mixed types—A European for Toru—Wilson stuck fast—An emissary from Ntali—Disturbing news—Rumours from Buddu—Cunningham's departure—An alarm—The Futabangi—The Albert Edward Lake—An unwelcome guest—Ntali's town—Blood brotherhood—Sango—Transport arrangements—Spire sent to Kavirondo—Sail making—Boat building—Our carpenter.

AS I expected that the troops which Thruston had found on the west of the Albert Lake would be rather in the rough, I had thought it better to bring them to Uganda, where we had more opportunities of drilling them than were to be found in Unyoro. I had therefore told Thruston to send them down by the first opportunity, in charge of Mr. Forster, who was to accompany them as far as Makwenda's. On hearing of Cunningham's approach, I wrote to him, telling him to go straight to that place and take them over. He arrived there on the 18th of June, almost at the same moment that they did, and turned up at Port Alice on the 26th. On the following day I had a grand parade of them.

I have said before that our troops presented a curious appearance, and although I had got accustomed to rather strange turn-outs, I confess I was fairly startled by the bewildering variety of these warriors' costumes, equipments, and appearance. To begin with, they were of all possible ages, colours, and sizes,—doddering, grey-bearded old men, fine strapping youths, and pigmies, apparently from Stanley's forest, Abyssinian, Egyptian, and pure-blooded negroes, and strange crosses of each and all of them. The variety of their clothing was infinite, ranging from the nearest approach to nothing in which a military-minded person will appear before his commanding officer, to cherry-coloured trousers and blue frock-coats with gold braid. And then their arms! breech-loaders, muzzle-loaders, double-barrelled "scatter" guns, some with locks and some without, all were duly brought to the present on my arrival, and all their owners seemed equally satisfied that they were in possession of highly effective weapons.

After inspecting the line, and making a short

speech to the officers, I left to Cunningham the task of weeding out the rubbish, expressing my opinion to him that the greater part of them were best fitted to be inmates of a workhouse. However, after getting rid of the more hopelessly decrepit, he drilled the rest into really very good shape, and by enlisting a good many of their hangers-on, we were able to increase the force in Uganda by four hundred men, thus bringing our total strength up to twelve hundred.

Cunningham, however, was not left long at this peaceful work, for a month after his arrival I had to send him off on an expedition to Ankoli.

Towards the end of June I had received a letter from Mr. Scot Elliott, the explorer, who, while I was in Unyoro, had passed through Kampala on his way to Ruonzori. As he said that the Swahili headman whom Owen had left in Toru was playing the fool, I determined to send a European there as soon as I possibly could.

This opportunity was offered by the arrival of Mr. G. D. Smith, who had been sent up as accountant, relieving Wilson of his duties in that department. I therefore gave Wilson orders to take charge of the Toru district, and to go there *viâ* Ankoli and make a treaty with its king, Ntali. He started on the 20th, with an escort of twenty Sudanese and a number of Waganda porters. On the 24th of July, however, I got a letter from him dated from Marongo, on the borders of Koki and Ankoli, saying that all his porters had deserted, and that he was lying up there, unable to move, and surrounded by hostile natives, whom he momentarily expected to attack him.

In the meanwhile, other complications had arisen. An envoy had come in from Ntali, saying that his kingdom had been invaded by the Ruanda people from the south, and asking me to send troops to help him. Also a deputation of Protestant Waganda chiefs had brought some very serious charges against the king; preparations for a rising were reported as going on in Buddu; and Gibb wrote that Mwanga had some canoes ready at Mununyu, had packed up his traps, and was on the point of migrating to the Catholic province; lastly came a letter from Mwanga himself, saying that he wished to turn Catholic at once. Luckily, all these various items of rather disturbing news pointed in the same direction, and most of them hinged on one matter—Mwanga's religious views. It having leaked out that he wished to change his religion, I had little doubt that the Protestant chiefs had followed their old tactics, and immediately brought accusations against him; that he, feeling that there was a conspiracy against him, and following the dictates of his timid nature, had determined to make a bolt of it: while the Catholics, knowing that he was going to take refuge in their province, and fearing that the Protestants would try to reclaim him by force, were preparing to resist a possible invasion.

Whether this theory of mine was right or wrong, it was evident that there were two things to be done—first, to prevent his embarking at Mununyu, and second, to stop any chance of a rising in Buddu. The first was a simple matter, and needed no very particular measures, and the second happened to fit in very conveniently with the double appeal for help from Wilson and Ntali.

Feeling pretty sure that the presence of troops in the neighbourhood of Buddu would at once stop any disturbances there, I merely sent Cunningham off with orders to assist Wilson and then take that officer's place as an envoy to Ntali.

Having reason to believe that a considerable trade in arms and ammunition passed through Ankoli on its way to Kabarega, I was anxious to place a small post there to stop it, and Ntali's demand for protection against the Ruanda seemed to offer a good opportunity for establishing one. I wished, however, to keep friends with Ntali, so told Cunningham that if that king showed any marked disinclination to the presence of a permanent garrison in his country, he was not to force the matter, but to establish a post instead in the south of Buddu. I afterwards sent after him more detailed instructions, letting him know what course I should pursue in the event of a rising, and how I expected him to co-operate with me.

Cunningham started on the 25th of July, with fifty-seven Sudanese and sixty-five porters, crossing the Katonga river, which forms the northern boundary of Buddu, on the 30th; and on the 5th of August reaching Marongo, where he found Wilson encamped. During his passage through Buddu he had found everything quiet, but once when he had fired at a hartebeeste, a number of

armed peasants had rushed out of the neighbouring villages, declaring that they thought the war
had begun.

He found that Wilson had been despoiled of
a large quantity of cloth and trades goods by
" Futabangi," or pagan Waganda, who had been
driven out of their own country during one of
the religious wars, and had settled down in the
more easy-going states to the west. Feeling that
depredation of this sort could not be allowed on
a Government convoy, he sent a message to the
" Futabangi " chief, demanding a tribute of goats
and food as repayment. On this being refused,
he despatched a party of forty Sudanese to enforce
the fulfilment of his demand. The troops
were resisted in some force by the natives, and
an engagement ensued, in which one of our men
was severely wounded and eight Futabangi were
killed.

Being convinced from what he had seen
that there was no immediate danger in Buddu,
and thinking that Wilson's force was not large
enough to be safely allowed to proceed alone, he
determined to escort it to its destination, and
arrived on the 19th of August at Fort George,
our station in Usongora, on the Albert Edward

Lake. He described the road as in parts very precipitous and difficult for loaded porters.

On the 21st he began his homeward journey, taking a more southern route, so as to pass by Ntali's capital. Following a good road over an undulating plain, he reached Ruampoko on the 26th, and was there met by the envoy from Ntali who had brought the message to me at Port Alice. This man was accompanied by another ambassador, and although, in addition to his message to me, Ntali had sent another to Cunningham on his way up, asking him to arrange an interview, they now had the cheek to ask Cunningham what he had come for. He answered that he had come to see Ntali, because he had been asked to do so; whereupon the two plenipotentiaries exclaimed that he was quite mistaken, that no such message had ever been sent, and earnestly requested him to turn off on to the Marongo road, promising that Ntali would send him a further communication to that place. Cunningham, however, answered that Ntali had asked him to go to his capital, and that to his capital he was going.

Various attempts were made to lead him astray, one guide taking him half a day's march into a desert, and all authorities assuring him that the capital lay in every possible direction except the right one. His sound common sense, however, enabled him to see through all these little devices, and, quietly marching along the principal track, he halted on the 28th within sight of Ntali's town, a spot which, I believe, no European had before succeeded in reaching. He reported that it is placed on all existing maps a good deal to the north-west of its proper position, being situated on the south-east corner of the great plain which is bounded on the south by the Ruampora range, under which it lies, and to the south of the Ruwezi river.

The town, which lies at the foot of a five-peaked hill named Katchika, was composed of the usual beehive-shaped huts, but the king had a large high square house. He was not, however, in occupation of it, having fled to the hills on Cunningham's approach, and a large body of spearmen, lining the pass through which he had gained them, showed that any attempt to follow him would have been resisted. Although he has a superstitious horror of seeing a white man, he was anxious to make "blood brotherhood" with Cunningham by proxy, but my envoy excused himself from taking part in that rather disgusting ceremony by saying that he would only do so in the actual presence of the king. He, however, signed a treaty with Magota the Katikiro, who stated that he had been given full powers.

After careful inquiries, Cunningham came to the conclusion that Ntali's story of a Ruanda invasion was all moonshine, and that he had asked for troops in the hopes of getting our help in a little marauding expedition which he was contemplating in the Ruanda country. It seemed that Ntali had never dreamed of a white officer being sent in command of the party, and had probably thought that a black one might have been tempted, by a promise of share in the loot, to help him in his expedition.

Seeing that Ntali was decidedly averse to the establishment of a post in his country, Cunningham withdrew his force and proceeded eastwards through Koki to Buddu, and built a fort at Sango, near the mouth of the Kagera river. He was, however, convinced that the trade in arms and ammunition could only be stopped by the establishment of a station in Ankoli, through which all caravans for the north pass ; but as

Ntali levies toll on these caravans, he would naturally object to any action on our part which would tend to stop them.

Cunningham then marched northward through Buddu, which he found perfectly quiet, and returned to Port Alice on the 22nd of September. He described the southern road through Ntali's as a far better one than that which he had followed on his outward journey, *viâ* Marongo.

While Cunningham was away, I heard from the Consul-General at Zanzibar that some new transport arrangements had been made which necessitated my having an officer in Kavirondo to receive and despatch caravans and collect food for them. He told me that the first of these caravans would arrive at Mumia's early in November. I had already one district without a European in it, and certainly could not withdraw one from any of the others; so the only person available for the place was Spire. Accordingly the first time he returned from the German end of the Lake, I told him that he would have to give up his water transport work and take charge of the Kavirondo district. This mattered the less now, as, with improved arrangements on our own route, I hoped that sufficient cloth for our requirements would come through Kavirondo.

Before starting him off, I took the opportunity of re-rigging the boat, which was a sort of deformed schooner very much undermasted, and turned her into a yawl. I had never in my life designed a suit of sails before, but after a few experiments we turned out a very creditable set, and when I took the boat for her trial trip, Spire assured me that she had never sailed anything near so well before.

Native canoes were very unsatisfactory as means of transport. Owing to the large crews which they required, they were expensive, and they also leaked profusely. Therefore, emboldened by my success as a sailmaker, I tried to build a wooden boat as an auxiliary means of water transport, but the only person who by any stretch of the imagination could be called a carpenter, unfortunately, took to getting drunk rather frequently. What with the many calls on him, and the time he spent in a state of intoxication and in the guard-room, the work progressed very slowly, and I never had the pleasure of seeing my first attempt in naval architecture afloat.

CHAPTER XXIII

A BRITISH PROTECTORATE

ON the 25th of August I received a despatch
informing me that a Protectorate had been
declared over Uganda, and directing me to make
this publicly known. I accordingly got a Union
Jack out of the store, and wrote to Dr. Ansorge
at Kampala, asking him to see that the king's
signal halyards worked, as I did not want a hitch
in the middle of the ceremony.

Next day I rode off to Kampala myself, and
on the 27th, in as full a uniform as I could collect,
proceeded to the palace with an escort of a
hundred men and the full band of the regiment.

The king and chiefs were all assembled in the long room in which he had first received me.

After explaining that Her Majesty had been graciously pleased to ratify the agreement which Mwanga had made with Sir Gerald Portal, I called upon the king to fulfil the promise he had made in one of the clauses of that document, and make a fresh one with me in the same sense. The treaty was then read out in Luganda, and on a signal from me the band struck up what they thought was "God Save the Queen," the troops presented arms, and the flag ought to have run up and floated bravely on the top of the king's flagstaff; but, in spite of my precautions, nothing had been done to the halyards, and after waiting a few minutes, I saw a small boy laboriously shinning up the mast with the emblem of England's protection in his mouth, making longer and more frequent pauses for breath as he got farther from the ground. When about half-way up he seemed inclined to stop altogether; and as the exuberant energy of the band not only made it impossible to go on with the proceedings, but even (from where I was) to stop the music, I had to send them a message to cease their braying. When this was accomplished, we discussed the terms of the treaty for a few minutes, and I returned to the fort, where Mwanga promised to follow me in a quarter of an hour to sign the documents.

A smaller and more select party assembled in my office at the fort, where the important ceremony of signature took place. The king, with much giggling, having scrawled his name, and I having followed his example, our hieroglyphics were duly witnessed by Dr. Ansorge and the Protestant and Catholic Katikiros; but before the documents could be considered legally complete, the Commissioner's official seal had to be affixed to them, and here the little difficulty arose that no sealing wax could be found. I knew that I had none, and the doctor had grave doubts whether any could be found among his possessions; however, he started off to search, and in about five minutes returned triumphantly with three broken stumps about the size of marbles.

The duties of a Commissioner in Uganda are many and sometimes perilous, but I did not feel that patriotism called upon me to burn off the tips of my fingers, so I asked for a penholder, and having been presented with one, tried to fix on to its end one of the little lumps of wax; but

here the architectural peculiarities of the building interfered. The day was a windy one, and
the air was rushing through all the windows
like water in a mill-sluice. First, the doctor
tried to screen the candle, but a gust puffed it
out before the wax could even get its outer skin
softened; next, Apollo volunteered his services,
and then Mugwania, and finally the candle
was surrounded by a hedge of dignitaries, black
and white; but all of no avail, that draught
whistled through the chinks between their bodies;
matches (which are precious in Uganda) strewed
the floor, and the treaty was no nearer being
sealed than when we began. In this predicament
there was only one thing to be done, and that I
did. I shut the doors and shutters, and after a
moment's suspense in inky darkness, a sigh of
relief escaped the assemblage as they saw the
flash of a Bryant and May and the ridiculous little
yellow flame of the solitary and very inferior
candle. The king giggled, but he also perspired,
a sure sign with him of emotion, and I do not
think he half liked it. Perhaps he thought the
whole thing had only been a trick of mine to
perform in darkness some unholy rite that
would not bear the light of day; or perhaps he

only thought that I was going to cut his throat and bury his body under the office table : but whatever his fears may have been, he looked distinctly happier when sunlight was again let into the room, and when a few minutes afterwards I presented him with a new saddle that I had sent for as a present for him, he seemed so delighted, that an awful dread crept through me, for one moment, that he might embrace me.

Whatever they may have before thought of the desirability or otherwise of British occupation, I think everybody was genuinely pleased that something was settled at last. At any rate, both Protestant and Catholic Katikiros asked leave for their respective parties to fire guns that night, a permission which I the more readily granted, knowing that before sunset I should be half-way on my journey back to Port Alice.

Since my return from Unyoro I had been pegging away steadily at house - building and road-making. My house was by this time pretty well finished. It consisted of a main block containing the hall, with dining-room and office opening out of it, and two bedrooms and dressing-rooms on the other side facing the garden and lake. Connected by a passage to the right front corner of this was a square room with bow windows which I used as my study; while a similar block attached to the left rear corner contained the kitchen and servants' rooms; a broad verandah ran round the whole.

Since my return to England friends who have seen photographs of this house have spoken of it in very disparaging terms, calling it a "hut" and all sorts of opprobrious names; but in Uganda it was looked upon as a residence of the very highest class, and chiefs made long pilgrimages to see it, and thanked me for having erected such a beautiful object in their country. There was one item in it which particularly impressed their fancy, and that was the material with which the windows were glazed. On my way up, while rummaging in Hall's store at Kikuyu to see what I could annex, I came across some old celluloid photographic films, which had been thrown away by Colonel Rhodes on his journey down, and it struck me that this material would be the very thing for glazing windows in a country in which difficulties of transport made it impossible to use glass; so I at once wrote home for a good quantity of it, and soon after my return from Unyoro it arrived. It was a great success, as, apart from its being unbreakable and light it had the great advantage of being capable of being cut with a pair of scissors, and could consequently be fitted without difficulty to the curiously irregular window-frames which native carpenters turned out.

In spite of the gloomy prophecies of my friends when I moved down to the lake, I never had a touch of fever during the six months I lived in this house, although I had had it pretty regularly up to that date; and I believe this immunity was chiefly due to the fact of having windows which could be closed, and having a fire in all rooms at night. The fireplaces and chimneys for these gave me an immense amount of trouble. There being no limestone in the country, we had to use mud instead of mortar, and consequently the chimneys and arches over the fireplaces had to be built with rather an extra amount of care and precision, just the points in which a Swahili workman is least strong. I had therefore to do a good deal of the work myself, much to the surprise of the Waganda chiefs, who, coming with great pomp and a numerous retinue to pay their respects to Her Majesty's representative, would occasionally find him sitting astride the ridge of the roof, putting a chimney-pot in its place, or mounted on a scaffolding, trowel in hand, laying a course of bricks over the dining-room fireplace.

The roads being now nearly finished, my attention out of doors was chiefly directed to a harbour which I was building for the reception of the long-expected steam launches. I had chosen as a site for this the corner of the little bay in the middle of which the house stood; it was an excellent position, sheltered from the prevailing wind by a long wooded promontory, but the water was shallow and overgrown with reeds, and some pithy trees which spring up with marvellous rapidity in damp situations. I had therefore to reclaim this marshy foreshore and then run out a pier beyond it. The reclaiming of the marsh was comparatively easy work; baskets and native hoes were plentiful, and so was unskilled labour, and I simply put half the men on to dig, and made the other half carry the results of their labours away in baskets and dump them down in the water; but the sea-wall to protect the reclaimed land and the pier were more serious matters. This part of the beach was strewn with huge boulders, weighing from one to five or six tons, and, having no blasting materials or tools with which to break them, we had to move them bodily. To do this I first of all laid a rough railway, and had a number of twelve-feet rollers made, and then, digging down under the stone, we built a wooden frame below it, beneath which we inserted the rollers, cutting a long ramp to give an easy gradient out of the hole. Once fairly on the rail and rollers, it moved along pretty easily, but before getting it out we had endless mishaps, and if, as often happened, I was called away to try a case or receive a deputation just as the stone was on the point of getting nicely into its place, I was pretty certain, on my return, to find that the workmen had given it a move with their long levers just when they ought not to have done so, and that it had slipped off its packing back into the hole. This often meant a week's work undone, and everything had to be begun from the beginning again.

Even when we had got it fairly under way on the rails, our troubles were by no means over, for the most difficult job of all was dropping it into its place in the sea wall. Having no cranes or machines with which to lower it, we simply had to roll it over, trusting to my eye and judgment to make it fall into the right place. We had two or three accidents, which it took all our strength and ingenuity to repair, when a great boulder rolled over into the wrong place and blocked the entrance to the harbour; but before I had left, I had cleared all obstacles out of the way, and Port Alice really deserved its name. In this work the "monkey ropes," or hanging creepers, which the forest was full of, were of great use to us, and formed an excellent substitute for real rope, of which we were almost destitute.

After the collapse of the Buddu bubble, and Thruston's victory over Kabarega, my life began to be rather monotonous, and one day was very like another. I generally began the day with a look round the works, to set the men going; then, after breakfast at nine, did a little office work with Cunningham, tried cases, and as far as possible got over interviews with natives. With an interval for lunch, the rest of the day was chiefly spent in looking after the works, which went on till five, when, after tea, I wrote till sunset, and then took half an hour's rest in the verandah, while the fires were being lit and the rooms shut up. This was the pleasantest half-hour of the day ; the breeze had dropped, and the sun sunk behind the forest, the lake was like a sheet of glass, reflecting the many hues of the wooded promontory to the right, and only broken here and there by the snouts of a family of hippopotami, or the dark body of a crocodile gliding slowly towards his favourite rock. With the withdrawal of the noisy workmen, the monkeys emerged from the inner depths of the forest, and chattered in the trees that bordered my garden. To the right, a greenish tribe, with soft brown eyes and confident manners, swung themselves among the creepers, or sat in groups on a branch, in earnest discussion on the affairs of the nation. Sometimes they would even descend into the garden, and, standing upright on some rock or root which I had left for a nest of ferns, carefully scrutinised their big kinsman lazily smoking his cigarette in the verandah. Once a bold patriarch, whose years ought to have taught him more discretion, jumped on to the window - sill and took a survey of my room.

To the left was a black, wiry tribe, with smooth, shiny hair, and chalk-white noses, at once more shy and active than the green ones. They never ventured to the ground, but, bounding from tree to tree in astounding flying leaps, disported themselves in acrobatic exercises of almost super-simian daring, and on the slightest movement on my part disappeared like a flight of arrows into the forest.

Although before my arrival the belt of forest had been continuous, and the two tribes must have encroached on each other's ground, they seemed to have accepted my garden as a scientific frontier, which was never crossed, and I never once saw a black monkey on the right, or a green one to the left of the house.

Besides these wild companions, I had two domesticated little friends, both of the green tribe. They had both been brought to me as babies, the little gentleman first, and the lady some few weeks later. They were my constant companions; when I was writing by day, they would sit on the window-sill and catch flies; but if, tired of work, I leaned back in my chair for a moment, two bounds would bring them into my lap ready for a little game of romps. All about the house, or in the garden, they followed closely at my heels; but when I went down to the pier, we found Lendus at work, and, as everybody knows, a Lendu eats monkeys, so

THE RESIDENCY GARDEN, PORT ALICE

(To face page 308)

while in this dangerous neighbourhood, Tootie, the little lady, would scuttle up my legs and hide her head under my coat, while Tootums ascended a tree and surveyed his natural enemies from a distance, scampering down again and following me as soon as I left the workmen. Unfortunately, in their wanderings about the house, they fell victims to that pest the jigger, and, not seeing my way to save them from this infliction, as long as they stayed with me, I hardened my heart, and, following the example of the notorious uncle of the Babes in the Wood, I deliberately lost them in the forest. Tootums I never saw or heard of again, but Tootie, yearning for human society, made her way to the camp, whence she was brought back to me. She afterwards learned to catch the jiggers before they had time to burrow in her little toes, and never suffered any further inconvenience.

After sunset I used to write till dinner-time, and then, having looked through the one newspaper a day which I allowed myself, again set to work. I found that, what with six districts reporting direct to me, the missionaries, the chiefs, and the English mail, and having to copy all letters, I had generally enough writing to do to keep me up to quite a European hour.

On the 4th of November Captain Dunning and Mr. George Wilson arrived from the coast. The former I put in command of Singo, which since Arthur's departure had been without a European officer; and the latter, whom I had asked for when Purkiss left, took charge of public works, thus relieving me of a good deal of labour.

On the 28th of November, Mr. Jackson, Captain Ashburnham, and Lieutenant Vandeleur turned up, and my cook made a bonfire in their honour. I had been expecting for some time that he would set the house on fire, and had just begun to build a new range, which afforded him less chance of igniting the ·thatched roof of the kitchen; but I started it just too late, and as I was coming up from the pier at about noon, I saw a volume of smoke coming out of the kitchen wing. As this was connected with the main body of the house, it would have taken very little to set the whole place in a blaze, but luckily there were plenty of men about, and in less than five minutes I had three hundred of them on the roof of the main building, stripping off the thatch; and although we made rather a mess, and the kitchen and servants' rooms were completely gutted, no very great harm was done. Of course everybody was very excited, and a good deal of unnecessary conversation went on; but above the roar of the flames and the shouts of the men, could be heard the cook's wailing, for a terrible misfortune had happened. In the excitement of seeing his kitchen on fire, he had rushed out, quite forgetting that the potatoes for my lunch were boiling on the hearth. In vain he tried to re-enter his fast-crumbling sanctuary, and, failing in this himself, entreated Sudanese, Lendus, Swahilis, and Waganda alike, to perform the heroic task which he felt was beyond his strength; for "What," he said, "will be done to me if the master has no potatoes for his lunch!"

Early in December I began to get very tired in the afternoons, and one day with a splitting headache found myself obliged to go to bed at four; the same thing happened the next day, and again on the third; but on the fourth morning, instead of getting up again fairly refreshed, and dressing for my day's work, I am told that I further reduced the light costume in which I took my rest, and began wandering about the place, as Tom Nubi expressed it, like "idiot man." I have no very clear idea of what happened after this, but I have a vague recollection of two distinct personalities in me, each of which was, in some mysterious way, bound to take its turn at being uncomfortable, and both of whom shirked their duties in a most unsoldier-like manner. My first distinct impression is that of being bobbed along in a hammock, and being told by the doctor that Christmas day was over, and that I was being taken home.

MORRISON AND GIBB, PRINTERS EDINBURGH.

37 BEDFORD STREET,
LONDON,
February, 1896.

Mr. EDWARD ARNOLD'S

LIST OF

NEW *and* FORTHCOMING WORKS

NOTICE.—Mr. Edward Arnold has now opened an Office at 70 Fifth Avenue, New York, from which all his new Books are distributed in America.

FIRE AND SWORD IN THE SUDAN.

A personal Narrative of Fighting and Serving the Dervishes, 1879-1895.

By SLATIN PASHA, Colonel in the Egyptian Army, formerly Governor and Commandant of the Troops in Darfur.

Translated and Edited by Major F. R. WINGATE, R.A., D.S.O.,
Author of ' Mahdiism and the Egyptian Soudan,' etc.

Fully Illustrated by R. TALBOT KELLY.

Demy 8vo., One Guinea net.

Slatin Pasha was by far the most important of the European prisoners in the Soudan. Before the Mahdi's victories he held the post of Governor of Darfur, and was in command of large military forces. He fought no fewer than twenty-seven pitched battles before he was compelled to surrender, and is the only surviving soldier who has given an eye-witness account of the terrible fighting that occurred during the Mahdist struggle for supremacy. He was present as a prisoner during the siege of Khartoum, and it was to his feet that Gordon's head was brought in revengeful triumph within an hour of the city's fall.

The narrative is brought up to the present year, when Slatin Pasha's marvellous escape took place, and the incidents of his captivity have been so indelibly graven on his memory that his account of them has all the freshness of a romance.

From a military and historical standpoint the book is of the highest value. Slatin Pasha's various expeditions penetrated into regions as yet almost unknown to Europeans, but destined apparently to be the subject of serious complications in the near future. The map of these regions is believed to be the first authentic one produced. There is also a careful ground-plan of Khartoum and Omdurman, which might be of immense service in case of military operations.

The work is furnished with numerous spirited illustrations by Mr. R. Talbot Kelly, who is personally familiar with the Nile Valley, and has worked under the direct supervision of Slatin Pasha and Major Wingate.

THE EXPLORATION OF THE CAUCASUS.

By DOUGLAS W. FRESHFIELD, President of the
Alpine Club,

Author of ' Travels in the Central Caucasus,' ' The Italian Alps,' etc.

In two volumes, imperial 8vo., £3 3s. net.   Also a Large-paper
Edition of 100 copies, £5 5s. net.

Illustrated by over 70 Full-page Photogravures and several
Mountain Panoramas, chiefly from Photographs by Signor
VITTORIO SELLA, and executed under his immediate superintend-
ence, and by more than 100 Illustrations in the Text, of the
Scenery, People, and Buildings of the Mountain Region of the
Caucasus, from Photographs by SIGNOR SELLA, M. DE DÉCHY,
Mr. H. WOOLLEY, and the late Mr. W. F. DONKIN.

These volumes, intended to form a record of the exploration of
the Caucasus since 1868 by Members of the Alpine Club, as well as
a narrative of the author's recent journeys in that region, will
constitute one of the most complete and lavishly illustrated works
on mountain travel ever published in this country.

The letterpress will include a concise account of the physical
characteristics of the central portion of the Caucasian chain, and a
sketch of the principal travels and adventures of the mountaineers
who have penetrated its fastnesses, and conquered summits, eleven
of which are higher than Mont Blanc.

The personal narrative will consist of the story of two summers
recently spent among the glaciers and forests of the Caucasus by
the author, who was a member of the Search Expedition which
went out to ascertain the locality and nature of the catastrophe by
which Mr. W. F. Donkin and Mr. H. Fox with their guides lost
their lives in 1888, extracts from the diary of Mr. Fox, and accounts
of the first ascents of Kostantau and Ushba by Mr. H. Woolley
and Mr. Cockin.

An Appendix will contain a mass of novel and systematically
arranged topographical detail, which, it is hoped, may prove of
great service to future travellers and mountaineers.

District Maps on the scale of the old official map (3 miles to the
inch), forming together a complete map of the chain from Kasbeck
to Elbruz, are being prepared for the book mainly from the unpub-
lished sheets of the recent Russian surveys, which have been
generously placed at Mr. Freshfield's disposal by General Kulberg.

WITH KELLY TO CHITRAL.

By Lieut. W. G. L. BEYNON, D.S.O., 3rd Goorkha Rifles.

With Map, Plans, and Illustrations.   Demy 8vo., 7s. 6d.

Lieutenant Beynon was Staff-Officer to Colonel Kelly during the famous march for the relief of Chitral. Although other writers have published accounts of the campaign as a whole, no description of the march has yet appeared from the pen of an eye-witness.   Lieut. Beynon's official duties gave him special opportunities of seeing all that went on, and his narrative not only contains a complete record of the military operations, but is full of graphic touches in matters of detail, which enable the reader to realize exactly what the officers and men had to go through as they struggled on day by day in forced marches to their goal.

THROUGH THE SUB-ARCTIC FOREST.

A Record of a Canoe Journey for 4,000 miles, from Fort Wrangel to the Pelly Lakes, and down the Yukon to the Behring Sea.

By WARBURTON PIKE,

Author of ' The Barren Grounds of Canada.'

With Illustrations by Charles Whymper, from Photographs taken by the Author, and a Map.   Demy 8vo.

Mr. Pike is well known as an explorer, and in the journey now described he traversed some entirely unknown country round the Pelly Lakes.   For many months he supported himself entirely by hunting and fishing, being absolutely cut off from any chance of obtaining supplies.   Such a journey could not fail to be productive of many exciting episodes, and though the author treats them lightly, the hardships he went through form a fine test of the true explorer's spirit.

THE ART OF READING AND SPEAKING.

By Canon JAMES FLEMING, Canon of York and Rector of St. Michael's, Chester Square.

About 256 pp., crown 8vo., cloth, 3s. 6d.

Canon Fleming's reputation as a preacher constitutes him an authority on elocution, and in this little volume he gives a series of practical hints and directions for speaking and reading in public, which ought to be very useful. The book is, however, written in such a style that it can be perused with pleasure by the general reader, for it contains many interesting anecdotes and reminiscences, suggested by the author's wide experience of men and manners. It will not be forgotten that his funeral sermon on H.R.H. the late Duke of Clarence reached a sale of nearly fifty thousand copies.

COLONEL KENNEY HERBERT'S NEW COOKERY BOOK.

FIFTY LUNCHES.

By Colonel A. KENNEY HERBERT,

Author of ' Common-Sense Cookery,' ' Fifty Breakfasts,' etc.

Crown 8vo., cloth, 2s. 6d.

NEW EDITION.

IN A GLOUCESTERSHIRE GARDEN.

By the Rev. H. N. ELLACOMBE, Vicar of Bitton, and Honorary Canon of Bristol.

Author of ' Plant Lore and Garden Craft of Shakespeare.'

Crown 8vo., cloth, 6s.

' The book may be warmly recommended to all who love gardens, while it also cannot fail to interest even the horticulturally unlearned. It is written in a style that is clear, bright, and simple, and from beginning to end there is not a dull or wearisome sentence.' —*The Guardian.*

' Altogether a charming book.'—*Westminster Gazette.*

NEW EDITION.

POULTRY FATTENING.

By EDWARD BROWN,

Author of ' Pleasurable Poultry Keeping,' etc.

With Illustrations, crown 8vo., cloth, 1s. 6d.

NEW WORKS OF FICTION.

A MASK AND A MARTYR.

By E. LIVINGSTON PRESCOTT

Author of ' The Apotheosis of Mr. Tyrawley.'

One vol., crown 8vo., 6s.

A RELUCTANT EVANGELIST,

And other Stories.

By ALICE SPINNER,

Author of ' A Study in Colour,' ' Lucilla,' etc.

One vol., crown 8vo., 6s.

WORTH WHILE.

By F. F. MONTRESOR,

Author of ' The One who looked on,' ' Into the Highways and Hedges,' etc.

HADJIRA.

A Story.

By a TURKISH LADY.

SECOND EDITION.

TOMMY ATKINS.

A Tale of the Ranks.

By ROBERT BLATCHFORD,

Author of ' A Son of the Forge,' ' Merrie England,' etc

Crown 8vo., cloth, 6s.

' A splendid narrative of the barrack life of the rank and file.'—*Bradford Observer.*

' There is not a dull page in the book.'—*Eastern Morning News.*

' Most vigorous and picturesque sketches of barrack life.'—*Glasgow Herald.*

' Entertaining throughout, and reveals high literary ability.'—*Scotsman.*

' A really vivacious book ; the incidents are so well selected that the reader never wearies from start to finish.'—*Dundee Advertiser.*

A LITTLE TOUR IN AMERICA.

By the Very Rev. S. REYNOLDS HOLE, Dean of Rochester,

*Author of 'A Little Tour in Ireland,' ' The Memories of Dean Hole,'
' A Book about Roses,' etc.*

With numerous Illustrations, demy 8vo., 16s.

' There is not a page that does not contain some good thing—a gem of wit, a touch of wisdom, a scrap of kindly counsel, a quaint anecdote, or a homely truth. The Dean is brimful of humour, and even when he is serious and preaches a little sermon he is never for a moment dull.'—*Graphic.*

' His pages ripple over with fun, but his humour is not fatiguing, because it is never forced, and rests on a firm foundation of shrewd observation and kindly, but not indiscriminating, appreciation.'—*Times.*

' There are chapters abundantly illustrated in the daintiest style of art. These are full of incident and racy anecdote, charmingly garrulous, and full of pictures with a true local colouring. The wanderings of the writer were wide, and the peruser cannot fail to be struck by the wealth and accuracy of his observations.' —*Irish Times.*

' We say to everybody, Get the " Little Tour," and thank us for indicating the extent of ground which the survey of American life covers. As we said at the outset, the author touches almost every subject of human interest, and in doing so he brings into use a keen and searching criticism, and, on less serious occasions, all the wit and humour of which his genius is so particularly possessed.' —*Church Times.*

MEMORIES OF MASHONALAND.

By the Right Rev. BISHOP KNIGHT-BRUCE, formerly Bishop of Mashonaland.

With Photogravure Frontispiece, cloth, 8vo., 10s. 6d.

' Bishop Knight-Bruce has had considerable experience of Mashonaland, and his book shows him a keen observer who has admirably gauged the characteristics of the natives, among whom his wanderings have taken him. He understands their failings, and does not overrate their virtues, and few authors have given us a better insight of the nature of the natives of Africa. The book is well written, and adapted to every kind of reader. Those who are interested in travel and ethnography will find many chapters full of instruction ; to those connected with mission work this volume will be no less valuable. Bishop Knight-Bruce's description of Mashonaland in the past is charming. The concluding chapter on the Matabele War is quite as good as the previous ones, and it is most satisfactory to find that a bishop of the Church of England renders full justice to the able and humane way in which the campaign was conducted. To review this book fully is impossible, as there is not a single page devoid of interest, and all those who take an interest in South African affairs should not fail to read it.'—*Pall Mall Gazette.*

TWELVE HUNDRED MILES IN A WAGGON.

A Narrative of a Journey in the Cape Colony, the Transvaal, and the Chartered Company's Territories.

By ALICE BLANCHE BALFOUR.

With nearly 40 Original Illustrations from Sketches by the Author, and a Map.

Large crown 8vo., cloth, 16s.

'Full of keen observation, of good stories and amusing experiences, and it is permeated throughout with a humour which, generally genial, is sometimes caustic, and which never fails to entertain the reader, as it obviously smoothed the difficult path of the writer.'—*Daily Chronicle.*

'Miss Balfour's book is of the kind which should rather be read than reviewed. Its charm consists in an absolutely natural style of narrative applied to a subject which has become one of general interest. Everyone now wants to hear about South Africa. Miss Balfour saw the greater part of the settlements of the new country, and the veracious charm of her sympathetic narrative can hardly fail to increase the interest which is already felt in these possessions.'— *Times.*

'Emphatically a volume to read.'—*Black and White.*

'An excellent book of travels. There is not a page of this capital book which is not at once instructive and entertaining.'—*Glasgow Herald.*

'Miss Balfour has given us a most interesting and valuable volume. As the record of an adventure so far, perhaps, unparalleled, it will be read with profound interest, and the volume, we are sure, will be universally received as one of the best, most pleasing, and instructive of the season '—*Irish Times.*

THE LAND OF THE NILE-SPRINGS.

By Colonel Sir HENRY COLVILE, K.C.M.G., C.B., recently British Commissioner in Uganda.

With Photogravure Frontispiece, 16 Full-page Illustrations and 2 Maps, demy 8vo., 16s.

'One of the most faithful and entertaining books of adventure that has appeared since Burton's days.'—*National Observer.*

'It is not often that men who do things can turn out such an interesting account of the things done as Colonel Colvile has written of his administration of Uganda. From beginning to end there is not a dull page in the book.'—*Daily Graphic.*

'It is, indeed, the reaction from the Blue-book, whose phraseology he continually uses with the happiest irony. And as the reaction it is probably more valuable in its way than all the Blue-books that ever came out of the Queen's printing press.'—*Pall Mall Gazette.*

'Delightfully lively.'—*Truth.*

STUDIES IN EARLY VICTORIAN LITERATURE,
1837-1870.

By FREDERIC HARRISON, M.A.,
Author of 'The Choice of Books,' etc.

Large crown 8vo., cloth, 10s. 6d.

CONTENTS.

VICTORIAN LITERATURE.	ANTHONY TROLLOPE.
LORD MACAULAY.	CHARLES DICKENS.
THOMAS CARLYLE.	WILLIAM MAKEPEACE THACKERAY.
BENJAMIN DISRAELI.	CHARLES KINGSLEY.
CHARLOTTE BRONTE.	GEORGE ELIOT.

' Mr. Harrison has given us a welcome and delightful book—an important and even memorable contribution to modern critical literature.'—*Saturday Review.*

' Mr. Frederic Harrison ought to give us more literary criticism than he does. In no branch of literary activity does he show to so much advantage. Knowledge and sense—those are the qualities Stevenson found in it, and those are just the qualities which mark his new essays in Early Victorian literature.'—*St. James's Gazette.*

' A book that will have a permanent value. It is not only good criticism—it could hardly be otherwise in view of the name on its title-page—it deals historically with a period that has passed away, and it must always remain of use to the student as a work of critical reference.'—*Daily News.*

THE ROMANCE OF PRINCE EUGENE.

An Idyll under Napoleon the First.

By ALBERT PULITZER.

With numerous Photogravure Illustrations, in two volumes, demy 8vo., 21s.

EXTRACT FROM THE PREFACE : ' By chance, glancing over the Memoirs and Correspondence of Prince Eugene, published, about forty years ago, by A. du Casse, in ten volumes octavo, I read with real pleasure the letters addressed by the prince to his wife, born Princess Royal of Bavaria, and considered one of the handsomest women of her time. These letters, written during the stirring transformations of the Napoleonic epoch, reveal, in the exquisite tenderness which they breathe, one of the most charming love stories which history has given us.

SECOND EDITION.

BENJAMIN JOWETT, MASTER OF BALLIOL.

A Personal Memoir.

By the HON. LIONEL TOLLEMACHE,

Author of 'Safe Studies,' etc.

Crown 8vo., cloth, 3s. 6d.

' Mr. Lionel Tollemache has never produced anything before so interesting or showing so much insight as his little monograph '' Benjamin Jowett.''   It is amusing, and at the same time gives the reader a better idea of Jowett than anything that has hitherto been written about him by his friends.'—*Athenæum.*

' Displays most fully that combination of Boswellian anecdote, acute criticism, and allusiveness tempered by scrupulous economy of style, which has already marked Mr. Tollemache's former essays with a manner unique among present-day writers.'—*St. James's Gazette.*

-' Rather Boswellian and extremely amusing.'—*Speaker.*

' Readers of this stimulating and uncommon volume will rarely find a page that does not carry something of intellectual tonic.'—*Literary World.*

SECOND EDITION.

ROBERT LOUIS STEVENSON.

By WALTER RALEIGH, Professor of English Literature at Liverpool University College.

Author of ' The English Novel,' etc.

Crown 8vo., cloth, 2s. 6d.

' Quite the best contribution that has yet been made to our critical literature in regard to the late Mr. Stevenson.   Mr. Raleigh's book, in fact, is full of happily-phrased and sensible criticism.   It is well worth reading, and the better the reader knows his Stevenson, the more he will appreciate it.'—*Glasgow Herald.*

'' A capital piece of work, written with great life, and curiously Stevensonian in mood and style, though by no means unpleasantly imitative.'—*Manchester Guardian.*

' Few more discriminating appreciations of R. L. Stevenson have yet been uttered than that which Professor Raleigh delivered as a lecture at the Royal Institution, and now published, with additions, by Mr. Edward Arnold.'—*Morning Post.*

' An admirable study of a great master of letters.'—*Irish Times.*

THE STORY OF TWO SALONS.
Madame de Beaumont and the Suards.

By EDITH SICHEL,

Author of ' Worthington Junior.'

With Illustrations, 8vo., 10s. 6d.

'There is really not a page in the book that ought not to be read, and neither skimmed nor quoted from; and as we turn its pages over, we can only feel that there might well be more of it.'—*Spectator.*

'This interesting book is written with a wit and vivacity worthy of its subject. Miss Sichel has a regard for her period, which is an invaluable quality for its chronicler. Above all things it is entertaining.'—*Manchester Guardian.*

'To the ordinary English reader Madame de Beaumont is less well known than is her contemporary, Madame Recamier, and therefore one welcomes all the more warmly this fascinating study of her and of the "little household" of the Suards.'—*Glasgow Herald.*

WAGNER'S HEROES.

TANNHAUSER. PARSIFAL. HANS SACHS. LOHENGRIN.

By CONSTANCE MAUD.

Illustrated by H. GRANVILLE FELL.

Crown 8vo., handsomely bound, 5s.

'An excellent idea well carried out. Miss Maud has done for the Shakespeare of music what Charles Lamb once did for the real Shakespeare.'—*Daily Telegraph.*

'Constance Maud has elected to convey into simple language the histories of "Wagner's Heroes" and has succeeded admirably.'—*Black and White.*

'The little folks who study the beautiful stories in this book will be absorbing not the inane inventions of a hack-scribbler, but world literature, the possession of which must be a pleasure through life.'—*Bradford Observer.*

'Constance Maud gives a delightful embodiment of "Wagner's Heroes" and narrates the story of Parsifal, Tannhauser, Hans Sachs, and Lohengrin, with the quaintness and spirit which pervades the Sagas. Even without relation to Wagner's masterpieces the stories would be delightful reading.'—*Leeds Mercury.*

HOW DICK AND MOLLY WENT ROUND THE WORLD.

By M. H. CORNWALL LEGH.

With numerous Illustrations, fcap. 4to., cloth, 5s.

'Perhaps the best of all the children's books of the season.'—*World.*

'A really excellent book for small children.'—*Guardian.*

'One of the best children's books we have seen lately.'—*Liverpool Mercury.*

'One of the most instructive as well as entertaining of narratives.'—*Pall Mall Gazette.*

'No better book or a present can be imagined, and the parents will equally approve of a book which teaches geography so delightfully.'—*Western Morning News.*

TRAVELS, SPORT, AND EXPLORATION.

Balfour—TWELVE HUNDRED MILES IN A WAGGON. (*See page* 8.)

Beynon—WITH KELLY TO CHITRAL. (*See page* 4.)

Colvile—THE LAND OF THE NILE SPRINGS. (*See page* 8.)

Custance—RIDING RECOLLECTIONS AND TURF STORIES. By HENRY CUSTANCE, three times winner of the Derby. One vol., crown 8vo., cloth, 2s. 6d.

'An admirable sketch of turf history during a very interesting period, well and humorously written.'—*Sporting Life.*

Freshfield—EXPLORATION OF THE CAUCASUS. (*See page* 3.)

Hole—A LITTLE TOUR IN AMERICA. (*See page* 7.)

Hole—A LITTLE TOUR IN IRELAND. By AN OXONIAN (the Very Rev. S. R. HOLE, Dean of Rochester). With nearly forty Illustrations by JOHN LEECH, including the famous steel Frontispiece of the 'Claddagh.' Large imperial 16mo., handsomely bound, gilt top. 10s. 6d.

Pike—IN THE FAR NORTH-WEST. (*See p.* 4.)

Portal—THE BRITISH MISSION TO UGANDA. By the late Sir GERALD PORTAL, K.C.M.G. Edited by RENNELL RODD, C.M.G. With an Introduction by the Right Honourable Lord CROMER, G.C.M.G. Illustrated from photos taken during the Expedition by Colonel RHODES. Demy 8vo., 21s.

Portal—MY MISSION TO ABYSSINIA. By the late Sir GERALD H. PORTAL, C.B. With Map and Illustrations. Demy 8vo., 15s.

Slatin — FIRE AND SWORD IN THE SUDAN. (*See page* 2.)

AMERICAN SPORT AND TRAVEL.

These books, selected from the Catalogue of MESSRS. RAND MCNALLY & CO., *the well-known publishers of Chicago, have been placed in* MR. EDWARD ARNOLD'S *hands under the impression that many British Travellers and Sportsmen may find them useful before starting on expeditions in the United States.*

Aldrich—ARCTIC ALASKA AND SIBERIA; or, Eight Months with the Arctic Whalemen. By HERBERT L. ALDRICH. Crown 8vo., cloth, 4s. 6d.

AMERICAN GAME FISHES. Their Habits, Habitat, and Peculiarities ; How, When, and Where to Angle for them. By various Writers. Cloth, 10s. 6d.

Higgins—NEW GUIDE TO THE PACIFIC COAST. Santa Fé Route. By C. A. HIGGINS. Crown 8vo., cloth, 4s. 6d.

Leffingwell—THE ART OF WING - SHOOTING. A Practical Treatise on the Use of the Shot-gun. By W. B. LEFFINGWELL. With numerous Illustrations. Crown 8vo., cloth, 4s. 6d.

Shields — CAMPING AND CAMP OUTFITS. By G. O. SHIELDS ('Coquina'). Containing also Chapters on Camp Medicine, Cookery, and How to Load a Packhorse. Crown 8vo., cloth, 5s.

Shields—THE AMERICAN BOOK OF THE DOG. By various Writers. Edited by G. O. SHIELDS ('Coquina'). Cloth, 15s.

Thomas—SWEDEN AND THE SWEDES. By WILLIAM WIDGERY THOMAS, Jun., United States Minister to Sweden and Norway. With numerous Illustrations. Cloth, 16s.

HISTORY AND BIOGRAPHY.

Benson and Tatham—MEN OF MIGHT. Studies of Great Characters. By A. C. BENSON, M.A., and H. F. W. TATHAM, M.A., Assistant Masters at Eton College. Second Edition. Crown 8vo., cloth, 3s. 6d.

Boyle—THE RECOLLECTIONS OF THE DEAN OF SALISBURY. By the Very Rev. G. D. BOYLE, Dean of Salisbury. With Photogravure Portrait. 1 vol., demy 8vo., cloth, 16s.

Sherard—ALPHONSE DAUDET : a Biography and Critical Study. By R. H. SHERARD, Editor of 'The Memoirs of Baron Meneval,' etc. With Illustrations. Demy 8vo., 15s.

'An excellent piece of journalism, the kind of personal journalism which is both entertaining and useful.'—*Saturday Review.*

'M. Daudet's many admirers owe a deep debt of gratitude to Mr. Sherard for his biography—a work which, after all, reflects scarcely less credit upon its author than upon its subject.'—*Scotsman.*

Fowler—ECHOES OF OLD COUNTY LIFE. Recollections of Sport, Society, Politics, and Farming in the Good Old Times. By J. K. FOWLER, of Aylesbury. Second Edition, with numerous Illustrations, 8vo., 10s. 6d. Also a large-paper edition, of 200 copies only, 21s. net.

'A very entertaining volume of reminiscences, full of good stories.'—*Truth.*

Hare—MARIA EDGEWORTH: her Life and Letters. Edited By Augustus J. C. Hare, Author of 'The Story of Two Noble Lives,' etc. Two vols., crown 8vo., with Portraits, 16s. net.

' Mr. Hare has written more than one good book in his time, but he has never produced anything nearly so entertaining and valuable as his latest contribution to biography and literature.'—*Saturday Review.*

Hole—THE MEMORIES OF DEAN HOLE. By the Very Rev. S. Reynolds Hole, Dean of Rochester. With the original Illustrations from sketches by Leech and Thackeray. New Edition, twelfth thousand, one vol., crown 8vo., 6s.

'One of the most delightful collections of reminiscences that this generation has seen. —*Daily Chronicle.*

Hole—MORE MEMORIES: Being Thoughts about England Spoken in America. By the Very Rev. S. Reynolds Hole, Dean of Rochester. With Frontispiece. Demy 8vo., 16s.

'There is not a page in this volume without its good thing, its touch of wit or wisdom, quaint drollery, apt illustration, or quick association, kind counsel, grave truth, or happy anecdote.'—*World.*

' Full alike of contagious fun and mature wisdom.'—*Daily Chronicle.*

Kay—OMARAH'S HISTORY OF YAMAN. The Arabic Text, edited, with a translation, by Henry Cassels Kay, Member of the Royal Asiatic Society. Demy 8vo., cloth, 17s. 6d. net.

Knight-Bruce—MEMORIES OF MASHONALAND. (*See page 7.*)

Lecky—THE POLITICAL VALUE OF HISTORY. By W. E. H. Lecky, D.C.L., LL.D. An Address delivered at the Midland Institute, reprinted with additions. Crown 8vo., cloth, 2s. 6d.

Le Fanu—SEVENTY YEARS OF IRISH LIFE. Being the Recollections of W. R. Le Fanu. With Portraits of the Author and J. Sheridan Le Fanu. A New Edition in preparation.

' It will delight all readers—English and Scotch no less than Irish, Nationalists no less than Unionists, Roman Catholics no less than Orangemen.'—*Times.*

Macdonald—THE MEMOIRS OF THE LATE SIR JOHN A. MACDONALD, G.C.B., First Prime Minister of Canada. Edited by Joseph Pope, his Private Secretary. With Portraits. Two vols., demy 8vo., 32s.

'This full and authoritative biography throws much welcome light on the course of public affairs in Canada, as well as on the interesting personality of one of the chief actors in an epoch of change and restlessness, as well as of progress and expansion.'—*Standard.*

Milner—ENGLAND IN EGYPT. By Sir Alfred Milner, K.C.B. Popular Edition, with an Additional Prefatory Chapter on Egypt in 1894. Large crown 8vo., with Map, cloth, 7s. 6d.

' No journalist or public man ought to be permitted to write or speak about Egypt for the next five years unless he can solemnly declare that he has read it from cover to cover'. —*Daily Chronicle.*

Milner — ARNOLD TOYNBEE. A Reminiscence. By ALFRED MILNER, C.B., Author of 'England in Egypt. Crown 8vo., buckram, 2s. 6d. ; paper, 1s.

'An admirable sketch, at once sympathetic and discriminating, of a very remarkable personality. It was only due to Toynbee's memory that it should be published, but it is equally due to its intrinsic merit that it should be warmly welcomed and appreciated. Slight as it is, it is a masterly analysis of a commanding personal influence, and a social force of rare potency and effect.'—*Times.*

Oman—A HISTORY OF ENGLAND. By CHARLES OMAN, Fellow of All Souls' College, and Lecturer in History at New College, Oxford; Author of 'Warwick the Kingmaker,' 'A History of Greece,' etc. Crown 8vo., cloth, 4s. 6d. net.

'This is the nearest approach to the ideal School History of England which has yet been written.'—*Guardian.*

Pulitzer—THE ROMANCE OF PRINCE EUGENE. (*See page* 9.)

Raleigh—R. L. STEVENSON. (*See page* 10.)

Ransome—THE BATTLES OF FREDERICK THE GREAT; Extracts from Carlyle's 'History of Frederick the Great.' Edited by CYRIL RANSOME, M.A., Professor of History in the Yorkshire College, Leeds. With a Map specially drawn for this work, Carlyle's original Battle-Plans. and Illustrations by ADOLPH MENZEL. Cloth. imperial 16mo., 5s.

Santley—STUDENT AND SINGER. The Reminiscences of CHARLES SANTLEY. New Edition, crown 8vo., cloth, 6s.

Tollemache—BENJAMIN JOWETT. (*See page* 10.)

Twining—RECOLLECTIONS OF LIFE AND WORK. Being the Autobiography of LOUISA TWINING. One vol., 8vo., cloth, 15s.

LITERATURE AND BELLES LETTRES.

WORKS BY THE REV. CANON BELL, D.D.,

Rector of Cheltenham and Honorary Canon of Carlisle.

DIANA'S LOOKING GLASS, and other Poems.

Crown 8vo., cloth, 5s. net.

POEMS OLD AND NEW.

Crown 8vo., cloth, 7s. 6d.

THE NAME ABOVE EVERY MAME, and other Sermons.

Crown 8vo., cloth, 5s.

Bell—KLEINES HAUSTHEATER. Fifteen Little Plays in German for Children. By Mrs. HUGH BELL. Crown 8vo., cloth, 2s.

Most of these little plays have been adapted from the author's 'Petit Théâtre,' the remainder from a little book of English plays by the same writer entitled 'Nursery Comedies.'

Butler—SELECT ESSAYS OF SAINTE BEUVE. Chiefly bearing on English Literature. Translated by A. J. BUTLER, Translator of 'The Memoirs of Baron Marbot.' One vol., 8vo., cloth, 5s. net.

'English readers should not fail to make themselves acquainted with the work of one of the clearest, most broadly tolerant, and sanest critics of their literature that France has produced.'—*Daily Telegraph.*
'The present translation is excellent.'—*Morning Post.*

Collingwood—THORSTEIN OF THE MERE: a Saga of the Northmen in Lakeland. By W. G. COLLINGWOOD, Author of 'Life of John Ruskin,' etc. With Illustrations. Price 10s. 6d.

Cook—THE DEFENSE OF POESY, otherwise known as AN APOLOGY FOR POETRY. By Sir PHILIP SIDNEY. Edited by A. S. COOK, Professor of English Literature in Yale University. Crown 8vo., cloth, 4s. 6d.

Cook—A DEFENCE OF POETRY. By PERCY BYSSHE SHELLEY. Edited, with notes and introduction, by Professor A. S. COOK. Crown 8vo., cloth, 2s. 6d.

Davidson—A HANDBOOK TO DANTE. By GIOVANNI A. SCARTAZZINI. Translated from the Italian, with notes and additions, by THOMAS DAVIDSON, M.A. Crown 8vo., cloth, 6s.

Fleming—THE ART OF READING AND SPEAKING. (*See page* 5.)

Garnett—SELECTIONS IN ENGLISH PROSE FROM ELIZABETH TO VICTORIA. Chosen and arranged by JAMES M. GARNETT, M.A., LL.D. 700 pages, large crown 8vo., cloth, 7s. 6d.

Goschen—THE CULTIVATION AND USE OF IMAGINATION. By the Right Hon. GEORGE JOACHIM GOSCHEN. Crown 8vo., cloth, 2s. 6d.

'Excellent essays.'—*Westminster Gazette.*
'Full of excellent advice, attractively put.'—*Speaker.*

GREAT PUBLIC SCHOOLS. ETON — HARROW — WINCHESTER — RUGBY — WESTMINSTER — MARLBOROUGH — CHELTENHAM — HAILEYBURY — CLIFTON — CHARTERHOUSE. With nearly a hundred Illustrations by the best artists. One vol., large imperial 16mo., handsomely bound, 6s.

Gummere—OLD ENGLISH BALLADS. Selected and Edited by FRANCIS B. GUMMERE, Professor of English in Haverford College, U.S.A. Crown 8vo., cloth, 5s. 6d.

Harrison—STUDIES IN EARLY VICTORIAN LITERA-TURE. (*See page* 9.)

Hole—ADDRESSES TO WORKING MEN FROM PULPIT AND PLATFORM. By the Very Rev. S. REYNOLDS HOLE, Dean of Rochester. This volume contains nineteen Addresses and Sermons delivered by Dean Hole to Working Men on Friendly Societies, Gambling and Betting, the Church and Dissent, to Soldiers, on Temperance, Unbelief, True Education, Work, etc. One vol., crown 8vo., 6s.

'A book of great interest and great excellence.'—*Scotsman.*

Hudson—THE LIFE, ART, AND CHARACTERS OF SHAKESPEARE. By HENRY N. HUDSON, LL.D., Editor of *The Harvard Shakespeare*, etc. 969 pages, in two vols., large crown 8vo., cloth, 21s.

Hudson. — THE HARVARD EDITION OF SHAKE-SPEARE'S COMPLETE WORKS. A fine Library Edition. By HENRY N. HUDSON, LL.D., Author of 'The Life, Art, and Characters of Shakespeare.' In twenty volumes, large crown 8vo., cloth, £6. Also in ten volumes, £5.

Hunt — Leigh Hunt's 'WHAT IS POETRY?' An Answer to the Question, 'What is Poetry?' including Remarks on Versification. By LEIGH HUNT. Edited, with notes, by Professor A. S. COOK. Crown 8vo., cloth, 2s. 6d.

Lang—LAMB'S ADVENTURES OF ULYSSES. With an Introduction by ANDREW LANG. Square 8vo. cloth, 1s. 6d. Also the Prize Edition, gilt edges, 2s.

Maud—WAGNER'S HEROES. (*See page* 11.)

Morrison—LIFE'S PRESCRIPTION, In Seven Doses. By D. MACLAREN MORRISON. Crown 8vo., parchment, 1s. 6d.

Schelling—A BOOK OF ELIZABETHAN LYRICS. Selected and Edited by F. E. SCHELLING, Professor of English Literature in the University of Pennsylvania. Crown 8vo., cloth, 5s. 6d.

Schelling—BEN JONSON'S TIMBER. Edited by Professor F. E. SCHELLING. Crown 8vo,, cloth, 4s.

Sichel—THE STORY OF TWO SALONS. (*See page* 11.)

Thayer—THE BEST ELIZABETHAN PLAYS. Edited, with an Introduction, by WILLIAM R. THAYER. 612 pages, large crown 8vo., cloth, 7s. 6d.

WINCHESTER COLLEGE. Illustrated by HERBERT MARSHALL. With Contributions in Prose and Verse by OLD WYKEHAMISTS. Demy 4to., cloth, 25s. net. A few copies of the first edition, limited to 1,000 copies, are still to be had.

WORKS BY RENNELL RODD, C.M.G.

FEDA, with other Poems, chiefly Lyrical.
With an Etching by HARPER PENNINGTON.
Crown 8vo., cloth, 6s.

THE UNKNOWN MADONNA, and other Poems.
With a Frontispiece by W. B. RICHMOND, A.R.A.
Crown 8vo., cloth, 5s.

THE VIOLET CROWN, AND SONGS OF ENGLAND.
With a Frontispiece by the MARCHIONESS OF GRANBY.
Crown 8vo., cloth, 5s.

THE CUSTOMS AND LORE OF MODERN GREECE.
With seven full-page Illustrations by TRISTRAM ELLIS.
8vo., cloth, 8s. 6d.

FICTION.
SIX SHILLING NOVELS.

TOMMY ATKINS. By ROBERT BLATCHFORD. (*See p.* 6.)

A MASK AND A MARTYR. By E. LIVINGSTON PRESCOTT.
(*See p.* 6.)

A RELUCTANT EVANGELIST. By ALICE SPINNER.
(*See p.* 6.)

ORMISDAL. A Novel. By the EARL OF DUNMORE, F.R.G.S.,
Author of 'The Pamirs.' One vol., crown 8vo., cloth, 6s.

' In this breezy and entertaining novel Lord Dunmore has given us a very readable and racy story of the life that centres in a Highland shooting, about the end of August.'— *Glasgow Herald.*

THE TUTOR'S SECRET. (Le Secret du Précepteur.)
Translated from the French of VICTOR CHERBULIEZ. One vol., crown 8vo., cloth, 6s.

' If Victor Cherbuliez did not already possess a great reputation, his latest production would have been quite sufficient to secure him renown as a novelist. From the first line to the last we recognise a master-hand at work, and there is not a page that even the veriest skimmer will care to pass over.'— *Westminster Gazette.*

FICTION—*(continued).*

THREE SHILLING AND SIXPENNY NOVELS.

WORTH WHILE. By F. F. Montresor. (*See page* 6.)

ON THE THRESHOLD. By Isabella O. Ford, Author of
'Miss Blake of Monkshalton.' One vol., crown 8vo., 3s. 6d.

'It is a relief to turn from many of the novels that come before us to
Miss Ford's true, penetrating, and sympathetic description of the lives of some
of the women of our day.'—*Guardian.*

THE MYSTERY OF THE RUE SOLY. Translated by
Lady Knutsford from the French of H. de Balzac. Crown 8vo.,
cloth, 3s. 6d.

'Lady Knutsford's translation of Balzac's famous story is excellent.'—*Scotsman.*

DAVE'S SWEETHEART. By Mary Gaunt. One vol.,
8vo., cloth, 3s. 6d.

'Of all the Australian novels that have been laid before readers in this country,
"Dave's Sweetheart," in a literary point of view and as a finished production, takes a
higher place than any that has yet appeared. From the opening scene to the closing
page we have no hesitation in predicting that not a word will be skipped even by the
most *blasé* of novel readers.'—*Spectator.*

MISTHER O'RYAN. An Incident in the History of a
Nation. By Edward McNulty. Small 8vo., elegantly bound, 3s. 6d.

'An extremely well-written satire of the possibilities of blarney and brag.'—*Pall Mall
Gazette.*

STEPHEN REMARX. The Story of a Venture in Ethics.
By the Hon. and Rev. James Adderley, formerly Head of the Oxford
House and Christ Church Mission, Bethnal Green. Twenty-Second
Thousand. Small 8vo., elegantly bound, 3s. 6d. Also in paper cover, 1s.

'Let us express our thankfulness at encountering for once in a way an author who can
amuse us.'—*Saturday Review.*

HALF-A-CROWN NOVELS.

LOVE-LETTERS OF A WORLDLY WOMAN. By Mrs.
W. K. Clifford, Author of 'Aunt Anne,' 'Mrs. Keith's Crime,' etc.
One vol., crown 8vo., cloth, 2s. 6d.

'One of the cleverest books that ever a woman wrote.'—*Queen.*

THAT FIDDLER FELLOW : A Tale of St. Andrews. By
Horace G. Hutchinson, Author of 'My Wife's Politics,' 'Golf,'
'Creatures of Circumstance,' etc. Crown 8vo., cloth, 2s. 6d.

COUNTRY HOUSE—PASTIMES.

Ellacombe—IN A GLOUCESTERSHIRE GARDEN. By
the Rev. H. N. ELLACOMBE, Vicar of Bitton, and Honorary Canon of
Bristol. Author of 'Plant Lore and Garden Craft of Shakespeare.'
Second Edition. Crown 8vo., cloth, 6s.

'The book may be warmly recommended to all who love gardens, while it also cannot
fail to interest even the horticulturally unlearned. It is written in a style that is clear,
bright, and simple, and from beginning to end there is not a dull or wearisome sentence.'
—*The Guardian.*

'Altogether a charming book.'—*Westminster Gazette.*

Hole—A BOOK ABOUT THE GARDEN AND THE
GARDENER. By the Very Rev. S. REYNOLDS HOLE, Dean of Rochester.
Second edition. Crown 8vo., 6s.

Hole—A BOOK ABOUT ROSES. By the Very Rev. S.
REYNOLDS HOLE (Dean of Rochester). Twentieth thousand. Crown
8vo., cloth, 2s. 6d.

Brown — PLEASURABLE POULTRY - KEEPING. By
E. BROWN, F.L.S. Fully illustrated. One vol., crown 8vo., cloth, 2s. 6d.

'Mr. Brown has established for himself a unique position in regard to this subject, and
what he has to say is not only sound counsel, but is presented in a very readable form.'—
Nottingham Daily Guardian.

Brown—POULTRY-KEEPING AS AN INDUSTRY FOR
FARMERS AND COTTAGERS. By EDWARD BROWN. Fully illustrated.
Second edition. Demy 4to., cloth, 6s.

Brown—INDUSTRIAL POULTRY-KEEPING. By EDWARD
BROWN. Illustrated. Paper boards, 1s. A small handbook chiefly
intended for cottagers and allotment-holders.

Brown—POULTRY FATTENING. By E. BROWN, F.L.S.
Fully illustrated. New Edition. Crown 8vo., 1s. 6d.

White—PLEASURABLE BEE-KEEPING. By C. N. WHITE,
Lecturer to the County Councils of Huntingdon, Cambridgeshire, etc.
Fully illustrated. One vol., crown 8vo., cloth, 2s. 6d.

'A complete guide for the amateur bee-keeper, as clear and concise as such a guide can
be made.'—*Glasgow Herald.*

Gossip—THE CHESS POCKET MANUAL. By G. H. D.
GOSSIP. A Pocket Guide, with numerous Specimen Games and Illustrations. Small 8vo., 2s. 6d.

Cunningham—THE DRAUGHTS POCKET MANUAL. By
J. G. CUNNINGHAM. An Introduction to the Game in all its branches. Small 8vo., with numerous diagrams, 2s. 6d.

'These two excellent little manuals may be mentioned together. Both will be found well worth study by those who are interested in the subjects which they discuss.'— *Spectator.*

Kenney-Herbert—COMMON-SENSE COOKERY : based
on Modern English and Continental Principles, Worked out in Detail. By Colonel A. KENNEY-HERBERT ('Wyvern'). Large crown 8vo., over 500 pp., 7s. 6d.

'A book which is sure to have a large circulation, since the author, the well-known "Wyvern," has been for some time generally accepted as perhaps the chief English authority on the art of cookery.'—*Times.*

Kenney-Herbert—FIFTY BREAKFASTS : containing a
great variety of New and Simple Recipes for Breakfast Dishes. By Colonel KENNEY-HERBERT ('Wyvern'). Small 8vo., 2s. 6d.

'All who know the culinary works of "Wyvern" are aware that they combine a remarkable conviction and excellent taste with an exceptional practicalness and precision in detail. His "Fifty Breakfasts" will well sustain this reputation.'—*Saturday Review.*

Kenney-Herbert—FIFTY DINNERS. By Colonel KENNEY-
HERBERT. Small 8vo., cloth, 2s. 6d.

'The book is eminently sensible, practical, and clear ; and as the author is a well-known authority on all that relates to the culinary art, the success of his latest venture as a caterer may be taken for granted.'—*Speaker.*

Kenney-Herbert—FIFTY LUNCHES. By Colonel KENNEY-
HERBERT. Small 8vo., cloth, 2s. 6d.

Shorland—CYCLING FOR HEALTH AND PLEASURE.
By L. H. PORTER, Author of 'Wheels and Wheeling,' etc. Revised and edited by F. W. SHORLAND, Amateur Champion 1892-93-94. With numerous Illustrations, small 8vo., 2s. 6d.

'Will be welcomed by all to whom the wheel is dear. The book is intensely practical, and it is a most useful vade mecum for the cycling tourist.'—*Daily Telegraph.*

SCIENCE, PHILOSOPHY, ETC.

Bryan—THE MARK IN EUROPE AND AMERICA. A Review of the Discussion on Early Land Tenure. By ENOCH A. BRYAN, A.M., President of Vincennes University, Indiana. Crown 8vo., cloth, 4s. 6d.

Burgess—POLITICAL SCIENCE AND COMPARATIVE CONSTITUTIONAL LAW. By JOHN W. BURGESS, Ph.D., LL.D., Dean of the University Faculty of Political Science in Columbia College, U.S.A. In two volumes. Demy 8vo., cloth, 25s.

Fawcett—THE RIDDLE OF THE UNIVERSE. Being an Attempt to determine the First Principles of Metaphysics considered as an Inquiry into the Conditions and Import of Consciousness. By EDWARD DOUGLAS FAWCETT. One vol., demy 8vo., 14s.

Hopkins — THE RELIGIONS OF INDIA. By E. W. HOPKINS, Ph.D. (Leipzic), Professor of Sanskrit and Comparative Philology in Bryn Mawr College. One vol., demy 8vo., 8s. 6d. net.

Ladd—LOTZE'S PHILOSOPHICAL OUTLINES. Dictated Portions of the Latest Lectures (at Göttingen and Berlin) of Hermann Lotze. Translated and edited by GEORGE T. LADD, Professor of Philosophy in Yale College. About 180 pages in each volume. Crown 8vo., cloth, 4s. each. Vol. I. Metaphysics. Vol. II. Philosophy of Religion. Vol. III. Practical Philosophy. Vol. IV. Psychology. Vol. V. Æsthetics. Vol. VI. Logic.

THE JOURNAL OF MORPHOLOGY. Edited by C. O. WHITMAN, Professor of Biology in Clark University, U.S.A. Three numbers in a volume of 100 to 150 large 4to. pages, with numerous plates. Single numbers, 17s. 6d. ; subscription to the volume of three numbers, 45s. Volumes I. to X. can now be obtained, and the first number of Volume XI. is ready.

' Everyone who is interested in the kind of work published in it knows it. It is taken by all the chief libraries of colleges, universities, etc., both in England and the Continent.'—PROFESSOR RAY LANKESTER.

' The *Journal of Morphology* is too well known and appreciated to need any praise from me.'—PROFESSOR MICHAEL FOSTER.

Morgan—ANIMAL LIFE AND INTELLIGENCE. By Professor C. LLOYD MORGAN, F.G.S., Principal of University College, Bristol. With 40 Illustrations and a Photo-etched Frontispiece. Second Edition. Demy 8vo., cloth, 16s.

Morgan—PSYCHOLOGY FOR TEACHERS. By Professor C. LLOYD MORGAN, F.G.S., Principal of University College, Bristol. Crown 8vo., cloth, 3s. 6d. net.

Morgan—THE SPRINGS OF CONDUCT. By Professor
C. LLOYD MORGAN, F.G.S.   Cheaper Edition.   Large crown 8vo., 3s. 6d.

Morgan—PSYCHOLOGY FOR TEACHERS. By Professor
C. LLOYD MORGAN, F.G.S.   With a Preface by J. G. FITCH, M.A.,
LL.D., late one of H.M. Chief Inspectors of Training Colleges.   One
vol., crown 8vo., cloth, 3s. 6d. net.

Young—A GENERAL ASTRONOMY. By CHARLES A.
YOUNG, Professor of Astronomy in the College of New Jersey, Associate
of the Royal Astronomical Society, Author of *The Sun*, etc.   In one vol.,
550 pages, with 250 Illustrations, and supplemented with the necessary
tables.   Royal 8vo., half morocco, 12s. 6d.

ILLUSTRATED GIFT BOOKS, ETC.

**** For further particulars of books under this heading see
special Catalogue of Gift Books for Presents and Prizes.

WINCHESTER COLLEGE. Illustrated by HERBERT
MARSHALL.   With Contributions in Prose and Verse by OLD
WYKEHAMISTS.   Demy 4to., cloth, 25s. net.   A few copies of the first
edition, limited to 1,000 copies, are still to be had.

GREAT PUBLIC SCHOOLS. ETON — HARROW — WIN-
CHESTER — RUGBY—WESTMINSTER— MARLBOROUGH—CHELTENHAM—
HAILEYBURY — CLIFTON — CHARTERHOUSE.   With nearly a Hundred
Illustrations by the best artists.   One vol., large imperial 16mo., hand-
somely bound, 6s.

A LITTLE TOUR IN IRELAND. By AN OXONIAN (the
Very Rev. S. R. HOLE, Dean of Rochester).   With nearly forty Illustra-
tions by JOHN LEECH, including the famous steel Frontispiece of the
' Claddagh.'

**** A New Edition in preparation.

WILD FLOWERS IN ART AND NATURE. By J. C. L.
SPARKES, Principal of the National Art Training School, South Kensing-
ton, and F. W. BURBIDGE, Curator of the University Botanical Gardens,
Dublin.   With 21 Full-page Coloured Plates by H. G. MOON.   Royal 4to.,
handsomely bound, gilt edges, 21s.

PICTURES OF BIRDS. For the Decoration of Home and Schools.

List of Coloured Plates :

Blue Tit.	**Bullfinch.**	**Skylark.**	**Waterwagtail.**
Thrush.	**Swallow.**	**Blackbird.**	**Starling.**
Chaffinch.	**Yellowhammer.**	**Sparrow.**	**Robin.**

The Pictures can be supplied in the following styles :

Unmounted—6d. per Plate. Set of 12, in envelope, 6s.

Mounted—Single Plates, mounted on boards, 12 by 15 inches, eyeletted and strung, 1s. each. Sets of 3 Plates, mounted together on boards, 34 by 15 inches, eyeletted and strung, 2s. 6d. each.

Framed—Single Plates, mounted and framed, 2s. each. Sets of 3 Plates mounted and framed together, 4s. 6d. each,

All the above prices are net.

WILD FLOWER PICTURES. For the Decoration of Home and School. Twenty-one Beautifully Coloured Plates, issued in the same style and at the same prices as the ' Birds.'

Honeysuckle.	**Poppy.**	**Foxglove.**
Forget-me-Not.	**Cornflower.**	**Cowslip.**
Convolvulus.	**Iris.**	**Bluebell.**
Hawthorn.	**Rose.**	**Primrose.**
Lychnis.	**Buttercup.**	**Violet.**
Harebell.	**Heather.**	**Daffodil.**
Daisy.	**Water-Lily.**	**Anemone.**

BOOKS FOR THE YOUNG.

SEVEN AND SIXPENCE EACH.

TALES FROM HANS ANDERSEN. With nearly 40 Original Illustrations by E. A. LEMANN. One vol., 4to., handsomely bound in cloth, gilt, 7s. 6d.

THE SNOW QUEEN, and other Tales. By HANS CHRISTIAN ANDERSEN. Beautifully Illustrated by Miss E. A. LEMANN. Small 4to., handsomely bound, gilt edges, 7s. 6d.

FIVE SHILLINGS EACH.

ERIC THE ARCHER. By MAURICE H. HERVEY. With numerous full-page Illustrations. Handsomely bound, crown 8vo., 5s.

THE FUR SEAL'S TOOTH. By KIRK MUNROE. Fully Illustrated. Crown 8vo., cloth, 5s.

HOW DICK AND MOLLY WENT ROUND THE WORLD. By M. H. CORNWALL LEGH. With numerous Illustrations. Fcap. 4to., cloth, 5s.

DR. GILBERT'S DAUGHTERS. By MARGARET HARRIET MATHEWS. Illustrated by CHRIS. HAMMOND. Crown 8vo., cloth, 5s.

THE REEF OF GOLD. By MAURICE H. HERVEY. With numerous full-page Illustrations, handsomely bound. Gilt edges, 5s.

BAREROCK; or, The Island of Pearls. By HENRY NASH. With numerous Illustrations by LANCELOT SPEED. Large crown 8vo., handsomely bound, gilt edges, 5s.

THREE SHILLINGS AND SIXPENCE EACH.

HUNTERS THREE. By THOMAS W. KNOX, Author of 'The Boy Travellers,' etc. With numerous Illustrations. Crown 8vo., cloth, 3s. 6d.

THE SECRET OF THE DESERT. By E. D. FAWCETT. With numerous full-page Illustrations. Crown 8vo., cloth, 3s. 6d.

JOEL : A BOY OF GALILEE. By ANNIE FELLOWS JOHNSTON. With ten full-page Illustrations. Crown 8vo., cloth, 3s. 6d.

THE MUSHROOM CAVE. By EVELYN RAYMOND. With Illustrations. Crown 8vo., cloth, 3s. 6d.

THE DOUBLE EMPEROR. By W. LAIRD CLOWES, Author of 'The Great Peril,' etc. Illustrated. Crown 8vo., 3s. 6d.

SWALLOWED BY AN EARTHQUAKE. By E. D. FAWCETT, Author of ' Hartmann the Anarchist,' etc. Illustrated. Crown 8vo., 3s. 6d.

HARTMANN THE ANARCHIST; or, The Doom of the Great City. By E. DOUGLAS FAWCETT. With sixteen full-page and numerous smaller Illustrations by F. T. JANE. One vol., crown 8vo., cloth, 3s. 6d.

ANIMAL SKETCHES: a Popular Book of Natural History. By Professor C. LLOYD MORGAN, F.G.S. Crown 8vo., cloth, 3s. 6d.

TWO AND SIXPENCE EACH.

CHILDREN'S HOUR SERIES.

MASTER MAGNUS. By Mrs. E. M. FIELD, Author of ' Mixed Pickles,' etc. With Four Full-page Illustrations. Small 8vo., 2s. 6d.

MY DOG PLATO. By M. H. CORNWALL LEGH. With Four Full-page Illustrations. Small 8vo., 2s. 6d.

FRIENDS OF THE OLDEN TIME. By ALICE GARDNER, Lecturer in History at Newnham College, Cambridge. Second Edition. Illustrated, square 8vo., 2s. 6d.

THE CHILDREN'S FAVOURITE SERIES. A Charming Series of Juvenile Books, each plentifully Illustrated, and written in simple language to please young readers. Handsomely bound, and designed to form an attractive and entertaining series of gift-books for presents and prizes. The utmost care has been taken to maintain a thoroughly healthy tone throughout the Series, combined with entertaining and interesting reading. *Price 2s. each; or gilt edges, 2s. 6d.*

My Book of Wonders.	My Book of Perils.
My Book of Travel Stories.	My Book of Fairy Tales.
My Book of Adventures.	My Book of Bible Stories.
My Book of the Sea.	My Book of History Tales.
My Book of Fables.	My Story Book of Animals.
Deeds of Gold.	Rhymes for You and Me.

THE INTERNATIONAL EDUCATION SERIES.

FROEBEL'S PEDAGOGICS OF THE KINDERGARTEN; or, His Ideas concerning the Play and Playthings of the Child. Translated by J. JARVIS. Crown 8vo., cloth, 6s.

THE EDUCATION OF THE GREEK PEOPLE, AND ITS INFLUENCE ON CIVILIZATION. By THOMAS DAVIDSON. Crown 8vo., cloth, 6s.

SYSTEMATIC SCIENCE TEACHING. By EDWARD G. HOWE. Crown 8vo., cloth, 6s.

EVOLUTION OF THE PUBLIC SCHOOL SYSTEM IN MASSACHUSETTS. By GEORGE H. MARTIN. Crown 8vo., cloth, 6s.

THE INFANT MIND; or, Mental Development in the Child. Translated from the German of W. PREYER, Professor of Physiology in the University of Jena. Crown 8vo., cloth, 4s. 6d.

ENGLISH EDUCATION IN THE ELEMENTARY AND SECONDARY SCHOOLS. By ISAAC SHARPLESS, LL.D., President of Haverford College, U.S.A. Crown 8vo., cloth, 4s. 6d.

EMILE; or, A Treatise on Education. By JEAN JACQUES ROUSSEAU. Translated and Edited by W. H. PAYNE, Ph.D., LL.D., President of the Peabody Normal College, U.S.A. Crown 8vo., cloth, 6s.

EDUCATION FROM A NATIONAL STANDPOINT. Translated from the French of ALFRED FOUILLÉE by W. J. GREENSTREET, M.A., Head Master of the Marling School, Stroud. Crown 8vo., cloth, 7s. 6d.

THE MORAL INSTRUCTION OF CHILDREN. By FELIX ADLER, President of the Ethical Society of New York. Crown 8vo., cloth, 6s.

THE PHILOSOPHY OF EDUCATION. By JOHANN KARL ROSENKRANZ, Doctor of Theology and Professor of Philosophy at Königsberg. (Translated.) Crown 8vo., cloth, 6s.

A HISTORY OF EDUCATION. By Professor F. V. N. PAINTER. Crown 8vo., 6s.

THE VENTILATION AND WARMING OF SCHOOL BUILDINGS. With Plans and Diagrams. By GILBERT B. MORRISON. Crown 8vo., 4s. 6d.

FROEBEL'S 'EDUCATION OF MAN.' Translated by W. N. HAILMAN. Crown 8vo., 6s.

ELEMENTARY PSYCHOLOGY AND EDUCATION. By Dr. J. BALDWIN. Illustrated, crown 8vo., 6s.

THE SENSES AND THE WILL. Forming Part I. of 'The Mind of the Child.' By W. PREYER, Professor of Physiology in the University of Jena. (Translated.) Crown 8vo., 6s.

THE DEVELOPMENT OF THE INTELLECT. Forming Part II. of 'The Mind of the Child.' By Professor W. PREYER. (Translated.) Crown 8vo., 6s.

HOW TO STUDY GEOGRAPHY. By FRANCIS W. PARKER. Crown 8vo., 6s.

A HISTORY OF EDUCATION IN THE UNITED STATES. By RICHARD A. BOONE, Professor of Pedagogy in Indiana University. Crown 8vo., 6s.

EUROPEAN SCHOOLS; or, What I Saw in the Schools of Germany, France, Austria, and Switzerland. By L. R. KLEMM, Ph.D. With numerous Illustrations. Crown 8vo., 8s. 6d.

PRACTICAL HINTS FOR TEACHERS. By GEORGE HOWLAND, Superintendent of the Chicago Schools. Crown 8vo., 4s. 6d.

SCHOOL SUPERVISION. By J. L. PICKARD. 4s. 6d.

HIGHER EDUCATION OF WOMEN IN EUROPE. By HELENE LANGE. 4s. 6d.

HERBART'S TEXT-BOOK IN PSYCHOLOGY. By M. K. SMITH. 4s. 6d.

PSYCHOLOGY APPLIED TO THE ART OF TEACHING. By Dr. J. BALDWIN. 6s.

PERIODICALS.

THE NATIONAL REVIEW.

Edited by L. J. MAXSE.

Price Half-a-crown monthly.

Among recent contributors to the Review have been :

H. O. Arnold-Forster, M.P.
Lord Ashbourne.
Alfred Austin.
Right Hon. A. J. Balfour, M.P.
Miss Balfour.
Sir David Barbour, K.C.S.I.
A. C. Benson.
Hon. St. John Brodrick, M.P.
Right Hon. J. Chamberlain, M.P.
Admiral Colomb.
E. T. Cook.
Rt. Hon. Leonard Courtney, M.P.
Hon. G. N. Curzon, M.P.
Sir Mountstuart Grant - Duff, G.C.S.I.
Dr. Symons Eccles.
Violet Fane.
Lord Farrer.
Earl Grey, K.G.
George Gissing.
Lord George Hamilton, M.P.
Benjamin Kidd.
Rudyard Kipling.
James W. Lowther, M.P.

Sir John Lubbock, Bart., M.P.
Hon. Alfred Lyttelton.
Hon. Mrs. Alfred Lyttelton.
The late Earl of Lytton.
J. A. Fuller Maitland.
Admiral Maxse.
Sir Herbert Maxwell, Bart., M.P.
Mortimer Menpes.
George Meredith.
Sir H. Stafford Northcote, Bart., M.P.
R. H. Inglis Palgrave.
Sir Frederick Pollock, Bart.
Stanley Lane Poole.
T. W. Russell, M.P.
The Marquis of Salisbury, K.G.
F. C. Selous.
Leslie Stephen.
St. Loe Strachey.
The Earl of Suffolk.
H. D. Traill.
Sir Richard Webster, Q.C., M.P.
Rev. J. E. C. Welldon.
Viscount Wolmer, M.P.

LONDON : EDWARD ARNOLD, 37 BEDFORD ST., W.C.
Publisher to the India Office.

THE PHILOSOPHICAL REVIEW.

Edited by J. G. SCHURMAN,

Professor of Philosophy in Cornell University, U.S.A.

Six Numbers a year.   Single Numbers, 3s. 6d. ; Annual Subscription, 14s.
post free.   The first number was issued in January, 1892.

The Review ranges over the whole field of Philosophy ; the articles are
signed, and the contributors include the names of the foremost philosophical teachers and writers of America, and many of those of England and
the Continent of Europe.

THE JOURNAL OF MORPHOLOGY :

A Journal of Animal Morphology, devoted principally to Embryological
Anatomical, and Histological Subjects.

Edited by C. O. WHITMAN, Professor of Biology in Clark University, U.S.A.

Three numbers in a volume of 100 to 150 large 4to. pages, with numerous
plates. Single numbers, 17s. 6d. ; subscription to the volume of three
numbers, 45s.   Volumes I. to X. can now be obtained, and the first
two numbers of Volume XI. are ready.

PUBLICATIONS OF THE INDIA OFFICE AND OF THE GOVERNMENT OF INDIA.

Mr. EDWARD ARNOLD, having been appointed Publisher to the
Secretary of State for India in Council, has now on sale the
above publications at 37 Bedford Street, Strand, and is prepared
to supply full information concerning them on application.

INDIAN GOVERNMENT MAPS.

Any of the Maps in this magnificent series can now be obtained
at the shortest notice from Mr. EDWARD ARNOLD, Publisher to
the India Office.

Index to Authors.

The following Catalogues of Mr. Edward Arnold's Publications will be sent post free on application :

CATALOGUE OF WORKS OF GENERAL LITERATURE.

GENERAL CATALOGUE OF EDUCATIONAL WORKS,

Including the principal Publications of Messrs. Ginn and Company, Educational Publishers, of Boston and New York, and Messrs. E. L. Kellogg and Company, of New York.

CATALOGUE OF WORKS FOR USE IN ELEMENTARY SCHOOLS.
With Specimen Pages.

ILLUSTRATED LIST OF BOOKS FOR PRESENTS AND PRIZES.

CATALOGUE OF INDIA OFFICE PUBLICATIONS.

CATALOGUE OF INDIA OFFICE MAPS.
Price 6d.

LIST OF AMERICAN PERIODICALS WITH SUBSCRIPTION RATES.

AMERICAN BOOKS.—The importation of all American Books, Periodicals, and Newspapers is conducted by a special department, with accuracy and despatch, and full information can be obtained on application.

London : EDWARD ARNOLD, 37 BEDFORD STREET, STRAND.
Publisher to the India Office.